LONG SHADOWS

LONG SHADOWS

Rowena Summers

severn
House

This first world edition published in Great Britain 2007 by
SEVERN HOUSE PUBLISHERS LTD of
9–15 High Street, Sutton, Surrey SM1 1DF.
This first world edition published in the USA 2007 by
SEVERN HOUSE PUBLISHERS INC of
595 Madison Avenue, New York, N.Y. 10022.

British Library Cataloguing in Publication Data

Summers, Rowena, 1932-
  Long shadows
  1. Triangles (Interpersonal relations) - Fiction
  2. Brothers - Fiction 3. Great Britain - Social life and
  customs - 1918-1945 - Fiction 4. Domestic fiction
  I. Title
  823.9'14[F]

ISBN-13: 978-0-7278-6538-0   (cased)

Except where actual historical events and characters are being
described for the storyline of this novel, all situations in this
publication are fictitious and any resemblance to living persons

One

A cross the flat Somerset fields, church bells rang out in the frosty moonlit night, heralding the start of another year. In one of the cottages on the edge of Bramwell village, Walter Chase beamed at his wife and family gathered around him, the young 'uns old enough to stay up late on this special night, all except for the babby. Rose, the eldest, was courting a shopkeeper's son and going up in the world; Lucy wasn't too far behind; and at fourteen, the boy was already at work with his father at the local sawmills. It was a matter of pride that Walter had finally got the boy he'd hankered for so long after the arrival of his two daughters, which was why he sometimes almost forgot that they'd christened him Tom after his own father. Now, at this special hour, Walter smiled the smile of a contented man.

'I've a feeling in my bones that 1939 is going to be a good year for all of us,' he declared. 'We've not done so badly, have we, Mother?'

Alice as always resisted the urge to say sharply that she was not his mother. She was his wife, and had been for the past twenty years, but she knew it wouldn't have done any good to protest. Walter had called her Mother since the day Rose was born, when they'd barely been married long enough to make it respectable. Long enough though, she'd reminded him keenly whenever he'd joked that it was a good thing the girl hadn't come early, or there would have been plenty of gossip in the village about the lusty young farmer he had been then, and his pert city wife.

When the war to end all wars had finally ended and things were getting back to normal again, Alice had come on a charabanc trip to the seaside for a few days with the girls from the factory in the East End of London where she lived and worked, monotonously sewing shirts. They had arrived on the very day that Walter Chase and his brother had been there too, larking about and flashing her that cheeky, arrogant smile that had both annoyed and fascinated her, and trailing around after the girls all day. When he'd daringly asked for her address so he could write to her, she'd asked him coolly if he was sure he *could* write . . .

How patronizing she had been, she had thought so many times after that, since he had turned out to be a surprisingly good letter-writer, filling her head with the delights of living in the country: the fresh Somerset air (when it wasn't imbued with the smell of cow dung); the rivers where he and his mates went fishing for eels; the caves beneath the Mendip Hills that were full of wondrous sights such as a city-dweller could never imagine. He filled her head with a world she didn't know – a world that was becoming more and more intriguing.

And it had eventually come to this, Alice thought now as she did on every New Year's Eve, with a mixture of contentment and restlessness. She was barely forty years old, but her once-slim shape was now rounded and matronly. Walter's lust was a far more temperamental thing after all these years as the gout irritated him into bouts of roaring temper, but what they had to show for it all were their two beautiful older girls and the late baby, Bobby – and of course Tom, the apple of Walter's eye.

'Mum's got that soppy look in her eyes again,' Lucy giggled.

'It's just New Year's Eve,' Rose told her indulgently. 'She always gets a bit dewy-eyed at the turn of the year. Did you make any wishes, Mum?'

'Only that the good Lord would keep my family safe and well as always,' Alice replied, crossing her fingers as she did so.

If she had her way, her dearest wish would be that Tom found himself a different job from the one he had with his dad. Sawmills could be dangerous places, and there was more than one of the men who'd had the top of a finger lopped off in the course of a day's work. Alice couldn't bear the thought of that happening to Tom – nor to Walter, she added, almost as an afterthought.

In any case, she suspected that Tom and his pals in the village had ideas of their own, and she wasn't sure that exchanging one dangerous job for an even more dangerous one would make a mother's mind any easier. Nothing had happened yet, of course, but talk of war was in the air, as heady and tantalizing to young lads as fragrant wood smoke. The mere thought of war was enough to get them over-excited, full of the idea of being heroes, even though Water pooh-poohed it, saying it was all pie in the sky and nothing would come of it. He and his brother had both been farmers and therefore in reserved occupations in the last war, but their father had needlessly joined up at his age, and had been killed very early in the war. It had turned both young men from any glorious feelings about war, especially Mick, who was more of a thinker than Walter. He liked the simple life, and he had no truck with warmongers or politicians.

As far as Walter was concerned, politicians spent their days sitting on their fat backsides, arguing and squabbling and lining their pockets with outrageous salaries while ordinary folk got on with their lives, earning a crust as best they could. Alice knew he never suspected that Tom was charmed by the idea of flying an aeroplane and zooming about the sky like one of the heroes in his comic papers.

'She's not dreaming now,' Walter said, noticing Alice's puckered brows for the first time. 'Is there something wrong, Mother?'

Her patience snapped. 'For heaven's sake, Walter, how many times do I have to say that I'm not your mother? I have a name and I wish you would use it.'

Lucy gave another nervous giggle, and Rose shushed her up. It wasn't often that Alice rebelled against the affectionate term, but when she did, they always knew there was going to be trouble.

'I know you've got a name, woman,' Walter snapped, adding insult to injury and not even realizing it.

Rose spoke up quickly, sensing that there might be fireworks brewing. 'I think I'm going to bed now. The shop's staying closed tomorrow and Peter's taking me to the seaside for the day, so I need to get my beauty sleep.'

Her mother was still biting her tongue after Walter's

insensitive remark, but thought to herself that her girl didn't
need any beauty sleep. She was beautiful enough already,
the echo of what Alice herself had once been, if it wasn't
immodest to think it. But she might as well think it, because
it was a certainty that Walter would never tell her as much.
She couldn't remember the last time he had paid her or any
of his womenfolk a compliment. It was only his boy who
could do no wrong in this house. Alice loved all her children, and she was sure Walter did too, and it annoyed her
that she had to feel even a mite resentful because of the way
Walter favoured Tom above his girls.

'Goodnight, Mum,' Rose said. She gave her mother a quick
hug. As a family they didn't go in for too much outward shows
of affection, even on special nights like this. 'Goodnight, Dad.
Are you coming up, you two?'

Lucy jumped up at once, followed by Tom. It was a shame
to spoil a happy night like this with a row, and if there was
going to be one between their parents, they all preferred to
be out of earshot. Lucy burst out at once when the two girls
reached their bedroom and closed the door behind them.

'He can be so mean and stubborn sometimes. I don't know
how Mum has put up with it all these years!'

'She puts up with it because he's her husband and she
loves him,' Rose said mechanically. 'You put up with a lot
when you love somebody.'

Lucy glanced across the bedroom to where Rose was
undressing and folding her clothes ready for the morning.
Rose had all the curves that Lucy longed to have. Their
brother sometimes teased her remorselessly that so far she
hadn't blossomed much larger than fried eggs, even though
she was nearly seventeen now. Rose had all the looks too,
together with the thick, glossy dark hair like her mother,
while she and Tom had hair like coarse sand. Even Bobby,
at three, was going to be a charmer with his big blue eyes
and mop of dark curly hair.

'What are you staring at?' Rose asked, pulling her cambric
nightdress over her head and jumping into bed.

'You. You're so lucky, Rose.'

Her sister looked at her in genuine astonishment. 'What's
that supposed to mean?'

'You've got the looks in the family, and you've got Peter Kelsey being all soppy over you as well. I wish I was old enough to go courting.'

Rose laughed, snuggling down beneath the bedcovers in the chilly bedroom. 'You'd better not let Dad hear you say that. He's only agreeable to me seeing Peter on our own because he's a respectable grocer's son. Just wait until you're old enough.'

Lucy jumped into her own bed and switched off her bedside lamp, so that the room was lit only by the pale moonlight through the small square of window. The ringing of church bells had long since ended. Now and then they could hear the noise of late-night revellers in the village as they went first-footing, but apart from that there was only the mournful sound of branches in the nearby trees, swaying and sighing, and somewhere the hoot of an owl or the call of a fox to split the silence.

'What's it like, Rose?' Lucy said eventually.

'What's what like?' Rose was already half-asleep, dreaming about tomorrow and the whole day she and Peter were going to spend together. It would be a public holiday, so nothing would be open – no shops or amusement arcades, except one or two of the tackier ones, perhaps – but the sea and the beach were free, and so were the sand dunes where a courting couple could cuddle in private, out of the wind. And if it got too cold for that there was always the back of Peter's van where they could ignore the lingering odours of winter cabbages.

'Courting, of course. What do you do? Do you kiss each other much? You don't have to tell me if you don't want to, mind,' Lucy added hastily.

Rose was jolted out of her dreaming, and she tried not to laugh as she realized how serious her sister sounded. How awkward too, genuinely wanting to know.

'Of course we kiss each other sometimes, and we talk a lot and walk a lot, and we just enjoy one another's company.'

And the rest, of course . . . but that was private, and she had no intention of telling Lucy any of it. She wasn't sure if her mother had told Lucy the personal and intimate things she had so painstakingly told Rose at sixteen, but if not then it was high time she did. It was their mother's place to do so, not Rose's. If the truth were told, she wasn't all that comfortable herself with the way her relationship with Peter was going. She had a young girl's romantic view of love, while Peter was far earthier, despite what her parents thought of his status as a grocer's son.

'If you don't already know about the birds and the bees, ask Mum,' she said sleepily now, turning over in her bed.

It wasn't the birds and the bees she wanted to know about, Lucy thought crossly. It was *people*. She wanted to know why Rose sometimes came home from working in Kelsey's grocery shop with Peter and his widowed father with her eyes sparkling more than usual and hot colour in her cheeks, and the explanation that Mr Kelsey had been away at the local farms picking up fresh produce, and that she and Peter had been extra busy all afternoon. She sometimes wondered just what they had been busy doing.

But Rose evidently wasn't going to tell her anything else tonight, and Lucy turned her back on her sister too, as frustrated as ever.

Downstairs, Walter was roaring at his wife.

'I don't know why you get so fussed up over nothing, Alice.'

'Oh, I'm *Alice* now, am I?'

'It's your bloody name, isn't it? I thought that was what all the fuss was about. For Christ's sake, you were only a jumped-up factory girl when I met you. A bloody cockney too, so you've got nothing to put on airs and graces about.'

Her cheeks burned. 'That just shows how ignorant you are, Walter. Not everyone who comes from London is a cockney, and I certainly wasn't. I don't know why you think somebody born with hayseeds sticking out of their mouth is so superior, when it's obvious from your lack of manners that they're not!'

Walter's face darkened. 'I was good enough for you when we met, wasn't I, woman? I seem to remember you couldn't wait to get away from the smoke fast enough when I offered to wed you.'

'*Offered?*' Alice spluttered. 'I seem to remember you practically begged me, and I couldn't even be sure if it was you or your brother who was writing to me, so don't flatter yourself.'

It wasn't strictly true, but when she'd made the long journey down to Somerset again to meet Walter's mother, her heart had given an uncomfortable leap at seeing them all in their own home – the two young men and their ailing mother. It had been obvious then who was the more caring of the two Chase boys, and it wasn't Walter. Mick was the older by a couple of years, and he was the one who made sure that his mother was comfortable, while Walter continued flapping around Alice like a moth around a flame. It was flattering, of course it was, but even then she had wondered how much of it was all for show – and how long it would last.

She had also realized, her heart sinking, that all this time she had been receiving letters from Walter she had thought they were from the other one – the more sensitive one who wanted to be a vet and work with animals. She knew the letters were signed 'Walter', but on that day at the seaside the two boys had been so close together, both teasing and joking with the factory girls, that she had somehow got their images mixed up in her mind.

'Well, this is a fine start to a new year, isn't it?' Walter growled now. 'The moon must have turned your head, so we'd best go to bed and sleep on it. Things will look better in the daylight.'

It was always the same whenever his brother Mick came into the conversation. Alice knew there was a lingering guilt in Walter's mind that it was Mick and his wife who had cared for their mother until she died, while he made the feeble excuse that with three children to care for at the time, it was up to Mick, the eldest, to do his duty. Never mind the fact that Mick and Helen had a boy of their own . . . However, the fact that, just sometimes, Alice also had a lingering question in her mind that maybe it should have been Mick that she married and not Walter made her bite back any more caustic remarks. It wasn't worth it, and tomorrow it would all be forgotten, anyway.

And the one thing she couldn't deny was that Walter had been a good husband all these years. He had never strayed, or gone boozing, and he was a good provider for his family.

Above all, she knew that he loved her, even if he never put it into actual words. She stood up now and moved across the room towards him, still graceful despite the fact that her figure wasn't as slim as it had once been.

'Things always do look better in daylight, don't they, Walter? And I don't want to fight with you.'

She put her hand on the back of his neck, and his response was quick and ready as his arms went around her, his change of tone telling her he was as eager for her tonight as he had ever been.

'Fighting's not what I had in mind either, girl. I can think of much better ways to start a new year.'

Tom Chase listened to his small brother's chesty breathing in the cot on the other side of the bedroom. They all made a pet of Bobby, but he wasn't keen on having to share a bedroom with a three-year-old, though since there was hardly room in the cottage to swing a cat, he had no choice. He wished he had a room to himself like his cousin Jack. Being an only child must be strange, but a darned sight better than being one of four, even if he knew damn well he was his dad's favourite.

Jack was four years older than Tom, but they shared the same dreams of flying up into the wide blue yonder, as the comic papers called it, soaring into the sun and practically reaching the stars. Those were Jack's words, Tom thought, grinning to himself. Jack was the poetic type, unlike himself, who couldn't string two words together without them sounding clumsy. His Uncle Mick was a bit poetic too, he thought now, which probably came from having to placate the old ladies who brought in their cats for injections and tablets, and to put them to sleep when they got old. Tom shuddered for a moment. It was an odd job, being a vet. He liked animals as much as the next chap, and Jack must like them too, working on a farm like his dad once did, but having to do some of the stuff that his Uncle Mick did with animals would turn Tom's stomach.

'When one of our cows was giving birth her calf got stuck,' Jack once told him. 'The farmer had to call my dad out, and he had to shove his arm right up the cow's you-know-what to get the calf out, or they might have lost them both.'

'For Christ's sake, Jack!' Tom said, using language he'd never dare to use at home as Jack put the graphic images into his head.

Jack shrugged. 'You get used to it,' he said.

Tom shuddered again in the darkness, quite sure that he'd never get used to it. Jack was tougher than he was in that respect, and his Uncle Mick must be too. It was like being a doctor, except that the patients couldn't tell you what was wrong with them, so you had to do all that investigating and prodding and probing, and there would be all that blood . . . Oh, no bloody thanks; he'd stick to the sawmills for now, until he was old enough to do what he really wanted.

He turned over in bed and let his mind drift skywards as it so often did, careering in and out of the clouds in a magical machine, being a hero – maybe even joining one of those flying circuses and performing daring tricks in the sky . . . looping the loop and skimming the treetops to the applause of thousands . . .

It was a dream he'd had for ages now, but he knew better than to let his dad in on it. He was the youngest worker at the sawmills, and he knew Walter was very proud of the fact that his son had followed him into the same trade. There could be the occasional bit of blood there too, Tom admitted, when somebody was careless and had an accident with a saw or a plane, but he'd been taught by an expert, and never took risks. He had no intention of being carted off to hospital with bits of himself missing.

Some time later Alice lay back in her husband's arms, wishing things could always be like this. Wishing Walter could always be gentle and considerate and not get into the black rages that she knew were only stirred up by the pain in his foot when the gout tormented him. At times like these, though, he was once more the lover she had always wanted, the one she had married, blocking out all thoughts of anyone else. He was her darling, her rescuer from the slavery of the shirt factory, as he'd often told her teasingly. He had caressed her skin, kissing her responsive mouth and every part of her, blinding her to everything but the love she felt for her man. She twisted her head to look at his silhouette now, his strong, rugged face already in repose, already asleep. She didn't blame him for that. She was the one who rarely slept immediately after they had made love, as if something deep inside her insisted that she reaffirmed in her mind that this was the life she had chosen for herself, and the life that she wanted. She had her man, and her four beautiful children, and she was truly blessed.

Inevitably, the longer these thoughts turned over in her mind, no matter how serene they were, the longer she knew she was going to stay awake. This particular night had been eventful, going down to the village to share the evening with Mick and his family. They had drunk cider to welcome in the New Year long before midnight and then come back home before the church bells rang out because Bobby was fretful and falling asleep in her arms.

'He could always stay here,' her sister-in-law Helen said. 'We don't have room for you all, but you could stay with him, Alice love, if you could bear to be away from your family for one night.'

'I couldn't do that,' Alice had said at once. 'Especially not on New Year's Eve. I'm sure Walter wouldn't like it if I did.'

'Damn right I wouldn't,' he'd said good-naturedly. 'A wife's place is beside her husband, especially in the marriage bed, and the babby's place is at home with us, but we thank you all the same for your offer, Helen.'

It was a comfortable enough conversation between folk who knew one another well, and no offence was taken. There was no reason on earth why two of the people in that warm and cosy room should suddenly be looking at one another as if to the exclusion of everybody else. No reason why Alice Chase's heart should suddenly beat faster because of a certain look in her brother-in-law's eyes. No reason why she should start to make a fuss of gathering up her smallest child and deciding that it was definitely time he was home and in bed and that the rest of them had better come too. No reason why she felt the need to get out of there as quickly as possible and to feel the cool night air on her flustered cheeks, perfectly sure that she couldn't possibly sleep easily under Mick's roof.

'Goodnight, then, all of you.' Once they were all ready to

leave, Helen and Mick stood at their front door to see them
off, with Jack calling out to Tom that he'd see him tomorrow
for a walk in the woods. 'And a happy New Year to you all.'

'To you as well,' Walter's family had chorused back.

Alice had carried the sleepy Bobby home in her arms,
almost crushing him to her as if to remind herself that he
was her cherished baby, the one neither she nor Walter had
expected after so many years. They had assumed their family
was complete with Tom, but then this late miracle had arrived,
bringing a renewed sense of fulfilment to Alice. The girls
had adored him from the moment they saw him, and Tom
had said grudgingly that he wasn't too bad, even if it would
be a long while before he could play football. Even longer
before he joined them at the sawmills, Walter had agreed
with a grin.

Was that the moment that Alice realized she wanted a
different kind of life for her baby? She wouldn't want him
coming home reeking of wood shavings, however sweet or
pungent they were. She wouldn't want him having to sluice
himself off in the yard to rid his body of every vestige of
the clinging splinters, or have problems with his breathing
when they got up his nose and down his throat, as both
Walter and Tom did occasionally.

She sometimes wondered if Bobby's snuffling breathing
at night had anything to do with sharing the bedroom with
Tom, who wasn't too fussy about dropping his work clothes
on the floor of the bedroom. The dust from the wood might
be washed from his body, but it was still in his clothes, and
Bobby had been vulnerable to coughs and colds from the
day he was born.

No, she wanted something different for her darling, Alice
thought fiercely now, as the thoughts drifted in and out of
her head in her sleepless hours. She wouldn't be disloyal
enough to call it something better, because the sawmills
provided a good and respectable living for them all, but there
were other jobs in the world. Her nephew, Jack, had a good
job on the farm, working in the open air, which must surely
be a healthier environment.

Without warning, the thought of Jack led her to think of
the moment earlier that night, when her glance had clashed

with Mick's, and her heart had began to beat faster. It was absurd. There was no reason for it. She had known Mick for as long as she had known Walter, and he was merely the older brother. It was Walter who had courted her, although most of it had been by long-distance letter-writing, but it was Walter she had fallen in love with and come to Somerset to marry. It was Walter she had loved then and whom she loved now. She didn't even want to think about anything else, and she refused to question why she was even thinking so forcefully about it now.

Two

Around ten o'clock the next morning Rose heard the toot-toot of the motor horn on Kelsey's grocery van in the lane outside the cottage. Peter never bothered getting out of the van, knowing she would be ready and waiting. One of these days, she thought without rancour, she'd surprise him and not appear until he got out of the van and knocked on the door. In one of her magazines she'd read that although you should always be polite and not keep him waiting, it didn't do for a girl to let a boy take her for granted. If you let him take you for granted for the small things, he'd expect to do it in every other way too.

She grinned as she called out goodbye to her parents and skipped out of the cottage to wrench open the passenger door of the van and climb in beside Peter. The warm scent of apples and the earthy smell of potatoes and winter vegetables that always lingered in the back of the van now greeted her nostrils. Peter leaned over and squeezed her hand, knowing better than to kiss her while her parents were still likely to be watching.

He smiled at her. 'You look good enough to eat,' he said predictably.

'You don't look so bad yourself,' she said pertly, wondering as she often did why people always said the same things.

She tried not to think about it. Peter often told her she thought too much. She was like her mum in that respect, Rose thought suddenly. Her mum could sometimes go off in a kind of dream for a few minutes, and then look quite cross with herself, as if she was thinking of something quite different from her ordinary life. Rose had never realized it quite so acutely before, and she didn't know why she was thinking about it now. Mothers didn't go off into dream worlds, did they?

'Did you go first-footing last night?' she asked instead, knowing that Peter's dad thought it the correct thing for a family greengrocer to do, if only to present himself in a jovial light to his customers.

'Oh God, yes; Dad never misses a trick like that,' he replied mockingly. 'I didn't see any of your lot doing the rounds, though. I looked for you, kid.'

'Did you?' Rose said, pink with pleasure at the thought that he was looking for her. 'We spent the evening at my uncle's as usual, and then Bobby fell asleep long before midnight, so we all came home again.'

Peter glanced at her as the van trundled along the country lanes and out towards the coast. She was quite naive in many ways, and he'd put money on it that she probably had no idea of the whiff of gossip that had surrounded her mother when she first came to Somerset from London.

Not that he had any real knowledge of it himself. He'd only been a babe in arms back then, but his dad had hinted on more than one occasion that the comely Mrs Chase could have had her choice of the Chase brothers, and that some reckoned she had picked the wrong one – and knew it.

'You've gone all quiet,' Rose told him now, gazing at his handsome profile.

He laughed. 'I'm concentrating on driving this old bus, sweetheart. I'll give you all my attention when we get somewhere more cosy, and that's a promise.'

She gave a small shiver. She liked it when he gave her all his attention. It made her feel important and wanted and womanly in a way she never did at home, where she was just the elder daughter and expected to help around the house and with the younger ones. Peter made her feel different, even if he also scared her a little when he got a bit too saucy for comfort.

'It'll be too damn cold for the sand dunes today,' he went on casually. 'We'll have to snuggle up on the rug in the back of the van and make our own amusement.'

She certainly wouldn't want to spend any time in the sand dunes with the keen wind from the Bristol Channel whipping up the sand and sending it stinging up into their faces. She didn't altogether fancy the back of the van as their love nest, either, nor going home with the aroma of stale cabbages on her clothes. But it was the best they could do if they wanted to be alone. Without thinking, she hugged Peter's arm, and the van swerved alarmingly as he yelled at her laughingly to save her amorous gestures until they found a secluded spot near the beach.

Alice always had misgivings about her daughter going off with the Kelsey boy for the day. It wasn't that she didn't trust Peter – or Rose, come to that – but she knew only too well how young peoples' feelings could get the better of them. Rose was a strong-willed young woman, and Peter was a lusty young lad. He also had what Walter called the gift of the gab, just like his father. You needed it in the grocery trade, she'd often heard Peter say cheekily, persuading all the old biddies to buy stuff they didn't know they needed.

He was as persuasive as Walter once was, or as Alice had thought he was from the lovely letters he'd written her. She'd kept them all, and if he knew they were in a box in the attic, he'd have said she was daft to keep such things at her age. As if she was in her dotage, instead of having a mind that was as sharp and lively as it had ever been, she thought indignantly. Her looks hadn't faded all that much, and she still had enough pride in her appearance not to let herself go.

With two pretty young daughters growing up, a mother had a duty not to let things slacken – or so Alice always told herself. There was nothing wrong in still wanting to look attractive for her husband; to not appear wearing a dreary overall and with unkempt hair when he came home from work at the end of the day. She still tried to be washed and changed into something tidier before she served up their evening meal. Whether he even noticed or appreciated it was something else, she thought now with an imperceptible sigh.

She plunged her hands into the washtub, scrubbing away at Walter's long johns as if her life depended on it. He was a good man, a good provider, she repeated to herself like a mantra, and she was a lucky woman. It was only sometimes, only very occasionally, that she wondered if there couldn't have been something better.

She felt something tugging at her skirt, and she looked around to see Bobby, his mouth wobbling and his eyes near to brimming over with tears, and then she saw the telltale dark stain on his little shorts. He was trying so hard to be clean and dry, but sometimes he just forgot. And Alice loved him so much, this little late arrival who had taken them all by surprise, that she always forgave him instantly. She scooped him up in her arms, regardless of the soapsuds on her hands, and kissed the tears away.

'Come on, my little man, we'll soon have you cleaned up – and we could go out for a walk later if you like.'

His face brightened at once. 'Can we go to the pond to feed the ducks?'

She laughed. 'All right. But I'll have to finish the washing first. Let's go and find Lucy and see if she'll read you a story until I'm finished.'

Lucy wouldn't be too pleased on the rare day off she had been given. When she wasn't working as a kitchen maid at the Grange, the local big house, Lucy spent far too much time in the bedroom she shared with Rose these days poring over books and magazines, and hardly seeing the light of day. Alice knew her second girl secretly had ideas to better herself, and she couldn't argue with that, even if Walter did. Walter said that too much book-reading was bad for you, and too much learning was wasted on a girl.

Alice bristled at the thought, sure that his brother Mick wouldn't say such daft things. Alice might have been a working girl herself in the days of long ago, but she still remembered how it felt to look up at the sky through the small grimy windows of the shirt factory and wish for better things. Mick had told her of a world away from smelly old London and the rancid stink of the river – and, yes, she was perfectly sure they had been Mick's words in those letters that Walter had sent. Walter might have written them, but they were Mick's words. She wasn't sure when the penny had finally dropped, but drop it did, and by then it was too late to do anything about it, even if she had wanted to. By then, she was virtually engaged to Walter, and you didn't turn a good man down, especially in favour of his brother. What a scandal that would have caused!

'Mama,' she heard Bobby say impatiently, and she realized she hadn't yet moved from the spot in the scullery where the steam of the washtub still surrounded them both.

Ten minutes later, with Bobby washed and dried and in clean clothes, they went in search of Lucy and, ignoring the girl's protests, Alice placed her youngest firmly on Lucy's bed and told her to keep him amused for a while. The washing was almost finished, and once she had hung it out to dry on the washing-line, she and Bobby could have an hour to themselves, feeding the ducks on the pond – if it wasn't completely frozen over.

The wind was blowing well by now and it was a struggle to hold on to the line while she hung out the clothes. Before very long, she knew that Walter's long johns would be frozen too, hanging as stiff as boards on the line, and Bobby would say in an awed little voice that there must be a ghost inside those empty legs.

Alice smiled, remembering his sweet nonsense. Yes, she was a lucky woman. She was definitely lucky to have a fine, healthy family and a man who loved her, even if he never said it.

If anyone had told Rose Chase that being in love could be compared to a constant wrestling match, she would never have believed it. But now, in the back of Kelsey's van in a small lane away from the sea front at Burnham, she tried to fend off Peter's octopus hands, and she could think of no better comparison.

'Please stop it, Peter,' she gasped with a nervous giggle, squirming away from his fumbling hands as he vainly tried to fiddle with the hooks at the back of her brassière. 'Somebody might see us!'

'Who's to see us?' he said, temporarily exhausted with the frustrating effort of contorting his hands and wrists. 'We're all alone, Rosie, and there's nobody about for miles. Anyway, you know you like it. At least, I thought you did.'

He frowned, because he was no longer sure of any such thing. She had always seemed as eager as himself for kisses and cuddles, and it hadn't gone much further than that. But hell, he was a red-blooded man and he wanted more from his girl. He wanted her to prove to him that she loved him.

He'd told her he loved her often enough. The words slid easily from his tongue without him ever considering them a permanent pointer to the future – without him having the faintest idea that girls might think differently from boys. According to everything he saw at the flicks, they were the words that girls wanted to hear from a bloke, and so he said them.

Her jumper had got all rucked up by now and he realized she was struggling to pull it down, dragging her coat around her with a shiver. Despite himself, his ardour was quickly dampening at her lack of response. He had to admit that this wasn't the best place to get up to things, especially with the stale smells wafting all around them in the van, but it was hardly summer outside. It was midday on the first of January, and already it had turned blisteringly cold. Sometimes the bloody van's engine wouldn't turn over in the cold weather. A fine thing it would be if they got stuck here. He wouldn't want to face old man Chase's wrath if that happened. Reluctantly he let go of Rose.

'Let's drive on and see if we can find a caff,' he said instead. 'We might find one that's open on the sea front if we're lucky.'

'All right,' Rose said meekly, knowing she had disappointed him.

She had to admit that she was relieved. Somehow this wasn't the right day or the right time. In the summer, when the sun shone and the birds sang, she could feel less inhibited than she did on a freezing winter's day. She had a young girl's romantic view of being in love, and sometimes she thought that she and Peter had very different ideas about it. She wanted to get married one day, of course she did. It was what all girls wanted. And married people were permitted to do all the things that Peter wanted her to do now.

'What are you thinking about now?' he said testily, when she had been silent for a few minutes on the drive down towards the coast.

'Do you think I'm frigid, Peter?' she said without thinking, and he gave a great guffaw of laughter.

'Well, that's a deflating question to ask a chap and no mistake. I bloody well hope not. Where'd you hear such a thing?'

'I read the word somewhere and I looked it up in a

dictionary. It said something about a female lacking warmth – and other stuff I'd rather not talk about,' she finished lamely, wishing she'd never brought it up at all.

Peter glanced at her. 'Don't worry, darling, you're not frigid – and if you are, I'll soon sort you out,' he added with a leery grin.

Once they reached the coast they parked the car and walked along the sea front with their coats firmly buttoned against the biting wind. There were plenty of other people around, getting some exercise, some walking dogs, others looking gloomily into the windows of closed shops. There was one small café open. It was crowded and it smelled of hot tea and baking and sweating humanity, but at least it was warm inside. They squeezed inside and fought their way to a corner table that had just been vacated.

'You sit here and I'll get us two cups of tea and a couple of currant buns to stave off the pangs of hunger,' he said, struggling back to the counter.

It wasn't Hollywood, Rose found herself thinking. It wasn't a beautiful restaurant at the top of some huge skyscraper overlooking a fabulous bay, she wearing an elegant gown and pearls and the love of her life looking at her adoringly and treating her to a wonderful meal . . . She blinked as the ludicrous thought crept into her mind. It wasn't that she was a girl who wanted everything, or was particularly dissatisfied with her life, but in that instant she knew that Peter was not the love of her life and never would be. She also knew that, just like a heroine in a romantic novel, she would be saving herself for the man she had yet to meet.

She saw Peter weaving his way through the other customers with a tray of tea and currant buns held high, mildly cursing anyone who got in his way. Rose fixed a smile on her face. It wasn't his fault that he didn't stir her as much as he thought he did, and nor did he know what was coming to him. He wouldn't like it, of course. He would sulk, like a small boy deprived of his favourite toy, but she couldn't go on letting him think that she was his girl when she didn't want to be. It was so strange to be thinking such a thing when she had so looked forward to this outing; she wondered if she was truly going mad.

'This is nice,' she said dutifully, biting into one of the currant buns while he slurped at his tea as if he had a cast-iron throat.

'This will warm the old cockles, anyway, whatever the hell they are. Isn't that what your mum says in that weird way of hers?' he said with a grin.

Rose smiled, on safer ground now. 'She says lots of things like that. Once a Londoner, always a Londoner, I suppose.'

Peter studied her. She was a beautiful girl, and he could imagine that her mother had looked just like her when she first came to Somerset. No wonder the Chase brothers had flirted with her. Chase by name and Chase by nature, he thought, admiring his own wit.

'She never went back though, did she, after she married your dad, I mean?'

He wasn't really interested. He was just making idle conversation, but he might have known she would take it seriously.

'She went once, to visit her old friends, and one of them came down here for a few days when I was little. They say that you can never really go back, though, can you? I don't mean just physically, I mean mentally too. Once you make your choice in life and burn your bridges, so to speak, that's it.'

'Christ Almighty, Rose, you're getting all book-learning again. I thought we were out to have some fun, not to talk about the meaning of life.'

'Well, you started it,' Rose said, taking a gulp of tea that was too hot and too strong and gasping at the sting of it.

For no reason at all, she was suddenly depressed. She had been very young when her mother's friend Tilly, with whom she used to work at the shirt factory in London, had come for a short visit to see Rose and the infant Lucy. Yet Rose could remember it as vividly as if it was happening right now. She could picture the pretty fair-haired Tilly bouncing Lucy on her knee while Rose was supposed to be having her afternoon nap. Instead, she had climbed out of her mother's bed and crept to the top of the stairs to listen to this vision and her mother talking in that rapid way they had that wasn't always easy to follow. But the words she had heard that day were easy enough to understand, even for a small child, and they had stayed hidden in her memory all this time. Until now.

'Are you feeling all right, Rose?' she heard Peter say sharply. 'Your face is all white and pinched. Drink up and let's get out of here. You need some fresh air, girl. We'll take our currant buns with us. We can't waste good money by leaving them behind.'

Meekly she did as she was told, feeling like an automaton as Peter pushed his way through the customers, making a way for her to follow. It had been hot and stuffy in the café, but once in the open air, the cold air hit her like blast of ice, and she felt momentarily faint.

'Peter, I need to go home,' she muttered, and he could see by her face that there was no point in arguing.

Half an hour later they were well on their way, and Rose hoped desperately that she wasn't about to throw up and disgrace herself completely. Peter's face was grim as he drove them along the frosted lanes towards home, and she knew this wasn't how he had wanted this day to turn out. Well, neither had she! The van had got cold standing in the wind, and it had been touch and go whether it would start at all, and he'd snapped that he'd be in queer street with his dad if it was out of action for his rounds tomorrow. Once he got it going, he said he had to keep it moving, but now there was a strong smell of petrol mingling with the stale vegetable smells in the back, not helping Rose's churning stomach.

By the time the van pulled up outside the Chase house, the engine still running and spluttering, she almost fell out of it, gasping that she'd be all right when she'd had a lie down and then she'd see him for work in the morning.

'I'll see you tomorrow then,' he called out as she tottered towards the front door. She didn't look back. She just waved her hand in his direction and fell into the house as soon as the door opened.

When Alice heard the door slam she appeared with a frown on her face. 'Couldn't you be a bit quieter, Rose? I didn't expect you back yet, and Bobby's having his afternoon rest on the sofa, and I don't want him waking up yet.'

On hearing her mother's words, the forgotten memory

Rose had been trying to ignore came back at her with such force that she almost reeled backwards, and probably would have done if she hadn't been leaning against the door. Alice's expression changed at once.

'What's wrong, love? Are you ill? Is it your little friend?'

Rose couldn't answer for a moment. Her 'little friend' was the way her mother referred to her monthlies. But it wasn't that. It had nothing to do with that. How could she say what was burning to be said? How could she ask the questions that were swirling around in her mind now? How could she possibly ask her mother if what a three-year-old child had heard all those years ago could be true, or if she had imagined the whole thing?

'It's probably something to do with that coming on,' she said in the end, knowing she was being a coward and unable to stop herself.

'I'll make you a hot-water bottle and a nice cuppa when I've got the washing in, then.'

'Oh, I don't need that, Mum, really,' Rose said quickly, feeling an idiot now. 'I'll help you with the washing.'

Alice looked at her thoughtfully. Something was up, but she didn't know what. She didn't have what some folk called the countrywoman's second sight. She was still a Londoner through and through, despite having lived here all these years, and if something was wrong she preferred to be told straight up, and not have to guess. But everyone was entitled to have secrets if they chose . . .

They walked outside to the washing-line in the yard, where Walter's long johns were so stiff and frosted they looked as if they could walk off the line by themselves. The two women wrestled with the wooden pegs, half of which were stuck fast to the clothes, when a new thought occurred to Alice.

'Peter didn't suggest anything you didn't like today, did he?' she said.

Rose gave an awkward laugh. 'No, of course not. It was just too cold and miserable at the beach today, so we decided to come home, that's all.'

'That's all right then.'

Rose hesitated. 'Mum, how do you know if you're in love?'

'Good Lord, what a question!' Alice said as they bundled

the solid collection of clothes into a basket and took it indoors to thaw out in the scullery. Bobby had just woken up on the sofa and was gazing vacantly into space with his thumb in his mouth as his senses slowly returned.

'Yes, but how do you know for sure?' Rose persisted, hardly knowing why she did so, but finding it somehow important to get her mother's opinion on this. 'It must be the most awful thing in the world to think you love somebody and then find out that you didn't. You might even marry a person and then find out you'd made a mistake. It would be too late then, wouldn't it?'

She blundered on, knowing she shouldn't be doing this, raking up suspicions that might mean nothing at all. Asking such questions in front of a three-year-old who wouldn't be taking any of it in, but who might store away the words in his little mind and remember them years later . . . She realized she was referring to herself as much as Bobby and she turned away from her mother in embarrassment.

Alice spoke quietly. 'All I can tell you, love, is that if you have to ask yourself the question, then you're probably not in love. If that's what's happening between you and Peter, then you've got your own answer, and it's much better to find out sooner than later. Now then, you go and make us that tea while I sort Bobby out and get him some milk.'

Rose did as she was told. Her mother hadn't been evasive and had answered her honestly, but she hadn't told her anything she didn't already know. She had spoken in such a general way that it would be shameful for Rose to let the suspicions from that newly remembered long-ago conversation nag away at her.

In any case, her mother had spoken in such a low voice at the time that Rose admitted she couldn't always hear her words clearly, but Tilly's voice had been higher and shriller, and it had carried easily to the ears of the small listener.

'I always wondered about it, you know, Alice,' Tilly had said in an anxious voice. 'There wasn't much to choose between 'em when we met, but it's too late now, ain't it? You've made your bed, as they say, and you've got two lovely little babes to show for it, so there's no use worrying about it, gel.'

Rose wished desperately that she could blot out the words.

They had meant little to a child, but she was hearing them from a woman's perspective now. All those years ago there had been a choice to be made, but Walter was the man her mother had married, and Walter was a loving husband and father, and it would be going against the Bible's commandment to honour thy father and mother if she let herself wonder for a single moment whether Alice had truly married the love of her life. Rose vowed that she would never think about it again.

Three

It was obvious to Rose that her sister was in a foul mood by the way she flounced about in their bedroom while she was getting ready for bed that night. She didn't say much, other than making loud tut-tutting noises and heavy sighs, but finally Rose could stand it no longer. She had come upstairs ten minutes earlier than Lucy, and now she lay in her own bed with her hands behind her head.

'If you've got something bothering you, why don't you come out and say it, Lucy? I'm not a mind-reader!'

'Who said I've got something bothering me, and why would I want to tell you if I did?'

'Because I usually get the brunt of it in the end, and the longer you delay it, the longer it will be before we go to sleep,' Rose said mildly, refusing to be ruffled.

The silence continued as Lucy jumped into the other bed and then thumped her pillow as if she had a furious grudge against it.

'Don't you ever want to better yourself, our Rose?' she said at last.

Rose twisted her head now, hearing the frustration in her sister's voice. They usually found night time, in the dark, was the best time for speaking their minds and airing their problems, and it was a sure bet that Lucy had one of major proportions now.

'In what way?' Rose asked cautiously.

'Well, we all know you think the sun shines out of Peter Kelsey's eyeballs, but he's only a grocer's son, isn't he? If you married him, you'd be just as much of a shop girl as you are now. It's still a step up from what I'm doing, though, and I hate it.'

Rose hid a small smile. For a kitchen maid, her sister

certainly had big ideas, but it wasn't fair to crush anybody's dreams. Instead, she spoke honestly.

'Well, you can be the first to know that I'm definitely not going to marry Peter Kelsey. We've had some good times together, but he's not the one I want to be my husband.'

Whatever was on Lucy's mind was forgotten instantly when she heard this important snippet of information. She sat up again, her long sandy hair falling about her shoulders, and her voice was eager. 'Does that mean I can have him, then?'

Rose burst out laughing at the question, not thinking for a second that she should take her seriously.

'Good Lord, Lucy, he's not a plaything to be passed from one girl to another. I thought you said he was "only a grocer's son"! Besides, I haven't told him yet – not properly, anyway.'

She hadn't told him anything at all, she thought uneasily. They had just spent a less enjoyable day together than usual and it had all ended uncomfortably. As far as Peter was concerned, though, she was still his girl, when she knew she definitely no longer wanted to be. The realization had hit her as keenly as a bolt from the blue, and she knew she would have to tell him very soon.

'Well, I don't suppose you'll want to go on working at Kelsey's if you've finished with him, so will you put in a good word for me to have your job for a start?' Lucy asked.

Rose's heart jolted. Her thoughts hadn't gone that far ahead, but Lucy was cuter than she was when thinking about the future – and capitalizing on it too. Rose had always liked working at the shop, but perhaps her sister had a point. How could she go on working there every day if she was no longer Peter's girl? It would be embarrassing for them both, and for his father too.

'I don't want to talk about it any more,' she said, 'and you're not to mention this to anyone, do you hear? Nothing's been decided yet, and I still have to choose my moment to talk to Peter about it properly.'

'He won't like it,' Lucy said slyly. 'He thinks a lot of himself, and he won't be pleased to think you want to finish with him.'

'Well, if it's going to upset his self-importance so much,

I'll just have to make sure he thinks he's doing the finishing, won't I?'

Pigs might fly, she thought. She had her pride too, just as much as Peter did. It hadn't occurred to her that Lucy, little Lucy, sweet sixteen, might not only be thinking that working in Kelsey's shop was a step up for her, but that going out with the boss's son could also be to her advantage.

She had given Rose something to think about, though. Peter was an arrogant young man, and it was obvious that she wouldn't want to continue working at the shop when she told him she no longer wanted to see him, any more than he would want her there. But she had to work somewhere. The question was: where?

The New Year festivities were quickly put aside as things got back to normal in the community. The weather was quickly turning colder, and the local housewives came into Kelsey's shop bundled up in coats and scarves and heavy boots.

'I think January's a foul month, Rose,' the butcher's wife commented as she came in for some potatoes and winter cabbages. 'Me and Herbert always look forward to the spring.'

'My mum always says we shouldn't wish our lives away,' Rose said with a smile, 'but I think it's good to have something to look forward to. I don't mind January so much, because it's my sister's birthday on the twenty-seventh and my mum's on the twenty-eighth, so we've always got a bit of celebrating to do then.'

'You've got a nice family, Rose. How old will young Lucy be?'

'Seventeen.'

'My goodness, almost a young lady, then. She'll be courting soon, I daresay.'

Rose laughed now. 'Not if Dad has his way. He still thinks we're all infants, and I think he'd keep us that way if he could.'

They were no longer infants, though. Lucy's figure might not be as well-developed as Rose's yet, but there was a lot of near-adult smouldering going on in Lucy's pretty head, even if Rose was the only one to see it.

'A penny for them,' she heard Peter's voice say softly as

the butcher's wife left the shop. She gave a start, remembering the conversation she and Lucy had had in bed last night, and knowing she had to get things sorted out between them soon.

'I was thinking I want to talk to you some time.'

'We're talking now,' he said, treating her to one of his dazzling smiles.

'Not here,' she said, as more customers came into the shop, rubbing their hands together and stamping their feet. 'I mean a proper talk, Peter.'

He looked at her oddly, as if he could see right through her and knew exactly what was going on in her head. But he couldn't know, she thought in panic. She hadn't been so standoffish yesterday that he could have had any inkling – could he?

'After work then,' he said at last. 'There's something I want to talk to you about as well.'

Her heart thumped as she turned to serve the next customer. Now that she had made up her mind to do the finishing, the last thing she wanted was the humiliation of hearing him say the same thing. She knew she was being a real dog in the manger, but she couldn't help it. She needed to be in control – which was ironic, because she was getting so flustered now that she gave the customer the wrong change for her purchases and had to start all over again.

'Hello, Rose love,' she heard a familiar voice say a little later, and she looked up to see her Aunt Helen enter the shop. 'I've come in for a few leeks, and a few other odds and ends while I'm here. I'm making a leek and potato pie for my menfolk on this cold day. It's your uncle's favourite.'

She was always cheerful, Rose reflected. She was very fond of her Aunt Helen, and her Uncle Mick too, and she refused to let any other thoughts about him come into her mind.

'I bet Jack finds it cold clearing the ditches in this weather, doesn't he?' she said, remembering what he'd told her he'd be doing at the farm today.

'He's young and fit, and a bit of healthy outdoor work never hurt anyone. We all need to breathe God's good clean air, even if most of it's scented with the smell of cow dung around here,' Helen ended, laughing at her own joke.

'Is that a dig at me for working in a shop, Mrs Chase?'
Peter put in lightly. 'Do you think it's woman's work?'
'You know me better than that, Peter. We all have our
place in this world, and if yours is being part of a family
business, then you're doing God's work as much as the next
man. I'll have a swede and a turnip as well, please, Rose.'
Rose saw Peter squirm. Her aunt wasn't overly religious,
but she had the uncomfortable habit of quoting the bible
whenever it suited her. She also rather fancied her status in
the community, being the wife of the local vet. And *that* was
a job he wouldn't want, thanks very much, Peter had once
said to her. Shoving his hand up some cow's backside when it
was giving birth wasn't his idea of a good time. Anyway, it
was a bit suspect, doing stuff like that, he'd added crudely,
making Rose go crimson with embarrassment at the implication.

'How's young Bobby?' Aunt Helen asked as she prepared
to leave the shop. 'I thought he looked a bit poorly on New
Year's Eve. Your mother should see that he's kept warm
through these winter months. Tell her to rub some goose
grease on his chest to keep out the cold.'

'Mum follows the doctor's advice for him, Aunt Helen,
and you know he's always extra snuffly at this time of year.'

'Yes, well, you can't be too careful with young 'uns,' her
aunt said as a parting shot. 'Give your mother my love and
tell her I'll pop round to see her soon.'

'Interfering old trout,' Rose heard Peter mutter.

Rose spoke defensively. 'I'm very fond of her, and she
just thinks she knows a thing about doctoring, whether for
people or animals, with my uncle being a vet.'

'She thinks she's a cut above the rest of you and that's
for sure. Her old man can keep his messy job, too.'

'We've been through all this before,' Rose said, becoming
irritated at his snide remarks, even though she partly agreed
with them. 'I don't know why you criticize my family. I
never criticize you and your dad, do I?'

'That's because the Kelseys are perfect,' he grinned, sliding
his hand around her waist while the shop was temporarily
empty. But he soon dropped his hand as his father came
bustling in from the back room.

'Now then, what are you two up to?' he said with a wink at Rose. 'Time enough for shenanigans when we've shut up tonight, my lad.'

'We're not up to anything, Mr Kelsey.'

Rose was suddenly annoyed with the pair of them. They could turn the simplest remark into something unpleasant and questionable. She didn't consider herself a prude, but it got very wearisome when everything had to have a double meaning.

'Oh-ho, Rose is getting on her high horse again,' Henry Kelsey said. 'Have you been saying things you shouldn't, Peter?' he added, poking his son in the ribs.

Rose gave a heavy sigh. She had intended to bide her time before saying what she had to say, but before she knew it the words were slipping out of her mouth. 'I might be leaving your employ soon, Mr Kelsey. I'm thinking of getting a different job, so it's only fair that you should know right away.'

It was hard to say which of the men was more astonished, but then Peter's face went dark with anger.

'What sort of a different job? And why didn't you say anything about this yesterday?'

She was agitated, already wishing she hadn't blurted it out so recklessly. 'I hadn't decided yesterday, and I don't know what kind of a different job yet. I just feel I'm in a rut – and besides, you don't really need a third person here, do you?'

The shop door tinkled as two women entered the shop, and Henry Kelsey spoke sharply to his two assistants. 'You two had better go into the back and settle your differences before you upset all our customers.'

Rose moved swiftly ahead of Peter, feeling her heart thump uncomfortably. She hadn't meant to do it this way at all, and she could imagine what her father would say if she went home and told him she was out of work, especially through her own stupidity. The Chases weren't poor, but they weren't rich either, and with Bobby constantly needing medicines, every wage packet was important.

'What's got into you, Rose?' Peter said savagely, grabbing her arm so tightly that it hurt. 'I thought we were all right – and a damn sight more than all right, if you know what I mean!'

'We were.'

'What does that mean?' Peter snapped, his hold on her arm becoming stronger and making her wince.

'It means I don't feel the same as I did, and to save any embarrassment, I think it would be best if I didn't work here any more. Is that so hard for you to understand?' she blurted, all in a rush.

The pain in her arm was making her close to tears now, but she'd be damned if she was going to let him see it. She blinked angrily, and finally shook herself free. But if she thought he was going to beg, she was mistaken. His eyes flashed as furiously as hers.

'Well, if that's how you feel, you can get your coat and clear out right now. You're right about one thing, too. Me and Dad don't need another assistant. You were only here under sufferance, because I fancied you.'

Rose gasped at his brutal words. At least it saved her the embarrassment of asking Henry Kelsey to take on her sister, she thought fleetingly, and a damn good thing. She'd hate to think that Lucy might succumb to Peter's flattery – or worse. For all Lucy's grown-up thoughts, she was still an innocent, and Peter's wiles were anything but. He'd made it pretty clear that Rose had never been more than a plaything to him. He'd said he loved her, but she doubted if he even knew the meaning of the word.

She held her head up high and reached for her coat from its peg with trembling hands. She had to keep control of her emotions now, even though she knew they would collapse as soon as she had time to think about what she had done.

'Please tell your father I've left from the back of the shop,' she said stiffly. 'I'm sure he'll be honest enough to see that the wages owed to me are sent round to my house.'

She fumbled with her coat buttons, rammed her hat on her head, and wound her scarf tightly around her neck to cover her shaking lips. Peter stood with folded arms now, and watched her go without saying another word. *So much for undying love*, Rose thought miserably. So much for the love of her life . . . But no, he was never going to be that, she reminded herself as she stepped purposefully out of the shop. She was still shivering inside, and she stood quite still for a few moments, unsure what to do next. She felt disorientated, knowing that in an instant she had not only burnt her bridges in the only job she had known, but had also ended nine months of being Peter's girl.

She swallowed the sudden lump in her throat. It had felt good to be half of a couple, and now she was on her own. No young man, no job . . . She wondered again what her parents were going to say. Perhaps she had been foolish to do what she had done, but the job was only part of the problem. The memory of the conversation she and her mother had had so recently came back into her mind. There could be nothing as soul-destroying as knowing you had committed yourself to the wrong man. And, for Rose, that man was Peter Kelsey.

She squared her shoulders and walked away from the shop. The ideal thing would be for her to find another job quickly, before she had to face her parents and tell them she wouldn't be bringing in a weekly wage for the time being. She had said she was sure Henry Kelsey would honour whatever wages were due to her, but in reality she couldn't even be sure of that, considering she hadn't even told him herself that she was leaving. It was turning into an awful mess, Rose thought, and she had brought it all on herself by being so reckless.

A soft fall of snow began to blind her eyes and she brushed it away quickly. The first snow of the new year was something to wish on, according to an old country tradition, but there were so many old country traditions around here that only the old folk paid any attention to them these days. This time, though, Rose found herself wishing hard that some good luck would come her way. She sent up a silent prayer to the heavens that everything would be all right . . .

She hardly noticed where she was going until her knees struck something hard, and she winced as she saw she had bumped right into a baby's pram.

'I'm so sorry, Mrs Stacey,' she gasped, recognizing the doctor's wife. 'I wasn't looking where I was going. I haven't hurt the baby, have I?'

She peered into the pram at the six-month-old infant, who gurgled up at her and made her give a hesitant laugh. Mrs Stacey smiled. 'No harm's been done, Rose, but what are you doing out here? Doesn't the shop have enough to keep you busy today?'

It was an innocent enough question, and one that Rose would normally have laughed off, except that right now she didn't feel like laughing. In fact she felt more like crying, and to her horror she felt her chin wobble. All she could think about was how awful it would be to cry in public, and the next moment she felt the woman's arm around her shoulders.

'This seems to be a good time for a hot cup of tea and a friendly ear. I've finished all I had to do this morning, so why don't you come back to the house with me and tell me all about it? Doctors' wives have to be good listeners, you know, so I won't take no for an answer,' she added kindly.

Rose nodded, although it seemed quite bizarre to be walking along with the doctor's wife and the baby until they reached the most imposing house in the village, as befitted a doctor's home and surgery. Rose had been here often enough before, when Bobby needed medicine, or when she was sent for something to ease her father's gout when he was bellowing that he couldn't put his foot to the ground, or when any of the Chase family needed medical advice. But she had never been to the Staceys' living quarters above the surgery and dispensary, and she felt awkward at being treated more as an equal than a patient.

Once they were inside, it was clear that the baby had had enough fresh air and was now fretful, waving her little fists about.

'Take off your coat and scarf, Rose, and then be a dear and pick her up for me while I put the kettle on, will you? I know you've had experience in handling little ones from your own brood at home.'

Mrs Stacey went through to the adjoining kitchen, leaving the door open between them, and Rose thought that neither Lucy nor Tom would care to be thought of as little ones, but Bobby was still at the sweet stage where he didn't object to being picked up and cuddled. She did as she was asked now, and lifted the Stacey baby out of the pram, breathing in her warm musky scent.

'That's better, isn't it, sweetheart?' Rose murmured. 'Now you can see what's going on all around you.'

The baby gazed back at her, wide-eyed, and then gave her a toothless smile.

'I think she's taken to you, Rose,' Mrs Stacey called out with a laugh.

'Oh, I think all babies respond to a kind word and a smiling face, don't they?'

'Not all of them, my dear. You should hear some of the bawling ones who come into the surgery sometimes. It takes more than a smiling face from my poor husband to placate them, but that's confidential, of course.'

'Oh, of course,' Rose said hastily, thinking it was the oddest conversation to be having with the doctor's wife. 'What's the baby's name, Mrs Stacey?'

'She's called Mollie, after my mother, and with any luck she's inherited her placid nature, although things will probably change once she starts crawling and asserting her own personality. I'll have my work cut out then, between looking after her and helping my husband with his paperwork and so on.' She smiled as Rose gently bounced Mollie on her knee and was rewarded by gurgles and more toothless smiles. 'Mollie's definitely taken to you, Rose. You wouldn't fancy a job as a mother's helper, I suppose?'

It was probably only said as an afterthought, not to be taken seriously, but Rose's heart began to thump.

'You don't mean it, do you?'

Mrs Stacey brought in two cups of tea and a plate of biscuits on a tray and put them on the table. She paused for a moment, and then she said slowly, 'You know, I rather think I do. Look, Rose, if you've got nothing else to do, let's have a bite to eat and then we could talk about it once you've told me your troubles and why you had such a sad face when we met in the village earlier on.'

An hour or so later Rose walked home feeling completely bemused. The snow had already stopped, and a brief, cold burst of sunlight had taken its place. There hadn't even been enough of a fall to make any slush; just enough to dampen the streets and then it was gone.

Just enough for someone to make a wish . . . and for that wish to come true.

She wasn't even sure how she really felt about it. She had managed to restrain herself from weeping on Mrs Stacey's accommodating shoulder, but still it had all come out, all the mixed-up feelings about Peter, the gradual realization that she didn't want to be his girl after all, and then those horrible final moments when she had flounced out of the shop and surrendered a good paying job into the bargain.

'I couldn't go on working there after all that, could I, Mrs Stacey?' she had said passionately. 'It would have been so embarrassing.'

'It would, and I doubt that Master Peter Kelsey would have made it any easier for you. He's a handsome enough young man, but he's got a sharp tongue on him. You made the right choice, Rose. And if you really would like to think about the job of mother's helper, go home and talk to your mother about it, and perhaps you can both come here in a few days' time to discuss it. Meanwhile I'll tell my husband I've found an angel to care for Mollie.'

Rose didn't think she deserved any such title, but it lifted her spirits all the way home. Her mother had been baking, and she looked up in astonishment when she saw her daughter come home in the middle of a working afternoon. The warm, homely smell of the fruit cake rising in the oven made Rose's mouth water, and it was such an idyllic scene after her traumatic day that the emotions simply washed over her and she burst into tears.

'What's happened, Rose?' Alice asked quickly.

The words poured out of Rose's mouth. 'I've walked out on my job at Kelsey's, I've finished with Peter, and if I have your approval I can have a new job as a mother's helper for the doctor's wife. It's all happened so fast I'm all at sixes and sevens now. I don't know what you're going to think, or if I've even done the right thing!'

Alice still had her Londoner's quick wit for evaluating a situation at once. She took her girl in her arms for a moment and then moved back from her, looking straight into her eyes.

'Well, for a start, is your heart telling you you've done the right thing in walking out on your job and finishing with Peter?'

'Yes, I think so,' she said hesitantly. 'In fact, I know so!'

'And a job as a mother's helper for the doctor's wife would suit you very well, Rose. It would also be very useful to have you on hand, so to speak, when we needed any medicines or special treatment for the family.'

She sounded so serious that Rose didn't realize for a moment that she was teasing. It was only when her mother's face broke into a smile that it became obvious that she definitely had Alice's approval for all that had happened that day.

'But what do you think Dad will say?' she said.

Alice was still smiling. 'You leave your dad to me, girl. Now go and get in some practice by getting Bobby up and giving him a drink.'

She watched her go upstairs, her lovely elder daughter, who had learned a valuable lesson so early in life. Alice didn't give a fig that the liaison with Peter Kelsey was over, no matter what his status in the community. It was far more important to know when your heart wasn't in a relationship and to have the courage to end it, and she applauded her girl for that. Not everyone had that courage.

Four

Despite Alice's assurances, Walter was not so ready to accept the new situation.

'I don't know why the girl couldn't be content with working for Henry Kelsey. Good God, the man's been a friend of this family since before Rose was born, so what's he going to think about her throwing a tantrum and storming out like that? And what about all the vegetables he was happy to send our way at half price, eh? She didn't stop to think about that, did she?'

'Walter, for goodness' sake,' Alice snapped. 'Can't you see there was more to it than that? Would you have wanted Rose to be embarrassed every time she set foot in the shop now that she and Peter are no longer walking out?'

Walter's eyes narrowed. His foot was giving him hell today and he was in no mood to be bothered with any adolescent nonsense that would probably blow over by tomorrow. But he knew his wife would expect some reaction and so he gave a disgruntled response.

'And why is that, do you think?'

'Perhaps she realized he was the wrong man for her.'

She didn't notice the uneasy look that flashed across his face. Walter wasn't the most articulate of men, but he loved his family with an earthy passion, and he loved his sparky wife the most of all. The fact that he knew very well that she was never quite sure which of the two Chase brothers she should have married was something he kept strictly to himself. Once such a thing was put into words there was no going back, so providing the thoughts were only inside his head, it was supposition and nothing more. But he also knew well enough to back away from provoking an argument when Alice was so defensive about Rose.

'Well, I daresay no harm's been done,' he went on less aggressively. 'Me and old Henry Kelsey have known one another too long to let the doings of our offspring get in the way of two old-timers having a drink and a game of skittles at the Pig and Whistle of a Saturday night. So what's your opinion on our Rose working for the doctor's wife then?'

Alice breathed more easily, knowing she had been in danger of making Rose and Peter's situation a mirror of her own. 'I'm quite happy about it. Mrs Stacey is a genteel sort of person, and Rose will be in good hands there. As for losing out on a few vegetables, it wouldn't hurt you to plant a few for our own use, would it? There's plenty of folk around here who have an allotment and grow their own.'

'Most of the folk don't work all hours the way me and the boy do, so don't start on at me with all that malarkey,' he growled. 'Where's he gone now, anyway?'

'He was going to see Jack, though sometimes I wonder why Jack bothers so much with him, our Tom being so much younger.'

'It's because the boy's got an adult head on young shoulders, that's why,' Walter said predictably. 'He can keep his end up with any conversation young Jack throws at him.'

Although if he could have heard the conversation Tom and Jack were having right then, Walter might not have been so complacent.

'How old do you think you've got to be before you can fly planes then, Jack?'

His cousin laughed indulgently. Although he'd sluiced himself thoroughly to rid himself of the underlying farm smells they still lingered, but in a family well used to animals it was considered a healthy smell, and right now he was happy enough to stretch out on his bed and answer Tom's eager questions.

'Older than you are, kid. About eighteen, like me, I daresay, unless there's another war. If that happened, they'd probably take anybody who looks old enough. You're tall for your age, so you might just about pass.'

'If a war comes then, that's what I shall do. I'll pretend

I'm eighteen and join up,' Tom said from his cross-legged position on the floor.

Jack sat up. 'For Christ's sake, you idiot, don't even think about it! People get killed in wars and I don't fancy being blown out of the sky. Our granddad was killed in the last lot, remember.'

'Well, since neither of us knew him, I can't get too het up about it.'

Jack threw a pillow at him. 'You're a callous little bugger, aren't you?' he said with half a grin. 'Don't let any of the parents hear you saying such things, or we'll end up having to listen to a lecture about having more respect for our elders, and how bloody terrible it was in the trenches and all that stuff.'

They'd heard it all before, anyway. On the anniversary of Granddad Chase's death, all the faded photographs came out, along with his one medal, and both Mick and Walter reminisced about their father and the hero he had been – at least to them. Whether he'd actually achieved anything spectacular during his few short months serving in the Great War was never explained, but after the ritual family get-together on that day, the brothers always went down to the Pig and Whistle later, excluding the rest of them, to drink a glass of ale in their father's memory.

'Our Rose has chucked in her job at Kelsey's,' Tom said idly, veering away from such gloomy reflections.

'What's she done that for? I thought she was courting Peter Kelsey.'

'Dunno. Perhaps he got too free and easy for her.'

'Oh yes. And what would a little whippersnapper like you know about a bloke getting free and easy with a girl?'

Tom threw the pillow back at him. 'I wasn't born yesterday. I don't need to watch farm animals doing it to know what goes on, either.'

'Tried it, have you?' Jack said, the grin spreading over his face now. At eighteen, he had far more knowledge than Tom about the birds and the bees – and about girls, too. He'd had a little dabble with the farmer's daughter until they both got tired of the sport and mutually decided to give it up. But he'd bet on it that this kid didn't know what day it was when it came to courting.

'No, I haven't tried it,' Tom said crossly. 'Only under the sheets at night.'

Jack laughed out loud now. He loved baiting the little squirt, and he knew damn well that Tom enjoyed their little spats, which were never serious. There might be four years between them but they had always got along very well, and the family ties between them were strong.

'Oh well, I always knew you were a handy sort of chap,' Jack mocked, and then got up off the bed. 'Look, I've got things to do now, but I might see you tomorrow night. Dad and me are going down to the church hall. They're having a meeting there and it might be worth listening to.'

'Oh God, it sounds as boring as hell. What's it about, anyway?' Tom said.

'About the bloody government, and the possibility of another war and what can be done to stop it, if anything. I bet your dad will turn up too. Interested now?'

Lucy's reaction to Rose's news was predictable. She brushed aside the reason why Rose had walked out of Kelsey's, and showed only a fleeting interest in the idea of her sister getting a new job with the doctor's wife. Instead, Lucy's eyes shone with the possibility that was open to her now.

'So there's no reason why I can't ask to take over your job at Kelsey's, is there?' she said. 'If Mum agrees, I could go this evening.'

'Not so fast, Lucy,' Rose said at once. 'I'm not sure Mr Kelsey will be taking on anyone else. Sometimes there's hardly enough work for two people to do, let alone three. It probably wouldn't be such a good idea.'

'Why not? Are you jealous because you think Peter might take a shine to me now that you're out of the running?'

Rose started to laugh. 'No, I'm not jealous of any such thing. I know you'll find a nice boy of your own one day, but Peter's too old for you, anyway.'

Lucy's eyes narrowed. 'What happened between you then, or is it a waste of time asking? Did he – you know – try anything?' Unknowingly she echoed her brother's thoughts, her voice dropping to a whisper that was both excited and nervous.

'For pity's sake, why do people instantly think something like that? I was the one to finish with him for the simple reason that it just didn't feel right any more. I was fond of him, but I didn't love him, and it wasn't enough.'

Even as she said it, she couldn't help feeling a pang. She had been his girl for a long time, and it felt odd to know she wasn't walking out with him any more. It would be even odder to see him with some other girl. Knowing how full of self-importance he was, Rose had no doubt that it wouldn't take long. Peter wouldn't want it known that he didn't have a girl hanging on to his every word, like a kind of trophy. It had taken her a long time to see it, but she saw it now, and she wouldn't want that new girl to be her sister.

'Trust me, Lucy,' she said more gently, 'he wasn't the one for me, and he's certainly not the one for you. Besides, what about that young stable lad you were telling me about who's just started work at the Grange? Len, isn't it?'

'It's *Ben*, as you very well know,' Lucy corrected her. 'Well, I suppose it would be a shame to leave there just as I'm getting to know him. And he is nice. He showed me around the stables the other day.'

'There you are then,' Rose said, knowing how easy it was for Lucy's thoughts to be diverted, and hoping that this Ben was as nice as he sounded.

In any case, she had other things to think about. She and Alice were going to see the doctor's wife in a day or two to discuss the offer of Rose's new job, which she was perfectly sure she was going to accept. The more she thought about it, the more she liked the sound of it. It would be almost like having a baby of her own to care for, but when she said as much to Alice she received a stern warning.

'The one thing you must never do, Rose, is to start imagining that the baby is your own. She's not yours and never will be. Of course you will care for her, but you must never get too attached to her. It's only a job, Rose, and you must always remember that.'

'I know that!' Rose said, surprised at her mother's vehemence.

'That's all right then,' Alice said more quietly. 'It's just that I wouldn't want you to blind yourself to a life of your own, because you became too attached to someone else's child.'

'You're not sorry I finished with Peter, are you, Mum? I know Dad made all those silly remarks about his friendship with his father, but you wouldn't want me to go on seeing Peter when I no longer cared for him in that way, would you?'

'Of course not; you know my feelings about that, Rose.'

Alice didn't intend to say any more, for fear she might give too much away about her feelings on another matter. They had been kept tightly under control for long enough now, and they were private.

'Your dad's going out to this blessed meeting tomorrow night,' she said, changing the subject. 'There's sure to be raised voices and probably a lot more when they get started on the government, if I know it. Tom says he's going with him, which has pleased your father, although it doesn't please me.'

She frowned as she said it. Young boys only saw the adventurous side of wars and fighting, when those old enough to remember what had happened in the last war knew far more, and never wanted such an atrocity to happen again. Too many young lives were lost. Too many young men never came back . . . and too many young women were left grieving because of it.

'Tom will be all right, Mum,' Rose said encouragingly. 'Anyway, I daresay Uncle Mick will be there as well, and he'll keep Dad's temper under control,' she added with a laugh.

'Oh yes, Mick could always calm things down,' Alice said. 'He was always more of a thinker than your dad. Walter acts first and thinks later.'

'I'm sure there won't be any trouble,' Rose went on, seeing her mother's frown deepen. 'If it's in the church hall, the vicar will be in charge, and he's not going to let things get out of hand.'

Alice looked at her daughter. Right now her face was glowing, the way it used to be when she was seeing Peter, but that was all over now, and Alice concluded that it could be that the prospect of a new job was enough to get her girl anticipating a different future, and she was glad for her.

'Let's forget them all,' she said with an effort. 'Whatever they decide, it will be mens' words that sort out the future, so there's no point in worrying about it.'

Bramwell church hall was anything but quiet by the time the Chase men and their sons arrived there the following evening. Posters had been stuck on trees and placed in shop windows in the village to announce the purpose of the meeting, and the hall was already more than half full, and not only with local men. The vicar and several speakers sat on the platform, shuffling papers and looking uneasily from time to time at the crowds who were filling the hall. It was intended to be a civilized and serious meeting, but there were known troublemakers infiltrating, and Mick noted the local constable taking up his position at the rear of the hall.

'A fat lot of good he'd do if things turn ugly,' Mick commented. 'He couldn't stop this mob in a month of wet Sundays if they began fighting.'

Walter had already made a nodding acknowledgement towards Henry Kelsey, who nodded back amiably enough despite the rumpus that had occurred between Peter and Rose, and then Rose walking out of her job. *Bloody kids*, Walter found himself thinking. Then he nudged his brother. 'The Collier boys have just come in,' he muttered. 'That doesn't look too healthy, either.'

The Collier boys were three brothers from a neighbouring village who could be relied on to turn up at any meeting where they could heckle and cause a fight. It was well known that they still engaged in bare-knuckle fighting, even though it was banned, especially when local fairs came to the area, and that they secretly organized the occasional cock-fight. Anything for a bit of a gamble, no matter how illegal it was, and since it was all done behind closed doors, so to speak, they were never caught. They were also known for breaking up meetings, whether it was just for sport or because they had been put up to it for a few bob.

Tom Chase was too busy looking around for his cousin to heed what his elders were saying and Mick now leaned forward to speak to the boy.

'You won't see our Jack here until later tonight, Tom. It's a wonder I got here myself. I was up at the farm where another of their cows had a difficult calving, and Jack's staying up there for a while in case he needs to call me back.'

'I only came because of Jack,' Tom said indignantly.

'Well, keep your mouth shut and listen, and you might learn something useful,' Walter growled. 'There's more to war than fancy ideas about flying aeroplanes about the sky.'

'Leave the boy alone, Walt,' Mick said mildly. 'He's only a babby still – let's hope he don't have to learn anything more than what's in his comic papers.'

Tom wasn't sure whether to be more aggrieved at being called a babby or the reference to his comic papers. They were far more than that to him. They told stories of heroes and villains, fighting against terrible odds. The heroes always won through in the end and returned home to an adoring public, and in his dreams Tom was always one of them.

From the platform the vicar rapped a gavel on the table to call order, and the meeting began quietly enough with speeches from one or two of the spokesmen, but it soon got out of control. Whenever individual government names were mentioned there was heckling and cat-calling from the back of the hall, and Neville Chamberlain's name produced the worst of it for being an ineffectual Prime Minister. What with running down the government and ranting with dire warnings about the rise of the German chancellor, Adolf Hitler, it was hard for the speakers to make themselves heard as other people tried to shout down the rabble-rousers, and the meeting quickly developed into an undignified slanging match.

'Get the bloody government out,' was one of the constant shouts. 'The bastards are nothing but warmongers, the lot of them.'

'Sit down and shut your noise, you stupid buggers,' returned others. 'Let the gaffers have their say.'

'We don't want no more wars!' came the retorts. 'We don't want no more women and children left fatherless just to fill the government's pockets.'

To a fourteen-year-old boy, half the comments didn't make sense, and it was more exciting than scary. Tom's heart thudded wildly with the thrill of it all as people kept leaping to their feet and waving their fists about, often connecting with those nearest them. After nearly an hour, when the meeting was becoming a farce and seemed to be going nowhere in terms of a resolution, Tom saw his cousin trying to push his way through the crowds towards him. He stood up, waving both arms furiously. Jack waved back, and for some reason the troublemakers saw this exchange as a signal for action. They leapt forward, pushing Jack in front of them, just as the more tolerant of the men decided they had had enough and it was time to leave.

Suddenly everyone was on their feet at the same time, ignoring the remonstrations of those up on the platform. The constable's futile whistle did nothing to stop the stampeding feet coming towards him. He bellowed that they should move out in an orderly fashion or they would all be arrested for obstructing a police officer in the course of his duty. Nobody heeded him. Those who were trying to get out were hindered by those attempting to get to the front of the hall and yank the speakers off the platform.

'It's a put-up job,' Walter yelled to his brother. 'We'd best get the young 'uns out of here before they get hurt.'

It was obvious now that the Collier brothers and their supporters were intent on fighting anybody who got in their way. They were a vicious crowd and there were going to be plenty of black eyes – and worse – by morning.

Jack had already disappeared, presumably having worked out what was happening, and was making his way outside. Mick tried to protect Tom by ushering him in front of him, while Walter, always the bigger and stronger one, lashed out at anybody who was in his way as they tried to reach the door of the hall.

They were almost outside when there was a new uproar accompanied by the sound of breaking glass, and the constable yelled to everybody to watch themselves as bottles were broken.

'Christ, let's get the boy out of here,' gasped Walter. 'We don't want to be witnesses to any injuries.'

The next moment he felt something sharp and jagged on his cheek, and he gave an agonized shriek as the hot blood spurted out. The perpetrator didn't stop to see the damage he had done as Walter clamped his hand over the wound and lurched outside into the fresh air. He almost collapsed with the sting of it as the cold air hit the gaping flesh, and then Mick was dragging him away from the hall, their terrified sons rushing behind them.

'My place is nearer than yours. We'll get you there until we see how bad it is,' Mick croaked. 'You may need stitches, but I can patch you up with some stuff from my surgery for now.'

'I don't want bloody horse remedies,' Walter roared. 'You can just stick a bit of tape over it and let me get off home.'

'Shut up, Uncle Walter,' Jack said sharply. 'Dad knows what he's talking about, and you'll probably need to rest after an attack like that.'

'I'm no bloody simpering woman needing to rest!' Walter roared again, and continued to rant until they reached the vet's house and surgery.

The sounds of shouting and police whistles receded into the background and, despite himself, he knew he was near to fainting. He gritted his teeth hard. He'd never fainted in his life and he didn't intend to start now.

The boys ran ahead and by the time the two brothers reached the house the door was open and Mick's wife was waiting with a damp cloth for Walter to press against his face until they saw how much damage had been done. He sank down heavily on a chair, refusing to admit how light-headed he felt, and asked Helen hoarsely for a glass of whisky.

'That's not such a good idea,' Mick said at once.

Walter glared at him. 'Well, if it kills me, at least I'll go out with a smile on my face, so don't argue for once.'

Mick nodded, and Helen fetched him a small glass of whisky, which Walter downed at once. It brought back some colour to his white face, but as yet they still hadn't seen what damage the broken bottle had done. Mick suddenly caught sight of Tom, shivering in the corner of the room, and realized how frightened the boy was. Maybe this was a lesson in just how brutal men could be to one another, he thought, but this wasn't the time to start moralizing.

'Tom, why don't you go home and tell your mother that

your father's had a small accident, but that he'll be fine when I've seen to him,' he said in the reassuring way he spoke to anxious owners of favourite pets. 'It may be best if your dad spends the night here, so that I can keep an eye on that wound, although he should really see the doctor.'

'No doctor!' Walter snapped at once, just as Mick knew he would. 'You can let your mother know what's happened, Tom, but don't alarm her. And we've never spent a night apart since we were married, so I don't aim to start now.'

'Go with him, Jack,' Helen said quickly, as the young boy hesitated, still shaking visibly.

The cousins left together, and then Mick gently removed the damp cloth from Walter's cheek. He tried not to draw in his breath too audibly as he saw the vicious wound. It definitely needed stitches, but Walter had an aversion to doctors, and he knew he would never agree to it. Not unless Mick did it himself . . .

'Let's get him into the surgery where I can clean him up,' he said to Helen, 'and then we'll decide what to do.'

'A bit of tape is all it needs, man,' Walter growled, but the words were becoming slurred – not only from the whisky, but from the shock of the attack, the loss of blood, and the stinging pain.

Mick and his wife helped the bigger man to the surgery, where he slumped on to a chair. Mick examined the wound, careful not to show too much alarm.

'You'd better lie down on the examining table,' he said finally. 'I'm going to give you a hefty injection in that cheek, because I've got to remove some bits of glass inside the wound and it won't be pleasant unless your face is numbed. You'll feel drowsy afterwards, especially after that whisky, but don't let it bother you.'

Somehow Walter found himself lying on the scrubbed table that had seen so many sick animals receive Mick's diligent attention. Mick put a small cushion beneath his head and prepared the injection. The sting of it momentarily halted his brother's muttering protests and moments later Walter's whole face went numb and he felt sheer panic.

'What the hell are you doing to me?' he mumbled. At least, he thought he was speaking, but his lips felt as if they no longer belonged to him, and Helen gently wiped away the dribble that he couldn't feel.

'Just lie still,' Mick ordered. 'Good God, man, I had less trouble with that cow in labour than I'm having with you.'

Walter tried to smile, but it didn't work. He felt increasingly light-headed after the injection, and his eyes felt so heavy that he could no longer keep them open, and he was obliged to close them for a few moments. He was vaguely aware of feather-like sensations on his cheek, and of muted voices nearby, but it was such a relief to feel the excruciating, raw pain diminishing that the need to sleep became overwhelming. In a last lucid moment he wanted to ask his brother what the hell had been in that injection that could put a horse to sleep, but it was all too much of an effort and he gave in to the inevitable . . .

Five

A lice and her daughters were listening to the wireless when Tom and Jack burst into the house that evening. Jack had warned his cousin to break the news gently, but as soon as she saw her son's ashen face, Alice dropped Walter's grey sock that she had been darning and leapt her feet.

'What's happened?' she gasped.

'It's Dad!' Tom couldn't contain himself any longer. 'He's been hurt and Uncle Mick's fixing him up, but there's a lot of blood, Mum . . .'

Jack shook his arm hard. 'It's not as bad it sounds. He got struck in the cheek with something when the meeting went wild, and Dad says he should see the doctor, but he won't, so he's gone to our house instead, and Dad thinks he should stay there for the night.'

Alice was already fetching her coat and hat, and the girls were also making for their coat hooks. Alice turned to them.

'No. You two stay here. It doesn't need all of us to crowd on your auntie and uncle, and remember that Bobby's asleep upstairs. We can't all leave him.'

They made token protests, but Alice was adamant. Inside she was shaking with worry, and with fury too. All these years she had faced the possibility of Walter being injured in a job that could often be dangerous, and now this. All because of a stupid fight at a meeting that was intended to establish community solidarity through wanting peace and not war.

'I'm coming back with you too,' Tom said at once and, seeing the determined look in his eyes, Alice knew it would be useless to forbid him.

They practically ran all the way back through the village, by which time Alice had a gnawing stitch in her side. The fury had subsided now, and she felt only a great fear for what state her husband would be in. These boys wouldn't have told her everything. They probably didn't know everything, anyway, and she was desperate to hear what Mick had to say. He wasn't a doctor, but he was the next best thing. As if he could see inside her head and share all the emotions she tried so hard to suppress, she felt Tom's hand grip hers as they neared the house.

'He'll be all right, Mum,' he said jerkily. 'You know our Dad. He's as tough as old boots.'

He couldn't think of any better way to put it, and Alice squeezed his hand in return, knowing he was doing his best to cheer her up.

Helen was waiting for them. 'Mick's still with Walter in the surgery, Alice, so when you've seen for yourself that he's going to be all right, I'll have a strong cup of tea ready for you. You go on through, and leave these boys with me.'

Alice did as she was told, feeling like an automaton now. Her feet were moving, and she knew the way into the surgery well enough, but she dreaded what she was going to see.

The smell of antiseptics and lingering animal scents assaulted her nostrils as soon as she opened the door. She prided herself on being a capable woman, able to deal with anything, but she hadn't felt so faint since she was expecting Bobby and feared that she must be ill rather than expecting a late baby.

Walter was still lying flat on his back, partially blocked by Mick, who turned at once and gave her a reassuring smile.

'Don't worry, Alice, he'll live, even if he's likely to sleep it off for a while due to the hefty dose of anaesthetic I gave him,' he said in a voice that was intended to reassure her.

He moved aside, and Alice could see her big, strong husband lying immobile on the examining table, with the jagged slash on his cheek stitched together and his whole cheek covered in some antiseptic red stuff. He looked as peaceful as a baby now, eyes closed and snoring gently. And without warning, Alice burst into tears and her legs felt as though they were turning to jelly.

The next moment she felt Mick's strong arms around her, holding her up.

'Sit down and put your head between your knees and take some deep breaths, Alice,' she heard Mick order. 'You've had a shock and it's only natural that it's taken you this way.'

She felt herself being led to the small couch where the anxious owners of Mick's patients could sit while he examined and treated their pets. She sat down without knowing that she did so, and felt him gently pushing her head down to her knees.

'That's right, deep breaths now,' he said. 'You wouldn't believe the number of times I've said that to people who are filled with relief that their pets are going to be all right.'

He didn't mention the other times, the far sadder and more emotional times, when the owners had to go home without their beloved pets.

Alice was vividly aware of the warmth of the arm around her shoulders, aware that someone was stroking her hair in a way that was surely far beyond the professional attentions of a vet. But this wasn't just a vet. This was Mick, whom she had known as long as she had known Walter . . . And as if to remind her of why she was there, Walter gave an involuntary snore that was louder than all the rest.

She straightened up slowly, but not before she thought – or imagined, or hoped – that she had felt the touch of Mick's lips on her cheek. Her heart thudded. He always kissed her in a brotherly way on occasions like Christmas and birthdays. Helen would kiss her and Walter too, because they were all one family, and it was never anything more than a gesture of genuine affection between them all.

'Are you sure that no real damage was done, Mick?' she mumbled, not knowing what else to say, but suddenly aware how piquant those words could be if she once let herself think too deeply of what might have been – and could still be in her guiltiest, wildest imagination, involving the three of them here in this room . . . and Helen too . . . and all their children . . . and breaking too many hearts.

'I'm quite sure,' he said, releasing her. 'But I'm going to stay with him for a while until he rouses, because if I don't get him off this table, he's likely to fall and make things worse. He'll need to stay here tonight so that I can see how things are in the morning, and you know you're welcome to stay too. Walter always boasted that you've never spent a night apart.'

'He'll have to do as he's told for once, then,' she said clumsily. 'I need to be at home with the children, Mick, and I'm sure Walter will be more comfortable sleeping on his own tonight. But I thank you for the offer.'

Did Mick really think she wanted to sleep under the same roof as him? And what madness was such a thought when her husband was lying here injured?

'Then you can be sure we'll do everything we can for him, Alice.'

'I know you will.'

As her eyes met his, she knew with certainty that however tenuous her feelings were, they weren't all on her part. In her heart she had always known that the sentiments in those long-ago letters were his words, even if Walter had written him. And she knew, as surely as she breathed, that nothing would ever come of those feelings now. It was too late, far too late, to ever think of breaking up two marriages and an entire family. The time for that was past – if it had ever existed.

'Thank you for all you've done, Mick,' she said steadily, back to being his brother's wife who was grateful for his expertise and his care.

She leaned over and kissed her husband's good cheek and heard his snuffling response. 'I'll be back in the morning, my dear,' she said softly, and then she left the brothers alone and went back to join Helen and their sons.

'Now then, Alice. You'll have seen that Walter's as well as can be expected, as they say, so just sit yourself down and have this cup of tea,' Helen said, pouring out the dark-looking brew at once. 'This has been a nasty shock for you.'

'For Walter too,' she replied, trying to smile. 'It's very good of you and Mick to let him stay tonight, Helen.'

'Nonsense. That's what families are for – to help each other. Mick's spent many a night caring for one of his patients, and he's always been a stickler for checking on them until they're well again. Walter will be as right as rain, though I'll guarantee his face will sting like billy-oh when the injection wears off.'

'You're good friends, as well as family, Helen,' Alice said.

'Are you staying here tonight, Mum?' Tom put in.

She shook her head. 'I'll wait until your dad starts to come round, but then you and I must get home to let the girls know he's all right. I'll come back to see him tomorrow, and you'll have to tell Mr Wakeman at the sawmills why your dad won't be there for a few days.'

'He won't like that – Dad, I mean.'

'Well, he'll just have to do as he's told,' Alice said for the second time.

Half an hour later they heard movements in the surgery, and then the two brothers emerged together. Walter was leaning heavily on Mick and his eyes were bleary.

'I don't know what the hell was in that stuff he put in my face,' Walter growled in a voice that was still doped and unlike his own.

'Whatever it was, it'll be a damn sight more comfortable for you than if I'd stitched you up without it,' Mick said smartly.

'So what do you think of me now, woman?' Walter said as Mick eased him gently into a chair where he sat, seemingly exhausted.

'I think you're still my handsome husband underneath it all,' she replied, not sure if she was reassuring him or herself.

Walter gave a lopsided smile and closed his eyes.

'Well, I think the sooner Jack and I get him upstairs and into a comfortable bed the better,' Mick said briskly. 'When you come back in the morning, Alice, I'm sure he'll be more alert, and ready to go home.'

She wasn't sure if she was being dismissed or not, but as Walter lumbered towards the stairs with the support of the two men, she felt useless and unnecessary, and she suddenly wanted to get out of there. She gulped down her tea, hardly noticing the scalding heat, and told Helen she must get back to her girls.

Once outside in the night air, she took some long deep breaths, and Tom gripped her arm again.

'Don't worry, Mum. You can trust Uncle Mick, and if he says Dad will be all right, I know he will be.'

Having got over the initial shock now, Alice's anger exploded.

'I don't know what the point of that blessed meeting was, anyway. What good do you think it will do? If the government decide to play at being soldiers, nothing we say will do anything to stop it. I thought they had all learned their lesson in the last war without sending more young men abroad to die.'

Tom was shocked at her vehemence. She was normally far more tolerant, and kept a lot of her feelings to herself – but normally she didn't have her husband lying injured on a veterinary examining table.

'Not everybody dies in a war, Mum,' he said uneasily. 'There are plenty who come back as heroes.'

'And there are plenty who don't come back at all, or are sent home in coffins,' she retorted. 'There's nothing glorious about it, Tom, so don't start thinking that there is.'

He kept his trap shut for the rest of the walk home, knowing that it was far too late to tell him to stop thinking about the glories of war. He wasn't daft. He knew people got killed, but they did it for king and country, because they believed in patriotism and the defence of the realm, and all that stuff that women didn't seem to see in the same way that men did. It was so exciting . . .

Rose and Lucy were waiting anxiously for news, and once they heard that Walter was going to be all right, Lucy burst into tears.

'Just like a girl,' Tom scoffed, having had plenty of time to get used to what had happened. 'Once they know he's all right, they start blubbing.'

'Shut up, you pig,' Lucy sobbed. 'Just because you have no feelings, don't think that we don't!'

It didn't come out quite as she meant it, but it shut Tom up all the same. You had to be hard when you were involved in a war, and now that all the drama of the evening was over, his thoughts reverted to the meeting and all that had been said. Even if it wasn't imminent, most of the men at the meeting had thought it was inevitable. Most of the older ones had dire predictions for it all, while the younger ones only saw the thrill of war, and the chance to be a hero.

But he knew well enough that these were also thoughts that were best kept private, and even though his sisters wanted to know more about what had happened at that meeting, he kept it brief, and told them shortly that he was going to bed. He had to be up early in the morning to let Mr Wakeman know why his dad wasn't with him that day, because he had no intention of letting the older chaps get there first and steal his thunder . . .

Rose lay awake far longer than her sister that night. Once Lucy had got over her tears and was assured that her dad was going to be all right, she seemed to adapt remarkably quickly to all that had happened. The real purpose of the meeting and all that it implied simply washed over her.

Rose wasn't nearly as complacent. She always thought Peter Kelsey's father was a bit of a warmonger on the quiet. It was odd that he and her dad got on so well, since they had such differing ideas, but presumably when men went to the pub for a game of darts and a few pints of ale, such differences were forgotten.

Her thoughts shifted to the treatment her uncle had been able to give to his brother that night. Rose had always admired her Uncle Mick, and in his way he was as clever as any doctor. Vets had to be, since they were doing the same kind of work with animals as doctors did with humans. They both made diagnoses, stitched up wounds and operated on the sick. They were special people, in Rose's opinion. All the same, she shuddered at the imagery of some of the unpleasant things they must have to do.

She thought instead about her prospective new job, and her spirits lifted. Caring for Mrs Stacey's baby would be a joy, and although this probably wasn't the right time to press her mother on coming with her to see the doctor's wife, she knew it had to be soon. Without a job to go to, she would feel oddly rootless – and besides, her mother would be glad of whatever money she could add to the family coffers from her wages. She had to earn her keep. It was a matter of pride as much as anything else . . . Finally she fell asleep, dreaming of the pleasure of caring for baby Mollie. It would be almost like having a baby of her own.

The following day, Mick Chase told his brother he would drive him home in his van at midday. Predictably, Walter insisted that he was all right and could walk home perfectly well, but Mick was having none of it.

'You'll thank me once you get a smell of the wind outside,' Mick snapped. 'It's bitter today, and once the cold air hits that wound, you'll know it! But I've got work to do this morning, so I can't do it until later.'

'You should listen to Mick, Walter,' Helen put in. 'He knows what he's talking about, so you just stay there on the sofa and put your feet up in front of the fire and be patient. Think of yourself as a man of leisure for once.'

Walter snorted. 'That'll be the day when I laze about like a woman all day,' he growled, which resulted in Helen slapping a bundle of newspapers on his lap and telling him he could occupy himself with making firelighters instead of riling her. 'You should count yourself lucky that Mick was on hand to help you,' she admonished him.

'Well, of course I do, woman. I know I've got a lot to thank Mick for.'

He started tearing the newspapers into strips, ready to start twisting them tightly and fashioning them into the slow-burning firelighters. There was never any shortage of wood in his own household, since he and the boy could always bring home the shavings and offcuts from the mill, and there was many a time when he'd brought a bag full for his brother's family. But Helen was a thrifty woman who never wasted anything, and throwing out newspapers once they had been read was definitely wasteful in her opinion.

'You're a good woman, Helen,' Walter said involuntarily.

She went pink at the unexpected compliment, but before they could both squirm with embarrassment he went on quickly, 'Anyway, I won't wait for Mick to drive me home in the van. As soon as Alice arrives, we'll be off, and I shall get back to work tomorrow.'

'I'm not sure that's such a good idea. In any case, you'll need to see Doctor Stacey about removing those stitches when the time comes.'

'Why do I need to see the bloody doctor?' he said, belligerent at once. 'Mick put the stitches in, so why can't he take them out?'

Helen sighed, sensing opposition. Sometimes she wondered

how Alice put up with him. 'It's really a doctor's job, Walter. Mick was there in an emergency, but I'm sure Alice will say the same, and I'm not going to argue with you about it. I've got beds to make – and please mind your language.'

Without giving him time to say anything more, she went upstairs. Leaving him to do women's work, Walter thought, savagely continuing with the newspaper firelighters. And why hadn't Alice arrived yet to see how he was doing? Or Rose, now that she had no job to go to? He wasn't a man who indulged in self-pity, but for a fraction of a second he felt as if his womenfolk had abandoned him as if he was already on the scrap heap because of one little scratch on his face.

He scowled and without thinking he brushed his hand across the wound, and then cringed as the action creased the stitched cut and sent shooting pains through his cheek. He was still smarting when Alice turned up at the house.

'Not too good then?' she said at once.

'I'll live,' he said shortly.

'I've made an appointment for you to see Doctor Stacey at three o'clock this afternoon.' Before she could say any more, Walter was bellowing at her.

'What the devil did you do that for? You women are all alike!'

Alice gave a small smile, relieved to see that his injury didn't stop him being his usual self. It was oddly reassuring in an irritating way.

'I see Helen's already mentioned it to you,' she said mildly. 'Well, it's done now, and Rose and I are also going to see the doctor's wife at the same time, so you've got no excuse for getting out of it, because we'll be coming with you.'

'I don't need a damn nursemaid, woman,' he muttered, the stinging pain of his wound taking away his self-confidence for the moment.

He looked so put out that Alice felt really sorry for him. She had no patience with hot-headed men who put themselves in the position they all had on the previous night, and she'd already given Tom a good lecture on the foolishness of it, but this was her man and he was hurt. She leaned forward and pressed a kiss to his forehead, squeezing his shoulder in sympathy.

'That you don't, love,' she agreed. 'But Rose is anxious to get her new job settled with the doctor's wife, and we thought it seemed like a good idea for us to go together. We'll have to take Bobby along too, of course.'

He gave a small scowl, aware that she was taking charge. Womenfolk! But Alice had a canny way of letting him know he wasn't getting out of this.

'Oh, God damn it, let's go home,' he grunted, and she knew she had won.

Tom had gone off to work full of importance that morning, and Lucy had left for the Grange, eager to cause a little stir of excitement by telling the new stable lad what had happened. Rose had looked after Bobby while her mother went to fetch Walter, but she was anxiously looking out for their return now, and had already warned Bobby that his dad would have a funny mark on his face. She hardly knew what to expect herself, but her eyes filled with tears when she saw the ugly wound, and the stitches that held it together.

'Now, don't start piping your eye, girl,' Walter said at once. 'It's nothing that can't be fixed, and your Uncle Mick made the best job he could of it.'

'Mick's a good man,' Alice murmured.

Bobby was staring at the red antiseptic stain surrounding Walter's injury, his lips puckering. 'Does your face hurt, Daddy?' he said.

Walter would normally have laughed off the child's fears, picked him up and swung him around, but he still felt a mite groggy after all the anaesthetic that Mick had pumped into him, and wisely he sat down and pulled Bobby over to sit him on his lap.

'Do you remember when you fell over and scraped your knee last week, and your mum washed it and put some ointment on it?' he said.

Bobby winced, remembering. 'It hurt!'

'But now it's better, isn't it? Well, my face hurt last night and it still hurts a bit now, but in a few days, just like your knee, it will be as right as rain again, so don't you worry about your old dad.'

Alice smiled at the undoubted affection between them, and the way Walter reassured his small son. How could she ever have thought he was unfeeling? She realized he was looking at her now, even though he was still talking to Bobby.

'Your mum's taking me to the doctor, same as she takes you when you're poorly, and that's nothing to worry about either, see? We're all going together, you and me, your mum, and Rose.'

'Is Rose poorly?' Bobby asked, his attention diverted.

Rose laughed, taking him off her father's knee, knowing that he'd soon start fretting that too many people in his family were getting ill.

'I'm not poorly, love, but I'm going to be looking after the doctor's baby instead of working at the shop.'

'Why can't the doctor look after it?' Bobby said at once.

'Because he's too busy looking after everybody else,' Alice put in smartly, before the questions got out of hand. 'Now let your dad get some rest.'

Truth to tell, Walter wasn't sorry to have a rare day off work. It was about the first time he'd done so in years, and he imagined that this was how a gentleman of leisure must feel, with nothing to do all day and no need to half kill himself in all weathers in order to earn a crust for his family. It took less than an hour before Alice was muttering about him getting under her feet, and for him to be bored from reading the newspaper twice and pottering in and out of the house – mostly indoors, because of the sting of the wind on his cheek. Mick had been right about that.

The morning dragged, but at last they were all ready for the walk through the village to the doctor's house, and Walter began to realize he was an object to be stared at and whispered about.

'What's wrong with folk today?' he grunted. 'Haven't they ever seen a man walking out with his family before?'

'Well, not one with stitches sticking out of his cheek, and the gossip about why you needed them,' Alice told him.

He clamped his lips together for a moment, but there were

things to be said, and he was never a man for keeping them in when they needed to be got out.

'Are you blaming me for getting hurt now, woman?'

Alice could be as outspoken as her man when need be. 'I'm blaming you for putting yourself in that position in the first place. Just as if a group of country folk could make any difference to the way the country's going, anyway. You should leave that to those who understand it.'

Rose knew the signs of an impending argument, especially when it came to the country versus the town, of which Alice was still very much a part, no matter how long she had been away from London. Rose walked on ahead of them, holding on tightly to Bobby's hand. As they passed Kelsey's shop she caught sight of Peter inside. She waved to him, and was shocked when he simply ignored her. But his father came outside as soon as saw the little procession, and asked his old friend how he was feeling today.

'Like a bloody peep show,' Walter growled.

'Well, it looks like the doc needs some new glasses,' Henry Kelsey agreed. 'I've seen better stitching on a bed quilt.'

Walter couldn't let this pass. 'He's not responsible. My brother patched me up, and thank God he did, or I'd be in a sorry mess by now.'

Henry Kelsey nodded. 'Your Mick were always a good 'un when it came to fixing other folks' pets, but I've never known him stitch up a man's face before,' he finished with a chuckle. 'Still, I suppose it's a kind of doctoring, and he made the best of a bad job.'

Alice couldn't stand any more of this oaf's patronizing. He may be able to weigh and sell vegetables, but he didn't have an ounce of Mick Chase's talent.

'We're all thankful Mick knew what to do, and did it quickly,' she snapped.

Henry turned his attention on her. She was a fine-looking woman, but a mite too outspoken for his liking. The daughter was the same, and he wasn't too sorry after all that his son had finished with her.

'Oh ah, Mick always knew what to do, even when he were a sprightly lad,' he said. 'He had the brains, while Walter here had the brawn – and we needed a bit of that last night, didn't we, old boy?'

He slapped Walter on the shoulder at the back-handed compliment, but his eyes still gleamed at Alice. She linked her arm through her husband's, making them a complete unit as she said they'd better not stand there gossiping or they'd be late for their appointment if they didn't get a move on. Anything to get away from the calculating eyes of Henry Kelsey.

Six

B y the time the Chase family left the doctor's house, they were in varying moods. Rose was ecstatic at having been welcomed so warmly by Mrs Stacey, and also by the fact that baby Mollie seemed to remember her at once. Alice was satisfied that her girl was being given a good opportunity in life, and starting her new job the very next day, and Bobby had been fascinated by the baby.

It was only Walter who stumped along in a black mood at having been kept waiting so long before he could see the doctor, and being subjected to whispers and stares from several old biddies who had appointments before him. And then he was told in no uncertain terms that he shouldn't return to work for at least a week until the stitches were out. Walter had exploded at once.

'There's nothing wrong with my hands, man. I can still use a saw and a plane, and do anything else the boss asks of me.'

'And if you do, you're quite likely to find flying splinters of wood striking your face,' Doctor Stacey said keenly. 'The wound has to knit together properly, and if any of those splinters worms its way into your cheek and causes an infection, you could be in for serious trouble. I'll give you a note to give to Mr Wakeman.'

'You'll be paying my wages as well then, will you?' Walter yelled. He wasn't overawed by a doctor as some folk seemed to be, and even though he knew the words made sense, he wasn't prepared to give in too easily.

Doctor Stacey gave a half-smile. 'Knowing your wife to be a thrifty woman, Mr Chase, I've no doubt she's regularly paid a few coppers into an emergency club to help you at such times. I doubt that the loss of a week's wages will mean that any of you will starve. Now then, I'll just write this note, and then you can leave me to see more appreciative patients.'

After that Walter had no choice but to rejoin his family, with the prospect of twiddling his thumbs at home for a week.

'There's plenty of things you can do,' Alice told him calmly when they were back at the house and had taken off their outdoor things, rubbing their hands together to get the circulation going again.

'Like what?'

'Well, for a start you can take Bobby out sometimes. If the pond's frozen, he'll enjoy watching the birds skim across it, scavenging for food.'

'What, and join all the other nursemaids? Our Rose, for one!' he roared.

Alice held her temper in check with an effort. 'Walter, I know this is hard for you, but did it never occur to you that I might even like your company at home for a week? I'm not saying I'd like it permanently, mind, but it will be nice to see you not being exhausted after a day's work at the mill.'

It was on the tip of his tongue to say that an honest day's work had never exhausted him in his life, but seeing how blue and sparkling her eyes were at that moment, she looked so much like the Alice he had first seen so long ago that he somehow resisted. Instead, he gave a rueful smile.

'I can be a right bastard sometimes, can't I, girl?' he said gruffly.

'Only sometimes,' she replied, squeezing his arm for a moment. 'But we've got something special to look forward to at the end of the month, and you did promise to do something about it.'

'Oh ah, and what was that?' he said, letting her go.

'You promised to make a sewing box for Lucy's birthday. It'll be a good chance for you to do it while she's at work, so she doesn't get wind of it.'

'So I did, and it's just like you to make the best of a bad job,' he said, with undisguised admiration. 'And if I'm in my shed for most of the day, I won't be under your feet, I suppose.'

'We'll both be happy then, won't we?' Alice said with a smile, thinking fleetingly that he would never know just how adept she had been at making the best of a bad job all these years. But that wasn't fair, she told herself. Walter was a good husband who was proud of his family and provided for them all, and she was lucky to have him. Luckier than her old friend Tilly, who had come to the seaside with her all those years ago. Tilly had always been a terrible flirt, but she had never managed to hold on to a man of her own, and was still doing the same kind of sweatshop work they had always done and earning her own living.

She didn't know why Tilly had come into her mind just then except that she fully expected to hear from her at the end of the month. For all that some folk thought her flighty, Tilly never forgot birthdays, and there were always cards for Alice and Lucy, since their birthdays were only a day apart, plus the occasional letters the old friends exchanged. Alice was touched at how she always kept in contact this way, even if there was never much news for Tilly to tell, and she always felt it pointed to the comparatively empty life Tilly led. When they were young, they had both confidently expected to be married with a brood of children. Alice had done that, and life was never less than busy, but it had somehow always eluded Tilly.

She shook herself and went to make Walter a strong cup of tea to keep out the cold, and later on she was going to make a beef broth for them all, to warm the cockles. She smiled again. Already she was reverting to her old London way of thinking, just by having thoughts of Tilly.

Lucy burst into the house like a whirlwind that evening, her eyes sparkling. She threw off her gloves and didn't even resort to the lanolin she studiously rubbed into her hands before she did anything else at the end of each day to cover the redness. Being a kitchen maid meant dealing with all kinds of dirty and wet jobs that took no account of tender young skin.

'Mum, I've been offered a different post by Mr and Mrs Frankley, and you've got to let me take it. You've just got to, or I'll die!' she ended dramatically.

Walter emerged from behind his newspaper and stopped her at once. 'Now just hold on, young lady, and don't start dictating to your mother about what she's got to do. Whatever it is, you've got to have my say-so before anything else.'

Alice put her hand on his shoulder. It was easy to see that Lucy was far too excited to consider any right or wrong way to go about things, and nor had she been expecting to see her dad sitting in an armchair at this time of day. She gulped, seeing his frown.

'I didn't mean to be disrespectful, Dad. But it's a great chance, and you've got to let me do it!'

Rose came downstairs from settling Bobby in bed and asked what all the fuss was about. Lucy turned to her in relief.

'Oh, Rose, you'll be on my side, won't you? Mrs Frankley's looking for a new parlour maid and the cook recommended me, and I had to see Mr and Mrs Frankley in the drawing room this afternoon, and they say I can have the job if Mum and Dad approve. It's a big step up, Rose, but the only thing is,' she gulped again and didn't dare look at her parents, 'I would have to live in.'

'You mean leaving home?' Alice exclaimed.

'That's what living in usually means, Mother,' Walter said dryly.

Rose took Lucy's hands in her own, her face as animated as her sister's.

'I think it's wonderful, and a lovely start to a new year, both of us with exciting new jobs. When do they want you to start, Lucy?'

Walter broke in at once. 'Now hold your horses, both of you. Nobody's agreed to any wild ideas about Lucy leaving home to go and live at some posh house and putting on airs and graces.'

Lucy turned on him. 'I've been working there for ages already and I haven't put on any airs and graces, have I, Dad? Anyway, I'll be seventeen in a couple of weeks' time, and quite old enough to leave home. Of course, Mrs Frankley will want to talk to you about it first, Mum.'

'Me?' Alice said. Her mind was in a whirl. When Lucy had got the job of kitchen maid, it was because she knew one of the other girls who worked there, and it had been Cook who had hired her, not the lady of the big house.

It was one thing to be talking to the local doctor's wife about Rose's new job, but it was another thing altogether to think about entering the Grange and having to sit twiddling her thumbs in a posh drawing room. It gave her a severe attack of the collywobbles, even though she knew an interview was inevitable – providing Walter agreed to it, and right now he was looking daggers at Alice.

'Quite right, too. You don't think a girl could take a live-in job without her mother seeing that everything's above board, do you, woman?' Walter snapped.

As if everything else that had happened in the past few days wasn't enough, he could feel the start of the telltale stabbing in his toe, and knew he'd be in agony before long, but as Lucy flung her arms around his neck he realized too late that he had virtually given his approval.

'Oh, thank you, *thank you*, Dad! As soon as I let Mrs Frankley know she'll arrange a proper appointment, Mum.' She laughed out loud as she danced around the room. 'I'm going to be a parlour maid and wear a uniform,' she almost sang.

'Well, right now you can come into the kitchen and help me dish out this beef broth for your family, miss,' Alice said, unaccountably irritated.

She should be pleased for Lucy, and in her heart she was. But she had the oddest feeling that this was only the first break in the family. She had always assumed it would be Rose to go first, marrying a nice young man in the natural order of things. That would happen in time, she was sure of it. But now it was Lucy leaving home, and one day it would be Tom, and then there would just be herself and Walter and Bobby. *Oh, thank God for Bobby*, she thought guiltily.

'Mum, are you all right?' It was Rose who was right behind her in the kitchen now, while Lucy was still chattering excitedly to her father.

'Of course I am.'

Rose hugged her for a moment. 'I'm sure she'll never change, whatever Dad says. She'll still be our Lucy, whatever she does, and you have to let her go, Mum. You can't hold on to any of us for ever.'

Alice flinched, wondering if Rose was a mind-reader now. 'I know that, and I'm glad for her. I'm more worried about myself, if you must know, having to go inside that big house and make small talk with the gentry,' she said.

It was true, but it also made her sound like a shrinking violet, and she had never been that. Coming to Somerset from London to marry a man she hardly knew had proved that. But she had been young then, not too much older than Lucy was now, and when you're young, you think you can do anything.

She was annoyed with herself for being so feeble now. Lucy must have spoken to Mrs Frankley before now, however briefly. Was Alice dumb enough to think she couldn't hold up her head as well as her own daughter? The next minute she felt someone else's arms around her shoulders.

'Thank you, Mum,' Lucy said breathlessly. 'I promise I won't let you down.'

Alice knew she was the one who had been in danger of letting her girl down, and she gave her a quick smile. 'I know you won't. Now, you slice some bread to go with the broth and let's get on with it, or your father will be saying I'm starving him.'

Later, as they all sat around the big table talking animatedly, with Tom home now, assuring his father that his workmates had all sent their good wishes to him, and with Bobby sleeping soundly upstairs, Alice wished she could somehow put their good humour into a bottle and keep it there for ever. Even Walter seemed resigned to the fact that Lucy would be leaving home, although she could see him wince now and then, and knew that the gout was troubling him again. A good thing, then, that he didn't have to go off to the sawmills for a week and drive all his workmates mad as well. Once he started spending time in his shed, working on the sewing box for Lucy's birthday, it would keep his mind and his hands occupied. And it would save her having to snap at him too often for getting under her feet.

'What are you staring at me for, woman?' Walter said, although she hadn't even realized she had been doing so. He left the table and hobbled over to the sofa to sit down heavily.

'I'm just thinking perhaps I could rub some embrocation

on your toe later, if you could bear it,' she said, just for something to say.

'Not bloody likely,' he said, then noting her seething look and hearing Lucy and Tom's giggles, he continued, 'sorry, but the farther away you stay from my toe, the better.'

'Perhaps Uncle Mick could give you something to put on it, seeing as how he did such a good job with your cheek,' Tom said helpfully.

'God damn it, I don't want nobody touching it!' he snapped. 'It's best left alone, same as me, and Mick can stick to his animal doctoring.'

'You didn't say that last night, did you?' Alice said. 'You were daft enough to put yourself in that position and as usual it was Mick who got you out of it.'

He looked at her without speaking for a moment, the only sounds being the ticking of the clock on the wall, the clattering of spoons against dishes as everybody continued with their meal, and Alice's heartbeats.

'What the hell is that supposed to mean?' Walter demanded. 'When did Mick ever get me out of anything "as usual"?'

Alice felt her face flush. She'd said it without thinking, and not for a moment was she referring to the letters from all those years ago, which she was sure had contained Mick's words in order to win her round to marrying his brother. She'd never said that she suspected it then, and she didn't intend doing so now, but from the look on Walter's face, something was making him feel less than comfortable, and she was quite sure it wasn't just the gout.

'It didn't mean anything,' she said finally. 'Just that brothers always rely on one another when things go wrong, and if they can't rely on one another, who can they rely on?'

'Well, Mick's the clever one, and sometimes I think you should have married him instead of me.'

Alice felt her heart leap. Had he really said those words or had she imagined them? Walter was trying to flex his foot now, and she knew he must be in pain. Or was it just an excuse not to look at her face at that moment, for fear of what he might see there? She sat beside him on the sofa and ruffled his greying hair.

'Sometimes I think you're an old fool,' she said softly.

She kissed the top of his head and felt an unexpected rush of love for him. He was far stronger than his brother physically, and she couldn't bear for him to sound so uncertain, however momentarily. She heard Tom giggle again, and then she heard Bobby call out, and she went upstairs quickly to see what he wanted.

She was oddly disturbed at that moment, not wanting Walter to think for a single moment that she had any fond feelings for Mick, other than sisterly ones. She didn't – no more than Mick had fond feelings for her.

And even if he did, she suddenly and irrevocably knew she didn't want them. Her mind cleared, knowing it was true. She was happy with her life, and complications like that were best kept for the fantasies on the silver screen. She swept Bobby's warm little body up in her arms and gave a small sigh, knowing she was definitely back in her proper place, having to change damp sheets and pyjamas as she kissed her baby's small, tearful face.

'Never mind, lovey,' she reassured him. 'We'll soon have you dry again.'

'I had a bad dream,' he said, still snuffling. 'Our Dad was in a fight, and he was all covered in blood, not just his face.'

'Well you can just put such thoughts out of your head. Your dad's not getting into any more silly fights and he's not going to get covered in blood! Now, let's get you sorted out so you can go back to sleep.'

Dreams were like premonitions, Alice thought resolutely. They didn't mean anything. They were best put out of your mind and left to those who believed in such things, while ordinary folk got on with their lives.

They got along surprising well over the next week, partly because Walter's gout had eased off, and partly because both of them were trying especially hard not to ruffle the other's feathers. Rose had begun her new job, and declared that she couldn't be happier in it. And on the appointed afternoon in the middle of the week, Alice was to go to the Grange with Lucy for the interview with Mrs Frankley. That was the only day when nerves almost got the better of her.

'You shouldn't let other folk think they're any better than

you, because they're not,' Walter advised her. 'In any case, you can always imagine them without any clothes on. Folk all look the same when they're as nature intended.'

'Walter!' Alice said. 'I could no more imagine Mrs Frankley – or anyone else – without any clothes on than I could imagine flying.'

He laughed at her pink face. 'Ah well, old girl, perhaps that's best left for the bedroom between man and wife, eh?'

Since Alice invariably undressed with the light out and was usually snuggled beneath the bedclothes in her night-gown by the time Walter came to bed, such talk made her go even pinker than before. It wasn't that she was averse to seeing her own body, nor Walter's, but neither did she think there was any need to do so. To her surprise, he suddenly put both arms around her and kissed her soundly on the lips.

'You go off and do your duty by our Lucy, my little puritan, and later tonight you can do your wifely duty by your husband.'

He must have too much time on his hands if he can think about such things, Alice thought in a fluster. But it was a nice fluster, for all that.

And, in the end, the interview went surprisingly well. It was obvious that the lady of the house was used to dealing with all kinds of folk, and although Alice felt all fingers and thumbs at first, she was soon put at ease as she and Lucy answered the questions that were put to them.

'And you'll have no objection to Lucy living in?' Mrs Frankley asked finally.

'Oh no, Ma'am,' Alice said, flustered again, wondering how anybody could object to living in such a lovely home, even as a parlour maid.

'Good. Then it's all settled. Now I'm sure Lucy would like to show you her room, and she'll be starting her new duties on Monday.'

They were dismissed, and Alice admitted she was relieved to get out of the drawing room with its lovely soft furnish-ings, highly polished expensive furniture, and the huge floral arrangements in what Lucy later told her were called jardinieres, a word Alice had never heard in her life before. It was an elegant room, but it was a world away from what

Alice would call homely. Even the doctor's sitting room where she had gone with Rose was far easier to live in, with its childish trappings and well-worn chairs. The Grange may be the envy of many folk with far less money, but for all that, Alice was quite content with her lot.

'So what do you think of her, Mum?' Lucy whispered when they had climbed the stairs to the servants' rooms at the top of the house. 'Isn't she beautiful?'

'I suppose she is. I hadn't really thought about it.'

Lucy laughed. 'You were more worried about not dropping your cup of tea and disgracing yourself, weren't you?'

Alice spoke sharply as they reached the top landing, holding her side after climbing the steep stairs. 'I certainly was not, and I hope you're not going to start getting above yourself now you're a parlour maid, my girl,' she said, thinking of Walter's words.

It didn't help to know that Lucy was quite right about her being worried, of course, and if it wasn't totally against her nature, she almost wished she'd done as Walter had teasingly advised and tried to imagine the beautiful Mrs Frankley sitting on her silk-covered chair without any clothes on. She shied away from such undignified thoughts at once, and her face now softened at Lucy's anxious look.

'Don't worry, if there's any danger of that, I'm sure your father will cut you down to size every time you come home. And you've got to be there for your birthday, mind.'

'Of course I will, Mum! Now then, this is my room, and I'll be sharing it with Sophie, one of the other maids.'

She flung open a door on the landing, revealing a fairly spartan bedroom, in complete contrast to the rest of the house, although it was furnished adequately enough. There would be no airs and graces from the two girls sleeping here, Alice thought with some relief.

She left Lucy at the Grange and walked home, ready to relate everything to Walter on her return, especially the appearance of the lovely carved wooden furniture, which she knew would interest him. It was always intriguing to see how other folk lived, but in the end there was no place like a body's own home.

She found him bouncing Bobby on his knee, telling him that his mother would soon be stewing the rabbit they had found in the woods for their dinner. Alice gave a small smile. Being a city child, she would once have been horrified to think that a rabbit found in the woods would have to be skinned and stewed before it could be eaten. But country children had no such fears. It was normal and natural to them.

'Did it all go well?' Walter greeted her.

'It was fine,' Alice said, with a sigh of relief. 'Lucy's a lucky girl to have a post in such a grand house.'

'She may not be satisfied with a sewing box her father made her, then,' he went on with a small frown.

'Of course she will! She'll want to take it with her, Walter, and you know she's been talking about it for ages. How is it going?'

The frown changed to a smile. 'Come and see for yourself.'

With all its sharp tools and implements, the shed was no place for a small child, so Alice sat Bobby on the sofa with his colouring books while she and Walter went outside. He removed the protective sheets of newspaper from the object on the bench, and Alice gasped in admiration. Walter was quite a craftsman when he put his mind to it, and the sewing box gleamed with the stain and polish that gave it the finishing touch. He lifted the lid, revealing the compartments beneath for all the cottons and silks, pins, needles and measuring tapes that a young girl could want for her craft.

'It's a real treat, Walter,' Alice said. 'I'll buy a few basic things for it in the village tomorrow, but I know she'll want to choose most of it for herself. I'm sure she's going to love it, my dear.'

It was a good end to a good day, she thought later. A good week, in fact, after the horror of the previous one when Walter had been injured and frightened them all so much. It just proved that you should never think fate was always against you, because better days might be waiting around the corner all the time.

Besides, she thought, cheering up still more, there were the birthdays to look forward to, when she would hear from Tilly again, and Tilly's letters could always make her smile.

*   *   *

The usual letter came with the birthday cards. They were a couple of days early, but that didn't matter. It just extended the birthday celebrations, Lucy always said. Alice opened the letter eagerly, glad to have the house to herself except for Bobby, and to have a bit of peace and quiet to read. Walter was back at work now, his stitches out and looking none too badly despite the scar on his cheek, which Mick said gave him the sinister air of a Hollywood gangster, and Helen said made him look quite dashing. Alice was just relieved that it didn't seem to bother him any more, though for a while it had itched and irritated him as it healed. Rose had suggested putting some cream on to ease it, only to be told that he wasn't going to be some dandy poncing around with face cream on his dial, thank you very much!

Alice forgot them all as she started to read Tilly's scrawling writing and her smile soon faded. This was not the Tilly she knew. This was a woman anxious about herself and about everything else, from the sound of it.

> The doc says I should give up the sweatshop on account of the dust from the wool and cotton getting down my lungs. I don't know what else I'm supposed to do, unless I work down the market, and I don't fancy that. Anyway, the cough's not that bad, but me chest tickles something wicked at times and I take that much linctus in the night it fair makes me head woozy. Still, you got to get on with things, don't you, gel? 'Course, if all the rumours are right and Jerry plans to bomb the hell out of London, it won't much matter either way, will it? There's more daft rumours going around that the government might give everybody some kind of air-raid shelter, just in case. A fat lot of good that would do if a bomb's got your number on it. But I won't go on about it, as it's your birthday and little Lucy's too, so have a good one, Alice.
> From your affectionate old pal, Tilly.

Seven

Tilly's letter put a cloud over Alice's birthday. It was unlike her to sound so anxious. Alice still remembered her as the exuberant girl she had been, not this seemingly downtrodden woman she had become. They had both grown older and their lives had changed, but even so . . . And as for Tilly letting the thought of illness affect her so much, it was almost unthinkable.

'What's got into you, Mother?' Walter asked irritably when she couldn't seem to shake herself out of the gloom. She was still so caught up in the tone and contents of the letter that she didn't even count to the usual ten at being addressed as Mother.

'I'm really worried about Tilly. It could be worse than just dust from the wool and cotton getting down her throat and into her lungs. You and Tom risk that sort of thing every day with the sawdust, but you're outdoors, and Tilly's stuck inside that awful place for hours on end with no air to breathe. I remember only too well what it was like,' she added with a shudder.

She had shown Walter the letter, of course, and he had said brusquely that Tilly should get out of London for a spell if she didn't want to end up in a worse state than she was already.

'She could come here if we had room, but we don't, so don't even think about it,' he said now, a warning note in his voice. 'I'm damn sure our Rose wouldn't want to share a bedroom with her, especially now she's preening herself at not having to share with Lucy any more. She wouldn't want to share a room with a stranger who's old enough to be her mother, especially one who's coughing her heart and soul out every night!'

'I know all that,' Alice snapped, and then said the thought

that had been taking shape in her mind. 'Mick and Helen have got room, though.'

Walter almost exploded. 'Why the hell would they want to take in a stranger who'd keep them awake all night?'

'Perhaps because they've got a bit more humanity in them than you have,' she snapped again. 'Anyway, Tilly's no stranger to them. You and Mick both liked her well enough when we first came to Somerset, and she's been here for a few visits since. Helen was always quite taken with Tilly, and she often asks after her.'

It was a little white lie, because Helen had only mentioned Tilly a few times, but it was true that she and Tilly had got along remarkably well considering their differences in temperament and background.

'I'm not going to ask them, anyway,' Walter said angrily.

'I don't remember asking you to, but unless you're thinking of putting a gag on me now, there's nothing to stop me doing so, is there?'

She glared at him defiantly, her eyes flashing, but even so, she saw his glint of admiration in return. She had never been a little mouse of a woman, and he had always loved her fiery spirit, and she knew darned well that riling him was often the best way to get him round to her way of thinking.

'Well, I seem to remember that when we were wed you promised to obey me, and I reckon any man should take good stock of a woman before he believes all that airy-fairy business! I daresay it wouldn't do me much good forbidding you to do anything you really wanted, would it?'

Her face relaxed as she laughed, and without warning he pulled her to him, and his muscular arms that cut such great planks of wood at the sawmills enveloped her now with surprising tenderness.

'Just as long as we both want the same things,' he said, breathing in the muskiness of her skin and the soft brown hair that she always kept well washed and fragrant. She was a damn fine woman, Walter found himself thinking, and she knew in her heart that he could rarely deny her anything. He might try, and he often did, but if he thought about it deeply enough, Alice usually got her way.

*   *   *

Alice always visited her sister-in-law with Bobby one afternoon every week. It was what they called their gossiping
time, when none of the men were around and they could put
the world to rights in their own way. She set out for Helen's
house that afternoon with Bobby in his pushchair, and her
thoughts were coincidentally along the same lines as Walter's.
The man of the house might be the breadwinner, but any
woman clever enough to want something badly always knew
how to wheedle her way around a man. It was a pity women
weren't in charge of governments and countries, she thought,
and then there would be no more wars. Well, probably not.
Somewhere in her memory she remembered hearing about
Boadicea, the warrior queen of the ancient Britons, and the
warlike Amazon women, so it wasn't always men who could
rouse such passions.

All the same, she was already regretting her reckless comment
about asking if Mick and Helen would let Tilly stay with them
for a week or two. She wasn't even sure whether to say anything
to Helen about it after all. It would be a lovely solution to have
her old friend so close at hand, and in the bosom of the family,
so to speak. But Tilly knew everything about Alice's old doubts
over who she should have married. Fond as Alice was of her,
Tilly could sometimes be a blabbermouth, and it would be
unbearable for Helen ever to suspect . . . But she knew she was
probably being ridiculous and letting her imagination go to
places that were unthinkable.

'A bit fresh today, isn't it, Mrs Chase?' she heard an oily
voice say close by, and she started, so deep in her thoughts
that she hadn't even noticed she was outside Kelsey's shop.
She gave a swift smile at Henry Kelsey, suddenly awkward
knowing Rose and his son had so recently parted company.

'It certainly is, but it's good to get some air in your lungs,
isn't it?'

'Oh ah, nothing better, providing it don't freeze the innards.
And how's your man going on after his little brush at the
meeting the other week?'

'He's back at work now, thank you for asking.'

'Good. Good.' He rubbed his hands together and Alice
realized again just how ingratiating he could be. 'And is Rose
well?'

She could see he was dying to hear that Rose was pining or looking for work.

'Rose is very well. She's working for the doctor's wife now, and it suits her very well indeed. We're all pleased abut it.'

To her annoyance she knew she was repeating herself like a parrot. It was a cold day and she'd stood there long enough with this nosy old fool, and Bobby was starting to fret.

'Excuse me, Mr Kelsey, but my sister-in-law is expecting me.'

'Oh, your sister-in-law, is it? Be sure to say hello to Mick for me, then,' he said, slyly enough to make her hold her breath for an instant.

'I will if I happen to see him,' she said coldly, and walked on stiffly with her heart thudding.

He was an odious little man, and she had never been too keen on Rose working at his shop – but it was Peter who had been the attraction, of course. But with those few words – those almost menacing few words – Henry Kelsey had managed to shake her confidence and made her think yet again of something that had happened years ago, and should have been dead and buried. It incensed and upset her to think that anyone else in the village could be thinking the way Henry Kelsey might. All these years she had been a good and faithful wife to Walter, and if her thoughts had strayed in the tiniest way, it had never been other than in her thoughts.

By the time she reached Helen's house she had got herself really worked up, and Bobby was complaining loudly that he was thirsty. Helen took one look at the two of them and ushered them indoors quickly.

'Come on, my lamb, let's get you a drink and then you can sit and draw some pictures by the fire while your mum and me have a cup of tea. And you can tell me what's wrong, Alice,' she added beneath her breath.

Well, that was something she absolutely couldn't do. She could hardly say that she had a horrible suspicion that Henry Kelsey was quite capable of spreading idiotic rumours about Alice and Mick in a fit of spite because Rose had finished with his precious son. It was a ludicrous thought, but smaller things had started rumours – and even wars. And now she couldn't get the blessed thought of war out of her head, either.

'What's wrong, Alice?' Helen said directly. 'I know there's something bothering you, so don't pretend this is your usual social call, pleasant though it is. Has Lucy said she won't be allowed home for her birthday tea or something? Or is it something more serious?'

Without knowing that she did so, Helen had given her the perfect opening, and Alice almost blurted out why she was really there.

'It's not Lucy. She's really fallen on her feet, thank goodness. It's my friend, Tilly, who I used to work with in London before I came down here. You've met her a few times when she came to visit.'

'Of course I remember Tilly. I liked her. She was always so bright and cheerful. There's nothing wrong with her, is there?'

It was obvious there *was* something wrong or Alice wouldn't be sitting on the sofa twisting her hands together like an idiot.

Alice tried to calm herself, wondering what the dickens was wrong with her today. One word from that hateful Kelsey man, which had probably meant nothing at all, and she had gone to pieces. It wasn't like her, any more than Tilly's current mood was anything like the girl she remembered.

'You read Tilly's letter while I get Bobby a drink and make the tea,' she said in a fluster. 'I know where everything is, and I need to be doing something, Helen.'

She was familiar enough with this house and with the kitchen, and so Helen took her place on the sofa and opened Tilly's letter. After a few minutes Alice carried in the tray of drinks and put them on the table, annoyed that her hands were not quite steady.

'Well, it's obvious the poor woman needs to get away for a rest,' Helen said, folding the letter after having read it. 'I'm sure she'll bounce back, because she's that sort, but they're often hit harder than other people before they do.'

'I know,' Alice said. 'I've never known her to be so down-hearted and anxious, though I do remember what it was like

in that sweatshop. I was thankful to get away from it, and
it seemed like heaven when I came here to live.'

Helen nodded as she handed Bobby a cup of lemonade.

'Well, if this is what years of working in that place has
done for Tilly, you made the right choice,' she said.

Alice thought wildly that she had to stop seeing double
meanings in everything that was said to her today. Of course
she had made the right choice in leaving smoky old London
and coming to live in the clean country air of Somerset –
and she had made the right choice in marrying Walter too.

'Why don't you invite her to come here and stay with us?'
Helen went on. 'We've got plenty of room and I'd love to
see her again. Write to her tonight, Alice, and before you
go, I'll write a little note for you to include with your letter,
so that she knows it's all above board.'

It was the solution that had been Alice's first thought, but
now she didn't know what to think.

'It's very kind of you to offer, Helen, but Mick might not
be so keen. Hadn't you better see what he thinks about it?
And there's Jack too, and if Tilly's going to be coughing all
night—'

'For goodness' sake, my dear, I can handle Mick and Jack,
and if Tilly has the bedroom at the back of the house, nobody
will hear her even if she does cough all night. No, this is
the best thing for everybody. Now, tell me all about the
Grange when you went there with Lucy. Was it posh enough
to scare you to death?'

By the time Alice left, she had Helen's brief note in her bag.
There was no help for it now, and of course she wanted to
see Tilly again. They had been closer than Siamese twins
once, and she had missed that old closeness for a long time
when she first came to Somerset. But that was many years
ago. She and Walter were an old married couple now, with
four children, and Tilly still seemed strangely rootless.
Besides, it would be Helen who would gradually become
Tilly's friend and confidante and, despite everything, Alice
felt a surprising stab of jealousy at the thought. She began
to wonder if she was going completely mad. She had a loving
family around her, so why begrudge her old friend the chance

to recover from whatever ailed her? But of course she didn't, she thought, and she would write back to Tilly that very night.

But before Alice had a chance to write to her friend, the January birthdays were upon them. As usual Helen put on a lovely spread of food for the two families, and she was eager to hear about her nieces' new jobs. Not having daughters of her own, Helen was very fond of them both, and not too unhappy that Rose had finished with Peter Kelsey, whom she considered as uncouth as his father.

'I'm really enjoying looking after the doctor's baby,' Rose told her. 'She's a real sweetie, and it's almost like having one of my own.'

'Well just remember that she's not, my love,' Helen said lightly. 'Don't get too attached to her, Rose, or you might never want one of your own.'

Rose laughed. 'I'm sure that won't happen, but since I'm not thinking of anything like that for ages, it's the last thing on my mind, Aunt Helen.'

'She's got to find a husband first,' Tom put in cheekily.

Alice held her breath for a moment at his thoughtlessness. She was reasonably sure Rose had got over Peter Kelsey, but she could never be certain. She was reassured by seeing Rose give her brother a playful slap on the arm.

'When I do, you little twerp, I'll make sure he's nothing like you.'

'And how about you, Lucy?' Helen turned her attention to her. 'You're not thinking of marrying anyone yet, I hope!'

She said it in a teasing way, since her niece was just seventeen that very day, but to her surprise Lucy coloured up at once.

'Not for ages,' she said, echoing Rose's words. 'I do like somebody though, and I think he likes me.'

'What's that?' Walter barked at once. 'I'll have no goings-on at that big house, my girl, and if I thought there was anything shady about it, I'd have you out of there at once.'

Alice could see that the two of them were about to clash, and this was not the time or place to do it. She intervened quickly. 'Now, Walter, keep your hair on. Lucy has already mentioned this nice young lad who works in the stables, and I'm sure Mr and Mrs Frankley wouldn't employ anyone less than respectable. Having spoken to the lady myself, I'm even more sure of it.'

All the same, it was high time she had a talk with her younger girl, Alice thought. She was becoming a young lady now, and needed to know certain things, whether or not Alice relished the thought of explaining it all to her. It was a mother's duty, and that was the end of it. She baulked at the thought of seeing Lucy's wide-eyed, unblinking gaze at learning about the facts of life, or alternatively being reduced to fits of nervous giggles which would only make Alice stumble over her words. Perhaps it would be better coming from Rose . . .

By the time the family walked home from Mick and Helen's house that night, they were replete with good food and lively conversation. Tom and Jack had disappeared to Jack's bedroom while the women dealt with the washing-up, and the men yarned about the ominous possibility of war. The boys too, had thoughts of war on their minds, but were in a very different mood.

'It's definitely coming,' Jack assured his young cousin jubilantly. 'The only question is – when? The minute it does, I'm signing up. You'll probably still be far too young for it, Tom, so don't even think of lying about your age. Your dad will only haul you back.'

'He'll have to find me first!'

Jack looked at him thoughtfully, wishing now that he'd never been quite so enthusiastic about the glories of war and the chance to shoot enemy planes out of the sky. Because of course they weren't just inanimate pieces of metal. There were men inside them, who would burn and scream and be blown to bits . . . But Tom could only see the chance to be a hero, and in that respect he was still wearing rose-coloured glasses about war.

'There's no point in risking your life while you're still a kid,' Jack went on. 'Anyway, if a war does come, it might go on for years, and then you'll get your chance, like everyone else.'

'You can't say it would go on for years,' Tom argued. 'We'd soon whip the Germans, and it might only be a few months, not years.'

'Grow up, Tom. We whipped them in the last one all right, but it took us four years to do it, and thousands died, including our granddad, don't forget.'

Tom glared at him. 'Why are you trying to put me off?'

'I'm not. I'm just trying to make you see sense, that's all.'

'Well, don't. My dad's bad enough for that, and my mum wouldn't even let me work at the sawmills if it wasn't for him saying I won't come to any harm while he's there to keep an eye on me. They treat me like a kid, but I didn't think you did, and I'm not listening to any more of it.'

They rarely argued seriously, let alone almost come to blows, but right then Tom couldn't get out of the bedroom fast enough. In his eyes he wasn't a kid any more, and he didn't want Jack, who was another sort of hero to him, telling him that he was.

He ran downstairs to join his family, who were already preparing to go home. He was glad. He'd had enough of being made to feel like an infant for one night, he thought resentfully. Now that Lucy was seventeen, she would be more snotty towards him than before, and he still had to share his bedroom with the real kid in the family.

'What's got your goat, boy?' Walter asked him as they marched home in a small convoy.

'Why can't you ever call me by my name?' he retorted.

After a few seconds of genuine astonishment, Walter burst out laughing, not seeing the resentment behind his son's words. Referring to his son as 'Boy' was his own way of expressing his pride in him.

Alice pressed Tom's arm, feeling affable and prepared to be generous after the enjoyable evening they had all spent. 'Don't fret, love. He's called me Mother for years, and no matter how often I tell him not to, he still does it.'

Tom shook her off. 'Well, I wish he wouldn't. It's not respectful, and you're not his mother. You're mine and Bobby's and the girls', not his. And I'm more than just a *boy*. I'm almost a man.'

Lucy smothered a giggle as Rose shushed her, sensing how their father's mood was rapidly changing.

'A man, is it?' he roared. 'While you live under my roof, boy, I'm the only man in the house and don't you forget it.'

'It'll be a good job when I leave then, won't it?' Tom yelled back, to be rewarded by a cuff around the ears that started Bobby wailing.

'Now see what you've done, Walter,' Alice seethed. 'Why do you always have to spoil everything? Let's get home, for goodness' sake, and stop making a show of yourself in public.'

Tom was already striding ahead of them, and for all Walter's furious words, Alice had to admit that her son did have the stance of a young man. It was mean of Walter to make him feel small, especially when he had always felt somewhat undermined by the teasing of his older sisters. She comforted Bobby and walked swiftly ahead to catch up with Tom, leaving the other three behind.

'You shouldn't bait him so, Tom,' she said, finally catching her breath. 'You know he thinks the world of you.'

'Well, he's got a funny way of showing it. He's a pig, Mum, and I'm not apologizing for saying so.'

'Then I won't ask you to,' she murmured.

'And why do you let him call you Mother? I know you don't like it.'

Alice sighed. 'After all these years, I'm not sure I'll ever change him. I do try, even though I wonder if it's really worth the bother. It's a kind of endearment, anyway. He doesn't actually treat me like his mother!'

There were times when he certainly didn't. Times when the loving was so tender and sweet it brought tears of joy to her eyes. And times when it was wild and passionate enough to make her feel like a young girl again . . . But these were private, intimate times that were between husband and wife, and had nothing to do with the children they had created. She cleared her throat, thankful that they were nearing home now and the others were catching up with them.

'Make your peace with him, Tom,' she said quietly. 'He does love you, even if he thinks it's unmanly to show it. Do it for me, please.'

She didn't know what was said between them, and she didn't intend to ask. It was enough that all was calm by the time everyone finally went to bed. And much later, when Walter had locked up and come to bed, she found herself nestling in the warmth of his arms in the chilly bedroom, and felt his ready response to her presence.

'Whose birthday is it then, woman?' she heard him whisper teasingly against her cheek.

'Yours, if you like,' she whispered back.

Lucy went back to the Grange early the next morning, taking her prized sewing box with her. She was in a cheerful mood, knowing she would be seeing Ben again. Apart from her brother's stupid little tiff with her father they had all had a lovely day, and she and Rose had had a good gossip in bed.

'I think our Jack fancies you,' she told Rose solemnly.

Rose had found it hard to smother her chuckles under the bedclothes. Was her sister turning into some kind of idiotic matchmaker now?

'Don't be daft! He's our cousin!'

'Makes no difference. I reckon he does, anyway. I saw the way he kept looking at you when we all sang "Happy Birthday" to Mum and me.'

'What way was that?' Rose looked across the room to the other bed. In the dim light from the window she couldn't see Lucy's expression, but she guessed that the little squirt was laughing at her now. It was just like her to make such a daft statement, just to see somebody else's reaction.

'Sort of shiny-eyed, as if he'd never seen you before. It must have been that blue dress you were wearing that made you look all curvy and film-starry.'

'Well, that just shows how daft you're being. I didn't look in the least film-starry, and I certainly don't want Jack Chase to think of me as being all curvy either, thank you very much! You want to wash your mouth out with soap, Lucy.'

'There's no need to go all prissy on me. I know what I saw, and I do reckon he fancies you, so there.'

She turned over in bed to face the wall, effectively ending the conversation, leaving Rose alternately fuming at her stupidity and wondering if it could possibly be true. Jack and she were the same age, but she had never thought of him as anything but her cousin who she liked enormously, and that was all. The last thing she wanted was to think of him as anything else. After Peter, she didn't want any kind of attachment for a long while, but now Lucy had spoiled all that, and she was going to feel really awkward when she saw Jack again.

She banged her pillow into a more comfortable shape and buried her head in it, wishing her sister would learn to keep her mouth shut. She certainly took after their father in that respect, Rose thought savagely.

Eight

Alice wasted no time in writing to Tilly, knowing that if she put it off, she might start thinking too much about why it wasn't such a good idea. Last night had ended so sweetly for her and Walter, reminding her of just why she loved this cantankerous, complex man, who could be so loving and gentle, and everything she ever wanted. She had everything . . . and, by comparison, Tilly had so little.

> I'm enclosing Helen's note, Tilly. It was her idea to
> invite you, and I was thrilled that she did so. I would
> love to have you staying with us, but with all of us here
> now, it would be like squeezing you into a shoebox.
> Helen's got plenty of room as you know, and she is
> really looking forward to seeing you again, so please
> say you'll come. I'm concerned about you, and I think
> you should get away from London as soon as possible.
> It's lovely down here in the country and it will do you
> a power of good. It's a bit cold at this time of year, but
> once the spring comes, everything looks so clean and
> green and smells so good.

She stopped writing the letter and read it back, wondering if she was being too gushing for her own good. And what was all this talk of spring, for goodness' sake? How long was this visit of Tilly's supposed to last? Helen hadn't said anything about how long she wanted Tilly to stay, and it would surely only be for a week or two. She screwed up the letter and started all over again, leaving out the bit about the wonders of the countryside in spring.

It was the middle of February before Alice received a reply. By then, with the country now aware of the truth about the government's plans to install air-raid shelters in London homes, the tone of it was predictably abrasive. And underneath it all, Alice could sense something else: Tilly was scared. Being brasher than usual was her way of hiding her true feelings.

> Bleedin' government! Pardon my French, Alice, but they scare the living shite out of ordinary folk, making us all think we're about to have bombs raining down on us like fly droppings. I don't mind telling you that the sooner I get away from here the better, so your letter was like a godsend, and Helen's note too. You know how I hate going to the doc for anything, but I mentioned it to him when I got my last lot of medicine and he said it was the best thing I could do for me chest. With all this stuff going on up here, I'm thinking I'd do better to up stakes and move down to the country for good, though God knows how I'd cope with all the smells and all that. I've written a note to Helen saying I'll take up her offer for a couple of weeks, and then I'll see how I go. I've finished with this bleedin' factory, anyway, so while I'm there I might look around for a little place to rent, and I'd need to find a job too, not having a husband to look after me in me old age like some people, ha ha. Watch out, gel, it'll soon be the old team again!
>
> From your loving pal, Tilly.

Alice was a bit startled by this letter. It wasn't what she had expected, and her feelings were mixed. Tilly had always been outspoken, but Alice had forgotten how coarse she could be when she wanted to be. The thought of her moving down here permanently hadn't been what she expected, either, but even as she found herself frowning anxiously, she was asking herself what kind of a friend she was if she didn't welcome the idea.

As Tilly said, it would soon be the old team again . . . Except that it wouldn't be, and never could be again. They were older now, and both of them had changed. They weren't the same carefree girls they had been when they'd first set

eyes on the two good-looking Chase brothers all those years
ago. She fingered the small envelope with Helen's name
scrawled on it that Tilly had enclosed with her letter, and
before she had time to think any more about it she buttoned
Bobby into his thick winter coat and told him they were
going to see Auntie Helen again.

'Well, we'll do all we can to make her comfortable while
she's here,' Helen said when she had finished reading the
short note Tilly had written her.

'I think you'd better read my letter as well,' Alice said.

Helen was a good friend, but she was also fairly strait-
laced and Tilly had never let her hair down with her the way
she did with her old workmate. It was as well for Helen to
be warned in advance, and easier to do it this way than by
putting a damper on Tilly's character, however delicately
Alice tried to do it.

'She doesn't hold back from saying what she thinks, does
she?' Helen said at last. 'It's refreshing in its way, of course.'

'But it might not go down so well with the vicar,' Alice
added for her.

Helen smiled. 'How likely is she to come into contact with
the vicar, Alice? Is she a churchgoer?'

'She's like a lot of people. When times are hard and there's
nobody else to turn to, they suddenly find there's a God after
all. I'm not saying Tilly's going to get all churchified, mind,
but it wouldn't surprise me if she didn't sing hymns more
loudly than the rest of us in the hope of catching God's ear.'
She let out an unexpected laugh. 'Actually, remembering
what Tilly's singing voice is like, it wouldn't take much to
catch anybody's ear!'

'Do you really think she'll consider moving here for good?'
Helen asked.

Alice shrugged. 'I doubt it. She was always a city girl,
but there's no knowing what she'll decide. She was always
more unpredictable than me.'

'I wouldn't say that, Alice! You were the one who left
London all those years ago to marry a man you hardly knew,
apart from the letters he wrote you. They must have been
pretty powerful to lure you away from everything you knew.'

'They were,' Alice said, starting to feel uncomfortable.

'But that's not the point now, is it? What are we going to do about Tilly?'

Helen laughed now. 'I think we already know the answer to that. Of course she can come here for a few weeks in the hope that it will do her some good, and if she wanted to stay longer, well, we'd have to see.'

'You don't mean you'd offer her a permanent home, do you?' Alice said, her heart jumping now. 'Oh, I don't think that's a good idea, Helen.'

'Probably not, although it would be nice to have another female in the house instead of two hulking males. You've always had the luxury of that, Alice, but I never have, and you know how I've always envied you your daughters. You needn't worry that I'd take away any of your friendship with Tilly, though. You two have a long history that nobody can take away.'

Alice felt uneasy. Helen was certainly right about that, and she was probably making mountains out of molehills. Of course it would be lovely to have Tilly close at hand again and to renew a friendship that had lasted over the years, albeit spasmodically and from a distance. She was being utterly selfish, and she should remember that the main reason for all this was that Tilly wasn't well. She gave a small shiver, as if suddenly realizing their mortality. Nobody lived for ever, and she quickly pushed such thoughts out of her mind.

'I think it's best if you write to her properly this time – Helen, separately from me, I mean – to offer the invitation. I know she'll appreciate it.'

Walter had been surprisingly expansive about the possibility of Tilly moving out of London for good. It started him thinking about the time they had all met that long-ago day at the seaside, and he became quite salty-eyed as he recalled it over the supper table that evening for the benefit of Rose and Tom.

'You never saw such bright-eyed girls as those two,' he chuckled. 'They were both as light as feathers, and cheeky too. You could span your mother's waist with two hands in them days, and the minute me and Mick caught sight of them we set out to court 'em.'

'What, all in one day?' his daughter Rose said with a grin, while clearly the thought of his well-rounded mother looking bright-eyed and as light as a feather was making it hard for Tom to stifle his laughter.

'Well, no, not all in one day, and I don't think Mick was as taken with Tilly as I was with your mother. She was the one for me, and I knew it straight away.'

'Shut up, Walter, you'll make me blush,' Alice said with a laugh.

Rose was clearly enchanted by what she was hearing, especially since it was so unlike her father to reveal his feelings in this way. But looking at her mother now, flush-faced and with her eyes sparkling, she got a glimpse of what her father had seen all that time ago. And Uncle Mick too, perhaps . . .

'Do you think she'll want to stay with Auntie Helen, Mum?' she asked before her thoughts strayed too far along those lines.

'I'm sure she will, though I've no doubt she'll have plenty of complaints at first about the country smells and being woken up at dawn by the sound of roosters and birds, and the slow pace of life down here, but Tilly will fit in well enough.'

'Well, you did, old girl, didn't you?' Walter said. 'And what's slow about the pace of life in the country anyway, I'd like to know?' he added defensively.

'Nothing at all when you've got a brood of children to look after,' Alice said smartly. 'But compared with London, she's bound to see a difference.'

She hadn't thought nostalgically about her early life in London for years, and she had never been back, but at that moment it all came flooding back to her. Not just the miserable back-to-back where she had lived with her gran after her parents died, nor the hectic hours in the sweatshop where the girls had to shout to one another above the sound of the machines. She remembered the way they had all spilled out of that place after work, breathing in air that wasn't so different from country smells, except that in London it was the whiff of the river that was so pungent when it was sluggish, and sometimes downright evil. She remembered how lively life had been, going to dances or the pictures, and flirting with young men who all spoke the same way as she did, quick and witty and sometimes a bit daring. It hadn't meant anything. It was all harmless fun, and neither she nor Tilly had thought seriously abut any young man until the day they had gone on a work charabanc outing to the seaside for a few days, and they had met Walter and Mick Chase. From then on their lives had changed for ever.

'Where have you gone, Mother?' she heard Walter say impatiently. 'That's the second time I've asked if you heard our Bobby yelling.'

She almost fled from the table, glad to take her mind off the confusing images that were coursing through it now. What was past was past, and it was pointless to waste your life wondering if you had done the right thing with it. It wasn't as if she constantly wondered. It was only now and then, and the presence of Tilly was bound to stir up memories. But now, cuddling Bobby's warm little body in her arms and thankful that he only wanted a drink of water, she wondered how anybody could ever want anything more than the life she had, with a husband who loved her and a strong and healthy family.

By the time she went quietly downstairs again, Bobby had already fallen asleep, and her hand froze on the banister as she heard Walter's jocular words.

'Oh ah, there was a time when it was a toss-up which of the four of us would get wed. 'Course, of the two of them, your mother was always the best looker, and both me and your uncle Mick had a fancy for her. But I was the one she chose, and a good job she did, or none of you would be here!'

Alice heard Tom snigger, and she made more noise as she reached the bottom of the stairs, knowing her son would be feeling awkward at any hint as to how they came to be here. Young men might lark about such things between themselves, for all she knew, but none of them would want to imagine their parents doing the very act that brought children into the world.

'Let's get this table cleared,' she said briskly now. 'I promised Tom a game of draughts tonight, and it's my turn to win.'

Being competitive, she knew this would turn Tom's thoughts to other things, and rightly so. She was surprised that Walter had become so talkative about their personal lives, and it surprised her even more when they went to bed later that night when his arms went around her again in the special way they did when he wanted more than a goodnight kiss.

'You know, I meant what I said earlier, Alice,' he mumbled against her cheek. 'You were always the best looker out of you two girls, and for a while I was half afraid you were going to choose Mick over me.'

Her heart jolted. 'Why on earth would you think such a daft thing?' she mumbled back.

'Oh, no special reason, just a feeling. But we ended up with something good, didn't we, girl? Something that's lasted.'

In the darkness, aware that his hand was gently stroking her breast now, she caught the slight uncertainty in his voice. Ever since they had been together he had never mentioned wondering if she had had any feelings for Mick rather than himself, not even in jest, and she felt a great wave of protectiveness towards him, not wanting him to think for a moment that he'd ever had anything to worry about.

'You're a big softie sometimes, aren't you, Walter?' she whispered. 'We've got a good life, and a lovely family, and I'd never want anything different.'

She knew he was reassured, because for the second time in two nights she felt the familiarity of his love-making, and it was a reinforcement of all they had been to each other for all these years.

Tilly told Alice in her next letter that she had finally given in her notice at the factory, and that she didn't intend working there again anyway, since it wasn't doing her chest any good, and she would see how she felt after a couple of weeks in the country. It seemed a reckless thing to do, but that was Tilly all over. Act first and think later.

'How long is she planning to stay then?' Walter said. 'Helen won't really want her moving in permanently. It's only meant to be a visit.'

'I know, but I rather think she's burned her boats now. She'd wanted to get out of the factory for ages, and this has given her the chance to do something different. If the country doesn't drive her mad, I think she may do as she says, and look for somewhere to rent in Bramwell.'

Alice knew it should have made her happier than it did, and it annoyed her that she couldn't feel more enthusiastic about it. What kind of a friend was she, if she didn't welcome the thought of Tilly being so close?

She was due to arrive at the end of February, and it was arranged that Mick, Helen and Alice would meet the train from Paddington at Bristol Temple Meads railway station in Mick's car. Alice was thankful Helen was there as well, and that she was also obliged to take Bobby with her. She and Bobby waited on the platform for her friend while the others stayed in the car. She hadn't seen Tilly for several years now, and it was with a little shock when she saw the thin, gaunt woman stepping out of the railway carriage with a large suit-case. But the moment her friend's face lit up at the sight of her, Alice knew she was still the same old Tilly.

'My Gawd, you're a sight for sore eyes after that long journey, gel,' Tilly said, wheezing audibly as she dropped the heavy suitcase at her feet. 'Let me look at you, and at the little 'un too. He's the spit of his dad, ain't he, poor little dab!' she added teasingly.

The two women hugged one another, while Bobby hung back behind his mother's skirts. Tilly had always been a bit of a snappy dresser, and even though her clothes hung on her more than they used to do, she still emitted a waft of the glamorous scent that had always impressed Lucy. But the railway station was draughty and they were all starting to shiver now.

'Come on, Tilly, let's get you into Mick and Helen's car. They're waiting outside for us.'

'Blimey, I always knew he'd come up in the world.'

Alice laughed. 'A vet has to have a car to get around to visit his patients, just like a doctor does.'

'I suppose so,' Tilly said, linking arms with Alice while Bobby looked on silently. Finally, he said the thing that was clearly in his mind.

'Is she a film star, Mum?' he whispered.

Tilly burst out laughing, while Alice said hastily that he'd been looking at too many of Lucy's film-star magazines. Lucy had always thought Tilly could have been a film star, and she was looking forward to seeing her again.

'Oh, don't apologize for him, Alice,' Tilly trilled. 'He's a real cutie, and it's a long time since anybody compared me with a film star!'

The cold air caught her throat as they went outside the station to Mick's waiting car, and as she desperately tried to suppress the coughing that began immediately, Alice made a mental note to try to get her to see Doctor Stacey while she was here.

Mick and Helen got out of the car at once and greeted Tilly warmly.

'Let's get your suitcase in the boot,' Mick said briskly. 'And by the sound of it a good hot cup of tea is just what the doctor ordered as soon we get you indoors.'

It was funny that they should also be thinking of the doctor at that moment, though in a completely different context, thought Alice. Helen flinched at the touch of Tilly's cold hands now as she hurried her inside the car.

'You're really scrammed, my dear, but some of my nourishing rabbit stew will soon put the colour back in your cheeks.'

Tilly smiled weakly as the fit of coughing subsided. 'I wouldn't bet on it, Helen. I'm always this colour, but it'll be worth a try. I must say none of you have changed much. Alice is a bit more buxom these days, but Mick's still as handsome as ever. Good job his patients are all of the animal variety and not human, eh?'

They all laughed, but Alice found herself hoping that Tilly wasn't going to get over-familiar with Mick while she was staying with him and Helen. It would be no more than harmless flirting, but none of them knew her as well as Alice did, and the last thing she wanted was to be always wondering what Tilly was going to say next, or to find herself apologizing for her. The more these things kept entering her head, the angrier she was at her own thoughts, but she just couldn't get rid of them.

'Lucy will be home at the weekend, Tilly, and she's longing to see you, so we'd like you to come to us on Sunday,' she said now. 'Is that all right, Helen?'

'Of course it is,' her sister-in-law said comfortably. 'Tilly's your friend, and we shall all do what we can to make her visit a happy one.'

So why did Alice feel that it was a slight reprimand? Of course Tilly would want to spend time with Alice and her family. She was only lodging with Mick and Helen, for heaven's sake. She caught Mick's glance in the driving mirror, and felt her face flush, as if he could read everything that was going on in her mind. She was reacting like a ruddy schoolkid now, she thought angrily, and it had to stop.

'Will you stop at Kelsey's shop on the way home, please, Mick?' Helen said. 'I need some flour and sugar, and it will only take a few minutes. Do you want to come and meet one of our local characters, Tilly? Rose used to work there until quite recently.'

'Why not?' Tilly said easily. 'I might as well get into the spirit of the countryside while I'm here, and I like the sound of a local character.'

Alice prided herself on being a down-to-earth woman who wasn't given to premonitions. But even though Tilly was being her usual chatty self, at that moment Alice felt an odd little shiver run through her. There was no reason for it, and nor could she imagine the fastidious Tilly ever taking to the coarse Henry Kelsey, but she couldn't get out of her mind the image of his podgy fingers curling around Tilly's narrow hand in greeting. How ironic it would be for the mean-minded Henry to set his cap at Alice's old friend. He was just the type to be cock-a-hoop at getting one over on the family whose daughter had snubbed his precious son.

'You've gone very quiet, Alice. Cat got your tongue?' she heard Tilly say.

Bobby swivelled round to peer anxiously at his mother's mouth, and Tilly laughed out loud as Alice assured him there was no cat biting her tongue.

'He's a sharp one for a babby and no mistake. I can see I'll have to mind my Ps and Qs in future.'

Alice could only hope that she did so. She felt ridiculously defensive on Tilly's behalf. Part of her was anxious that Tilly wouldn't make any gaffes about her feelings for Mick, and another part of her really wanted Tilly to be liked and not thought of as some slick Londoner who'd be making fun of these quaint country folk. They had reached Kelsey's shop now, and Tilly left the car and went inside with Helen.

'So it's the two pals together again,' Mick said after an awkward moment's silence. 'Tilly certainly doesn't look well, Alice.'

'No, and I hope it's not going to be a worry to you and Helen. Having her to stay with you, I mean. It's very good of you both.'

They were talking more like strangers than family, Alice thought. It wasn't often they were alone together. They were usually in the midst of a big, noisy family, and she felt suddenly strange with him.

'Helping each other out is what families do, isn't it?' he said. 'Don't worry, I'm sure we'll cope, and Helen can get along with anybody.'

Even somebody as bolshy as Tilly could sometimes be? Alice wondered silently. But she was sure she'd be on her best behaviour – at first, anyway. When the two women came back to the car Tilly's eyes were sparkling.

'He's a proper card, that Henry, isn't he? He's looking for a new assistant, and he said if I'm free, I could apply for the job any day,' she finished with a chuckle and a cough.

At that moment Bobby decided he felt sick, which was enough of an emergency to cover the need to comment on Tilly's words. Mick said they'd best get to the house promptly before the child threw up, and they reached it without mishap. Helen took Bobby off to the kitchen to watch her make some drinks for everybody, while Mick took Alice and Tilly upstairs to the guest bedroom.

'I'll leave you to it,' he said, putting Tilly's case on the floor. 'Come down when you're ready.'

The two old friends looked at one another and Tilly gave a crooked smile. 'Alone at last,' she said jokingly, and held out her arms.

Alice hugged her quickly, feeling how thin she was, despite the thickness of her clothes. When she removed her coat, it was even more evident that this was a sick woman.

'Let me help you unpack,' Alice said, stumped for words for once.

'I can do all that later. Sit on the bed with me and tell me the latest about your kids. Are the girls courting yet? And what about Tom? Is he still the apple of Walter's eye? I must say you're looking well, mate, which is more than can be said for me, so don't try saying anything different or you'll make me pipe me eyes, and I don't aim to put everybody in a gloomy mood.'

She paused for breath and Alice had to smile, despite her sombre last words. She was still the same old Tilly, wanting to know everything at once, covering her feelings with a cheerful manner, no matter what might be going on inside her.

'The girls aren't courting – at least, not as far as I know! Rose finished with Henry Kelsey's son recently, and Lucy's too young for courting, although you may not think so when you see how she's blossomed lately. Tom and Walter are still as thick as thieves, and you've seen Bobby and me, so that's all of us,' she finished.

Tilly grinned. 'And how about you and Mick?' she said mischievously.

'Don't go thinking about any of that old nonsense, Tilly,' Alice said sharply. 'We've all moved on since those days, and that's the way it is. But never mind all that. I'm going to say what I think, and you've never known me to do otherwise, so while you're here, I think it would be a good idea for you to ask our Doctor Stacey what he thinks about you. He's a good man, even if he's not a Londoner,' she added, forestalling Tilly's objections on that score.

Tilly scowled. 'Blimey, gel, I thought I'd come down here for a bit of peace and quiet, not to be nagged by my old mate.'

Alice squeezed her hand. 'A bit of nagging never did anyone any harm, and it's always good to have a second opinion. But I'd better tell you what happened to Walter before you see him, and why he's got a lovely scar down his cheek now!'

She changed the subject neatly, and when they went downstairs for a cup of tea and some of Helen's freshly made ginger cake, Tilly was full of admiration for Mick's skills in patching up Walter's face, and even more admiration for

Walter for sticking up for his rights. But by the time Alice took Bobby home, she was starting to feel exhausted. It was wonderful to renew their old friendship, but remembering all they knew about one another had been more of a strain than she realized, evoking some memories that were best laid to rest. It was absurd to feel that way, but she had never been happier to be inside her own front door.

Nine

Lucy was full of excitement at the thought of going home that weekend. It was quite true that she had always thought her mother's old friend was what the picture papers called a glamour-puss. Admittedly, she hadn't seen her lately, but she could always picture a laughing Tilly in her head. She considered her to be someone quite exotic and sophisticated. She would surely have had her fill of gentlemen friends too, and Lucy hoped they would get the chance to talk without anyone else being around. Quite how she would manage that in a small house that was always full of people she wasn't sure. But there were certain things a girl felt too embarrassed to ask her mother – most importantly how to go about letting a young man know she liked him without appearing too forward.

She felt deliciously shivery just thinking about Ben. They hadn't managed to talk too much either, she thought ruefully, since they were always busy with separate duties at the Grange, but when they had, she knew he liked her. A girl could always tell. She liked him too. He had an earthiness about him that came from working in the stables, but he wasn't a roughneck, and she liked that too. He was wholesome, that was the word. A nice, wholesome young man.

'Daydreamin' again, Lucy?' her roommate asked when she paused in her bed-making that morning. 'You'll go blind if you do too much of that – or is that only for boys?' she added with a snigger.

Lucy bent to straighten her bedclothes, her face red. Sophie was a little older than herself, and she often seemed to talk in riddles, as far as Lucy was concerned. Whenever she asked what she meant, Sophie just burst into peals of laughter and told her she'd find out when she was older. As if there was a special club for girls over eighteen, which Lucy wouldn't reach for another year yet.

'I'm going to see my mum's old friend at the weekend,' she snapped now. 'I told you about her. She's come down from London and she's very smart.'

Sophie sniffed. 'I don't like them people. They're all stuck-up.'

'You don't know any!'

'Do you, apart from this flashy whoever-she-is?'

Lucy's eyes sparkled. 'I know my mother, and she's from London too, and she's an old friend of Auntie Tilly's, so don't you say a word against Londoners. You don't know everything, Sophie, even though you think you do.' She shook her pillow furiously before slapping it down on her bed.

'Well, that's telling me, isn't it, kid?' Sophie said after a moment's silence. 'Look, I didn't mean to upset you, and I'm sure this Auntie Tilly's going to turn out to be a smasher. Forget I said anything, all right?'

Lucy supposed that she should, even though the remarks still stung. But she had to share a room with Sophie and there was no point in them being at loggerheads all the time.

'All right,' she said sullenly. 'Just stop calling me a kid.'

Sophie's face broke into a smile. 'I'll try to remember. Now you've turned seventeen you're not such a kid any more, anyway. You'll be courting soon, I daresay, so if you need to know anything about the birds and the bees, just ask your Auntie Sophie.'

She spoke airily, and it was probably meant to be an olive branch, Lucy thought as they departed from their room to go about their duties. It was tempting to do as she said and mention her feelings for Ben, but something told Lucy not to give in to the temptation. Sophie had a loose tongue, and the Grange was like a little community of its own. Lucy couldn't bear it if her feelings were broadcast for all to hear. No, she decided, Tilly was the one she would go to go to for advice.

With her time off on Sunday Lucy cycled home eagerly, knowing she would be the last one in the family to see Tilly again. Everyone else would have been to Mick and Helen's in the last couple of days, and she was sure Tilly would be coming to the house to see Alice. Above all, Lucy was keen to know what her sister thought about the visitor. She hadn't arrived yet, and once they had got beyond the usual greetings among the family, she cornered Rose in their old bedroom and plumped down on her old bed.

'So what's she like?' she asked eagerly. 'Is she as beautiful as ever?'

Rose frowned slightly, knowing that Lucy had always seen the image of Tilly through rose-coloured glasses.

'You know she hasn't been well lately and that's why she's here, so don't expect to see her as robust as Mum.'

'She's not *dying*, is she?' Lucy said, with youthful disregard for the word.

'I don't think so, but she does have an awful cough, and it would probably be a good idea if she got a second opinion about her condition.'

'Just because you look after the Staceys' baby, you're a blooming doctor now, are you?' Lucy said, not wanting to think that anything could be wrong with Tilly.

'Of course not, but it doesn't need a doctor to see that she's ill, Lucy, so don't be upset when you see her. I know you've always idolized her in a way, but she's flesh and blood like the rest of us. And, by the way, she wants us to call her Tilly. She says it makes her feel too old to be called Auntie.'

'Well, there you are then,' Lucy said, oddly relieved at this touch of sophistication, and pushing the rest of Rose's words to the back of her mind.

'How are you, anyway?' Rose went on. 'Enjoying your new job?'

'Yes, thanks. Are you enjoying yours?'

Rose coloured. 'Very much so. I love looking after Mollie, and Mrs Stacey is a lovely employer. The doctor seems quite different too, now that he's not treating me as a patient. His brother moved in a while ago, and I think the plan is for him to share the practice with Doctor Stacey as it's so busy in the village, especially at this time of year.'

'What's he like?' Lucy asked, although she was not really interested in the doctor's brother, and was just filling in time until Tilly arrived.

'He's very nice. He spent quite a bit of time playing with Mollie, which not all young chaps could be bothered to do. He's a lot younger than Doctor Stacey, and he's only recently qualified as a doctor, but I think the patients will like him when they get to know him.'

If Lucy hadn't been so wrapped up in her own thoughts about how to get Tilly alone to ask her advice about Ben, she might have been aware of the softening of her sister's voice and the sudden look of pleasure in her eyes.

Rose hadn't mentioned the newcomer's name, but nonetheless it was going round and round in her head at that moment. Matthew. Matthew Stacey, who had told her to call him Matt, as all his friends did. She could visualize him as clearly as if he was right there in the room with her, laughing into baby Mollie's eyes and making her gurgle back at him. His hair was dark, matching his eyes, and she thought he must be extraordinarily clever to be a doctor. It gave her a warm feeling, just thinking about him, and being able to count herself as his friend . . .

'They're here,' Lucy said, jumping up from the bed and racing towards the stairs. 'I can hear Uncle Mick's car. I hope they're not going to stay or we won't have room to move downstairs.'

'How gracious,' Rose murmured with a grin. 'Don't worry, Mick's just bringing her here and coming to fetch her later. Remember what I said, Lucy . . .'

But Lucy was no longer listening. She couldn't wait to see Tilly again, and when she flew down the stairs to meet the visitor as she entered the house she felt an enormous shock. This was no glamorous film star. This was a sick woman, with none of the good looks that Lucy remembered. She felt let down, as if Tilly had done this deliberately, even though she knew how stupid that was.

'My Gawd, is this little Lucy?' Tilly shrilled. 'I always knew Alice would produce a couple of beauties, and I wasn't mistaken. Your mum and dad will have to wrap you in cotton wool when the boys come sniffing around.'

Her shriek of laughter ended with a bout of coughing and Lucy felt hugely disappointed again. She had been building herself up for a tête-à-tête with Tilly, looking forward to

being treated like a woman of the world, but in an instant
Tilly had made her feel even younger than ever, and she
knew there was no way she would ask her for any advice
about Ben now.

'I won't stay, Tilly,' Mick was saying now. 'I'll see you
later on.'

'Now don't you worry about me, Mick. I'm not kicking
up the daisies yet, and I'll walk back when Alice has had
enough of me!'

She laughed again as if she had made an enormous joke,
and Lucy was perceptive enough to know that Mick was glad
to get away from this screeching woman. Her Aunt Helen
was so placid, a real countrywoman, and despite Tilly's illness,
it must feel as if a hurricane had invaded their house as Tilly
became ever louder and jumpy and talkative. Lucy wondered
how long they could stand it, and by the time Tilly decided
she was going to walk back to Helen's house, they were all
glad when she left. Her scent, which Lucy had once thought
so elegant, still permeated the room, making her wrinkle her
nose. Walter and Tom had long since gone off on pursuits of
their own, and Lucy suspected the reason for it now.

'She wasn't always like that, was she, Mum?' she asked
her mother.

'Like what?' Alice said, busy in the kitchen now.

'Well, so . . . so *awful*.' Lucy was unable to think of a
better word at that moment, and she flushed as her mother
looked at her.

'And you weren't always so snobbish, Lucy, and if that's
what your new position at the Grange has done for you, I'm
sorry you ever went there.'

'I'm not being snobbish! I just think she's embarrassing.
I know she's your old friend, Mum, but Auntie Helen will
hate it if she comes out with some of the words she uses.
You never use them, do you?'

Rose intervened, seeing how angry her mother was
becoming. 'Leave it, Lucy.'

Lucy rounded on her sister at once. 'Don't tell me what
to do. I'm not a child any more. I think Tilly's common and
I hope she doesn't stay for long. I don't want to see her
again, anyway.'

Walter and Tom returned home to find their womenfolk
getting heated, and Bobby was starting to fret at the atmosphere in the house.

'What's going on?' Walter demanded. 'I thought you were
settling in for a cosy afternoon with Tilly.'

'She's gone back to Helen's, and a good thing too, since
this little madam has decided that she's common,' Alice told
him in a frozen voice.

Walter began to laugh. 'Well, she's not wrong there,
Mother. I always thought the same, and you were always a
cut above her.'

This was too much for Alice. 'You know something? I'm
starting to be ashamed of the lot of you. Tilly's my friend
and she's ill, and I won't have you saying such horrible
things about her. I'm going for a walk to cool off, and you
can look after Bobby. And don't call me Mother!'

In her heart, she knew they were saying no more than the
truth, but she wouldn't have it. Not when she and Tilly had
spent so much of their youth together, and been as close as
any two friends could ever be. She wasn't prepared to stay
there and listen to any more slights against her friend. She
pulled on her coat and hat and thrust her hands into her
gloves, blocking out her ears to their remonstrations as she
left the house.

Didn't she know Tilly was no longer the girl she remembered? Was *she* the same person? Was anybody? Time didn't
stand still for any of them, but that didn't mean she was prepared
to listen to her slip of a daughter saying such things . . .

'Mum, wait.'

As she heard her name being called she was obliged to
stop walking, tightening her lips. She was in no mood for
apologies, and she stood quite still without looking around
until Lucy caught up with her. But it wasn't Lucy who linked
her arm through her mother's. It was Rose.

'She didn't mean it, Mum. I think she was so shocked to
see her idol with feet of clay that she had to lash out in any
way she could. She's upset about it now.'

'It's a pity she didn't think before she spoke, then. Tilly
was always fond of you children, not having any of her own,
and she didn't deserve this.'

'I know. But you must admit she looked dreadful, and not at all what Lucy had expected. And that scent she wears – well, it is a bit overpowering, isn't it? I'm not criticizing her in a nasty way, but I can see why Lucy was disappointed.'

Alice's feet slowed down until they were walking at a more reasonable pace, heading towards the scrubland on the edge of the village where people walked their dogs and revelled in the open air.

'I think Tilly's more ill than she let on,' Alice admitted. 'I didn't want to say anything, but the change in her is far more dramatic than I had expected. I know why she wanted to come here. She has no family of her own, and even though we've lived so far apart, I know she always had a special affection for all of you. That's why it hurt me so much to see how Lucy looked down on her.'

'She'll get over it,' Rose said. 'She always does, doesn't she?'

Alice nodded, squaring her shoulders. 'Let's go home, Rose. I'm sure she'll want to make her peace by now. It's getting cold, and we've had enough gloom for one day.'

'Can I tell you something cheerful then?' Rose said. She'd had no intention of doing any such thing, but she wanted to put the smile back on her mother's face. 'It's about Doctor Stacey's brother. He's a doctor too. Doctor Matt. He says he wants patients to call him that, so that he and his brother won't get mixed up when he works with him at the surgery. I think it sounds really friendly, don't you?'

She knew she was talking too fast now, but the smile was definitely back on Alice's face. Doctor Matt may have only arrived a short time ago, but she couldn't help thinking about him, and liking what she saw. After seeing him with Mollie, Rose guessed he would have a lovely manner with children, and with older people as well. And anyone less like Peter Kelsey, she couldn't imagine, and easily put her former beau to the back of her mind, where he belonged.

During the next week, Tilly spent as much time with Alice as she could. She made a point of walking back through the village afterwards, if only to prove to herself that she could still do it. Tilly was so glad for Alice that she had a warm and loving family. Having a family around you always stood you in good stead, no matter what life threw at you.

But she was perfectly sure she couldn't fool Alice indefinitely, even if her bright and breezy manner was intended to fool everybody else.

On her last visit to the doctor before she left London, he had told her the worst of news, and bluntly advised her not to go too far from home. So although she had mentioned to Alice that she might think about moving down here for good, she knew it was never going to happen. It was a pipe dream, no more. This was merely a respite from facing the inevitable, and in any case, she had no intention of landing herself on the good folks here by dying.

She no longer flinched at the word, since she had faced it for some time now. Everyone had to face it sometime, and of course her time was nearer than she had wanted, but you couldn't argue when the grim reaper decided to call. She had always known that she was never going to make old bones, any more than her mother and grandmother had before her. But, Tilly being Tilly, she refused to let herself be scared. Instead she fooled herself into thinking of it as the next great adventure, as thrilling as the one she and Alice had shared when they came to Somerset as eager young girls all those years ago.

They hadn't known what was in store for them then, and she didn't know what would be in store for her when she saw the white light at the end of the long tunnel like some said you saw as you passed from this world into the next.

She wasn't religious in the true sense of the word. She wasn't a regular churchgoer, although she had been once or twice recently. Whatever else it offered, there was a sense of peace and serenity inside a church, and she liked that. In her own way she was quite prepared for what came next.

On her way back to Helen's now, with her feet beginning to drag, she saw Kelsey's shop ahead. Her eyes sparkled. She knew the old man's type. He was a rogue if she ever saw one, but any bloke who could give back as good as he got in the way of a bit of chatter was all right with her. On an impulse she went inside the shop, and saw his ready smile as the bell over the shop door tinkled.

'This is an unexpected pleasure,' Henry said. 'Miss Dilkes, isn't it?'

'It is, but you can call me Tilly,' she said breezily, vainly trying to suppress a cough and not to wheeze after coming inside out of the cold. Wheezing was hardly the most attractive thing when you were trying to vamp a bloke.

'So what can I do for you, Tilly? From the sound of it, some lozenges for that pretty throat of yours won't come amiss. Why don't you sit down while I get them for you? And perhaps a cup of tea to keep out the cold?'

Tilly smiled. 'Do all your customers get this treatment?' she asked.

'Only the ones I take a shine to,' he said smoothly.

Blimey, thought Tilly, *I could eat him up and spit him out for breakfast, and I've seen better specimens on a market stall in Portobello Road.* But she laughed dutifully and said a cup of tea would be just what the doctor ordered.

'Peter,' Henry yelled through to the back of the shop. 'Make the customer a cup of tea, please.'

'Nice to have a slave,' Tilly remarked.

'That's my son. He was lately courting your friend's daughter, Rose, as I'm sure you will have heard by now.'

'Really?' Tilly said, not missing the way the man frowned. He clearly didn't like the fact that Rose had thrown over his son, but she wasn't letting on that she knew anything. She knew when it was best to keep her own counsel, and you learned a lot more that way.

'So how long are you staying in Bramwell?' Henry went on.

'Just a couple of weeks. I wanted to see Alice again.'

'Not the best time of the year for it, though. Summer's the best time down here. You'll have to come again then.'

She nodded in agreement, keeping the smile on her lips. You didn't tell a total stranger that the only place you were likely to be in the summer was six feet under.

When Peter brought out her cup of tea, Tilly could see why Rose had been attracted to his fleshy good looks – and why she had probably found him a bit too lusty for her taste. Good for Rose not to give in too easily. But she quickly forgot Rose as she sipped her tea, and thought that this was just what she needed right now. She always overlooked how long a walk it was from one end of the village to the other. She was definitely starting to flag, and Henry didn't miss how her shoulders drooped.

'You look a bit done in, girl. I'll run you back to Mick's place in my van if you like,' he offered.

'Thanks. I wouldn't mind,' she said.

The familiar gnawing pains in her chest were returning and she needed a couple of her pills, quickly. The sooner she got back to Helen's and put her feet up so that they could do their work, the better. She had the bottle of pills in her bag but she wasn't going to take them here in front of old Kelsey.

Helen brought her a glass of water to help wash the pills down. Jack was home from the farm too. To Tilly, he seemed to work all kinds of strange hours. She was aware that farming wasn't a nine-to-five job, and apparently he'd been up all night with a cow that was calving, and in the end they'd had to call Mick out as well or they might have lost them both.

Jack's eyes looked like piss-holes in the snow now. Those were the only words Tilly could think of to describe them. But she knew better than to say them out loud. Helen's background wasn't as liberal as hers had been.

'Looks like you and me both need some sleep, ducks,' she said to Jack, opening the pill bottle with unsteady hands.

He grunted. He wasn't as keen on this old friend of his aunt's as everybody else seemed to be. God knew he was used to some coarse language at the farm or when he was with his mates, and it never bothered him, but sometimes this one let slip words that were far from ladylike. And that God-awful scent that she used filled the bloody house . . . He preferred the healthier smell of the farmyard.

'I might have a snooze before I go out with my mates tonight,' he agreed, since she seemed to be waiting for a reply.

'Don't go wandering along the landing, then,' Tilly said with a giggle, even though she felt less like giggling with every breath.

Jack gave her a freezing look and muttered something

under his breath. *Cocky little squirt can't even take a joke,* Tilly thought. She swallowed the pills, trying to stop the water from slopping about in the glass, but before she could make for the stairs and her bedroom, her hands had lost control of everything. There was a huge roaring in her ears and then the floor seemed to come up to meet her.

'One minute she was talking normally, and then she just collapsed,' she heard someone saying anxiously. 'These are the pills she was taking.'

She vaguely recognized the voice as Helen's, and someone else was muttering as well, but it was all very muzzy, and there seemed to be an awful lot of people standing over her, crowding her, filling the space around her and blocking out the light, making it difficult for her to breathe. She was lying down somewhere. Not in bed . . . no, on the sofa, that was it. On Helen's sofa.

Slowly, the jumble of thoughts unravelled. Helen and her family hovered around her, and she found herself looking into the eyes of a man she didn't know.

'Who the bleedin' hell are you?' she mumbled before she could stop herself.

Helen spoke quickly. 'Tilly, this is Doctor Stacey.'

'I don't need no bleedin' doctor. I've had me pills, and I'll be as right as rain in a few minutes.' She struggled to get up and fell back again as the room was spinning.

'Miss Dilkes, I'm afraid you're far from being as right as rain,' the doctor said. 'Did your own doctor say you were fit to travel?'

She glared at him. ''Course he did. Well, he didn't say I couldn't, and he said some fresh air would do me good.'

Her own doctor knew she wouldn't have taken any notice of him, anyway. When you reached a certain stage of your life, you had to follow your own feelings. This new doctor had her pill bottle in his hand and was writing something on a pad, and when he didn't answer immediately, she went on, more slowly this time.

'It won't do me no good, though, will it, Doc? I can dose meself up to me eyeballs, but no amount of fresh air's going to put me right, is it?'

She heard Helen draw in her breath. Tilly glanced at her, seeing the concern in her face. As if she could detach herself from the desperately sick woman that she knew she was, Tilly found herself feeling sorry for this nice countrywoman, who had no idea that her husband had always had a thing for somebody else, and didn't deserve to have a dying woman landing on her like this.

Somehow this thought gave her a small burst of strength, and she forced the familiar nauseous feelings down and sat up.

'I'm better now, and I think I'll have a proper lie down on my bed,' she announced. 'Don't worry; it was only a storm in a teacup. I've had 'em before.'

She felt Doctor Stacey pick up her limp wrist as he looked into her hollowed eyes. Her old gran used to say you could tell when a person was dying by the look in their eyes – they were the windows to the soul, or some such rot – and she knew this doctor would be seeing it now. He must have seen something else there too, because he gave a small shrug as he dropped her wrist.

'I suppose there's no use suggesting that you go into hospital for a short while, Miss Dilkes, but I've prescribed some stronger medication for you, and I'll come and see you again in a few days.'

In Tilly's opinion people went into hospital to die. Home was the place for that, she believed, with familiar things around you, and this wasn't it. Why had she been so reckless as to think this would be a respite, when she was only going to be a bleedin' burden now? It wasn't fair to anybody. It wasn't what she had come for, and she vowed to gather all her strength to make sure nobody knew just how ill she was – providing this doctor didn't tell them, of course.

'You just see me right until I go back home then, Doc, and we won't come to blows,' she said as breezily as she could, all the time glaring at him.

Ten

Helen took the prescription to the chemist straight way, and whatever the doctor had prescribed for Tilly, the stronger pills certainly seemed to perk her up a little over the next few days. On the surface she seemed almost as lively as when she'd first arrived. That was Tilly. But underneath it all she knew she had made up her mind now. Much as she had wanted to see Alice, she knew in her own mind that it had been for a very special reason. Tying up loose ends, in a way.

Of course, she knew Helen would have told Alice about her collapse, and Tilly was prepared for some questions the next time she went to see her friend – taken in Mick's car now, and with orders to stay there until he fetched her. She expected the questions, and she had prepared the answers. Alice demanded to know the truth, but the truth was going to be strictly moderated. In Tilly's opinion, a few little white lies never hurt anybody.

Alice sat beside her on her sofa and looked her straight in the eyes. 'You can't fool me that this is just a bit of a cough any more, Tilly, so just how bad are you, gel? If you can't tell me, who can you tell?'

As Tilly looked back at her, cuddling Bobby on her lap, she felt a sharp twist of envy for the way their lives had differed. But not for the world was she going to admit that this would almost certainly be the last time they would ever see one another. As she spoke, she remembered something Henry Kelsey had said.

'Get on with you; I'm not as bad as I look. The docs can sort me out, and come the summer I'll try to get down here again, and you'll see a different me then.'

Alice frowned. The words sounded cheerful enough, but she wasn't entirely taken in by them. 'Is that a promise?'

'As near as dammit. But much as I've enjoyed my visit, I think it's time I was getting back home. There's only so much fresh air a cockney like me can stand.'

'You won't go back to the factory, though, will you? You said you'd finished there,' Alice went on.

'No, I've packed up that place. I might find meself a little cleaning job, or a job in a caff, just to keep me hands busy.' The more she said it, the more she hoped to convince Alice that she would definitely be looking for a new job when she got back home. She might even do it. She wasn't dead yet.

Alice was relieved. 'That sounds a bit more like it, but we always expected to be married with kids long before now, didn't we, Tilly? Both of us, I mean.'

'Well, one of us managed it, anyway. You got everything you ever wanted, and you are happy, aren't you, Alice? I'd like to go away from here thinking that you were really happy.'

'Of course I am,' Alice said, giving Bobby an extra squeeze. 'I've got no regrets in my life.'

She added the last bit just in case Tilly was going to bring up the forbidden subject again, and she didn't want to hear it. Whatever lingering feelings she may have had for Mick, they had faded, and she fervently hoped it was the same for him. For goodness' sake, she didn't even know if he *did* have feelings for her, and it was far better never to know. Seeing Tilly again had inevitably brought some of the memories back, but somehow they had drifted away quite naturally, like the shadowy things they were always meant to be.

'I'm really glad I came, Alice,' Tilly said simply.

'So am I. It's been far too long,' Alice replied. 'And just keep in touch more often from now on. I'll want to know that your blessed cough has gone.'

'Oh, you'll be sure to hear about that,' Tilly said.

Tilly had things to do when she got back to London. Already she was mentally preparing the special letter she would write to Alice, to be posted after a certain event took place. She knew the motherly landlady at her digs could be relied upon to see that it was posted – or she might leave it with her doctor with all her other instructions. Either way, Alice would know.

As if she couldn't get away quickly enough now, Tilly's preparations were quickly made after her visit to Alice, and it was the same little group who took her back to Bristol Temple Meads railway station early one morning. Mick and Helen kept Bobby in the car, while Alice and Tilly moved out on to the windswept platform.

As the train steamed in, billowing smoke and smuts everywhere, the two friends hugged one another. There weren't so many other people around at this time of year. In any case, railway stations always seemed a good place for emotional goodbyes, but they were each determined not to shed any tears.

'You keep your promise and come back in the summer, Tilly, or I might just have to come up to London and fetch you,' Alice said as the carriage doors spilled out their few passengers, and others were urged to get on board.

'I can't see you doing that, gel. Your place is here now, and good luck to you,' Tilly replied. 'Look after yourself and your lovely family, Alice.'

'Just you remember to look after yourself as well. I'll be thinking of you, Tilly, and looking forward to hearing that all's well.'

The porters began slamming the carriage doors and there was no time for anything more. Whistles were blown and flags were waved, and the chug-chug of the engine started up, filling the platform with smoke again. Once it had cleared and the train had gone, the porters disappeared into their cubbyholes until Alice was the only person left on the deserted platform. She felt chilled and oddly bereft, as if there was so much that had been left unsaid. But it was too late now, and as she turned to go back to Mick's car she vowed to write more frequently to Tilly, urging her to follow the doctor's orders and to get well, and not to leave it so long before they saw one another again.

Jack Chase was getting a bit tired of the way his young cousin Tom kept coming round. The difference in their ages was becoming more marked to him, and not only for the simple fact of there being four years between them, either. Jack was a young man, feeling the stirrings of adulthood in every pore, while Tom was still a boy. It had been flattering at first to have Tom listening to his every word, sharing their mutual love of aeroplanes, and planning for imaginary deeds of derring-do if the war ever happened. But now it was becoming boring, especially as Tom had started reading stupid comics, and had become more fascinated with the idea of aliens from outer space. Such things were all rubbish as far as Jack was concerned, and he couldn't be bothered even to think about them. When you worked on a farm as he did, or as a vet like his father, you saw the everyday dramas of life and death, and he was scathingly uninterested in unearthly beings conjured up out of somebody's weird imagination.

Tom turned up at his cousin's house on the evening after Tilly had left for London. He was prepared for a long session of chat, and only gradually realized that he didn't have Jack's whole attention the way he usually did.

'I bet you're glad your visitor's gone,' he said at last, with a snigger. 'She could have been a stand-in for an alien if you ask me, what with her skinny arms like pokers, and all those gaudy colours she wore.'

'I don't know about that, but be glad you didn't see her when she passed out,' Jack said briefly. 'Mum said her face was white and her lips were blue, and her eyes just kept staring into space.'

'Crikey. Just like an alien, then,' Tom said, wishing he'd been there to witness it.

'More like a zombie,' Jack said.

Tom wasn't all that sure what zombies were – only that they were something ghoulish that he preferred not to know about. At least if aliens existed at all they were out of this world, and therefore no threat to anybody, as they only existed between the pages of a comic paper. Jack's knowledge was superior to Tom's, and he would probably go on at length about zombies if anybody cared to ask, but tonight Jack definitely seemed to have something else on his mind.

'Do you want to go out somewhere, Jack?' Tom said at last. 'I don't mind what we do really.'

'Look, kid, I didn't know you were going to turn up

tonight, and the fact is I'm meeting somebody at the pictures later.'

'That's all right. I'll come too, as long as you're paying,' he added cheekily.

'No, you can't, sorry. I'm meeting a girl, and you know what they say: two's company and all that.'

Tom stared at him, finally realizing that his cousin looked far tidier than usual. Jack's mother always insisted that he had a good wash and change of clothes when he got home from the farm. His Uncle Mick did the same to rid himself of any lingering smells of the vet's surgery, but tonight was different. Jack was wearing a dark Fair-Isle jumper over a nice white shirt and grey flannel trousers, and his hair was slicked down properly as if he'd just washed it. Tom hadn't really noticed how smart he was looking until now. He got up from Jack's bed where he had been sprawled out all this time, aware now of a not-so-subtle change in their relationship, and that it was probably here to stay.

'I'll be off then,' he said clumsily. 'I know when I'm not wanted.'

'Don't be daft. It's just that I've got a prior engagement. Perhaps I'll see you at the weekend, Tom.'

'Yeah. If you're not too busy.'

Bloody hell. *A prior engagement*, for God's sake. What kind of prissy talk was that for a farm boy? Tom couldn't get out of there fast enough now. When he got downstairs Helen called out and asked if he wanted a glass of lemonade. He said no thanks and escaped quickly. Despite the fact that he was big and brawny for his age, the question just seemed to emphasize to him how young they all thought him.

How very much younger than his cousin Jack, who was meeting a girl at the pictures, and would be drinking scrumpy, not lemonade. He marched home in a fit of rage, hardly knowing why it should upset him so much, other than the inescapable fact that he was fourteen, and that it was a bloody awful in-between age that he hated.

Tom wasn't the only one going through the torment of adolescence. Lucy whirled home on her next time off from work, barely able to contain her misery. She wouldn't normally have confided in her mother, but there was no one else now that Tilly had gone – and anyway, she had been nothing like as approachable as Lucy had expected. She had been so disappointed in Tilly – in fact, the whole world was one great big disappointment as far as Lucy was concerned right now.

'What on earth is wrong with you today?' Alice asked as her daughter shoved a newspaper off the sofa and flounced down on it with her arms folded, glaring at nothing in particular. 'You look as if you've lost a penny and found a ha'penny, so if you've nothing better to do than to sit there moping, you can help me change the bed sheets ready for Monday's wash.'

To her astonishment Lucy burst into noisy tears, curled up into a ball on the sofa and buried her head in a cushion. Alice sat beside her, putting her arm around her heaving shoulders.

'You'd better tell me what's happened, Lucy,' she said quietly.

She felt a flicker of fear. Lucy always gave the appearance of being self-assured, but underneath the veneer she could still be vulnerable. She might be seventeen and consider herself grown-up, but to Alice she was still a child, and any mother was aware of the pitfalls that awaited young girls leaving home. And, guiltily, she knew she had been remiss in not explaining to Lucy the things that she should have done.

'Has somebody hurt you, Lucy?' she asked delicately when she got no response at all. 'Whatever it is, you know you can tell me, and I'd never blame you for anything.'

She didn't know how else to say it, although if it was the very worst thing that could happen in a family – other than death – she didn't know how Walter would handle it. Nor the rest of her family. Nor the village. Her heart sank. There was no denying that what happened to one person in a family affected all the others. It was like the ripples in a pool. Once they began they were almost unstoppable. Which was why she had decided long ago that any thoughts she might have had about marrying the wrong man should remain a secret with her – always. The past cast long shadows, but too many people would have been hurt if it had ever been known . . . And anyway, she certainly shouldn't be thinking about it now, while her girl was sitting there looking so angry and upset.

Lucy sat up, her face blotchy, her voice sullen. 'I haven't done anything. It's *him*. How could he have been so awful, so wicked, when he seemed so nice, and I liked him so much? How can you ever tell what a person is like underneath? They always hide the real people they are behind smiles and flattery.'

Alice's alarm grew to nightmarish proportions. *Oh God, this wasn't going to be the worst news a mother could hear about a daughter falling for some rogue, was it?* Her heart was racing so fast she thought she would explode if Lucy didn't explain properly what was happening. She prayed it wasn't as bad as she feared, and she gripped her daughter's hands tightly and tried to keep her voice steady.

'Who is this person, Lucy, and what has he done to you?'

Lucy snorted. 'He hasn't done anything to *me*. His name's Ben and he's a stable lad at the Grange. We've chatted a few times, and I really liked him, Mum, and I thought he liked me too,' she added, her voice faltering. 'I never thought he'd be a thief, but he was caught red-handed and forced to return the things he had stolen. He's been dismissed without a reference from Mr Frankley, and warned that if he shows his face in the area again, he'll get the police after him.'

Alice could have wept with relief as she realized Lucy had been done no harm. But she could see how her daughter was truly suffering at what she clearly saw as a betrayal of Ben's position, coupled with the humiliation she felt that she had liked and trusted this young man. She hardly knew what to say for the moment, but she knew it was a situation that had to be handled carefully.

'How could he have done such a thing, Mum? The Frankleys are such good employers, and I never thought Ben could have been so mean,' Lucy continued, bewildered.

'Well, darling, you've always seen the world in black and white, but there are many shades of grey in it. We have to accept that people have flaws.'

'*You* don't.'

Alice flinched at the impulsive and innocent words. 'I'm not perfect, my love, any more than anyone else. I just try to do the best for my family, the same as I've always done.'

Lucy was silent for a moment and then she gave a heavy sigh.

'I always thought your old friend Tilly was perfect, but she has flaws too, doesn't she? That awful scent of hers was meant to be so sophisticated, but it was almost sickening, wasn't it? Dad said the house practically needed to be fumigated after she'd gone. I know you don't like hearing anything against her, Mum, but you have to agree with me on that!'

Alice laughed ruefully, thankful that at least Lucy's thoughts were diverted from Ben for the moment. 'I'm afraid I do, love. But if it makes her happy, and it cheers her up when she's obviously not well, I'm not going to blame her for it.'

It was obvious that Lucy wasn't going to be diverted for very long, and the frown soon returned to her face.

'Do you think I was a fool to take Ben at face value?'

'Of course you weren't. It's what we all do, until we learn otherwise. We can't know what goes on in someone else's mind, or what their background is, either. If it teaches you to be more cautious in the future, and providing he was no more than a friend, as you say, then be glad you haven't had your heart broken.'

Lucy wasn't prepared to tell her mother she had harboured secret thoughts of Ben being more than a friend. She hadn't intended blurting it all out, either, but the black rage she had felt when she learned the truth about Ben's shady little pilfering was disappearing now, and once she got over the hurt she felt, she knew she would count her blessings that she hadn't been more involved with him.

Alice confided the things Lucy had told her to Walter in bed that evening, being careful not to let him think there had been any romantic goings-on between the young couple. She was sure there hadn't been, so there was nothing shameful about repeating how Lucy had felt so betrayed by a friend's behaviour. She knew Walter wouldn't have any truck with a young chap who stole from his employers. He would just be glad that Lucy had had a lucky escape.

'I always wondered about letting her work in that place,' he said.

'I'm sure we need have no worries about Mr and Mrs Frankley as upright employers, Walter, especially hearing how they dealt with the boy so swiftly. They wouldn't want any hint of scandal attached to their good name. Lucy was very upset about the whole episode, but I think this little experience will have opened her eyes a little, and when she realizes she was lucky not to be involved with a bad apple, it will have done her more good than harm.'

'You're probably right, Mother. You usually are in such matters.'

'I know. And it's Alice.'

Walter gave a low chuckle and squeezed her to him, the warmth of his large body enveloping her.

'You know I only say it half the time to rile you, don't you, girl? I know how your eyes sparkle when I do it, and even if I can't see them in the dark right now, I can guess how they look. Your eyes were what I remembered most about you when you went back to London after we first met. Blue as the sea they were, and they're still as bright as ever.'

Alice felt her mouth open with shock as he affectionately smacked her rump and turned over in the bed to start snoring almost at once.

He was paying her a compliment! And not just any old compliment: a compliment about her eyes . . . It was one of the remarks that had cropped up more often than anything else in the letters he had written her at that time. The letters were always written in Walter's hand, but she had always assumed they were Mick's sentiments. She still did . . . And yet . . .

Women remembered those things, but men didn't, and it was so unlikely that Walter would remember phrases his brother had suggested he should write all those years ago. Wasn't it far more likely that they had been his own feelings after all? The thought took her totally by surprise.

Impulsively she snuggled into his back, rather than sleep back to back as they normally did, and she heard his sleepy grunt of approval at her closeness.

The next time she and Bobby went to see Helen, Alice asked her sister-in-law bluntly what she had thought about Tilly's condition.

Helen hesitated. She had never considered Alice as impulsive a person as she thought Tilly could be, but the two of them had a long history of friendship behind them, and the last thing Alice needed was to be torn between looking after her family and rushing off to London to care for her sick friend. But she had always been a truthful person, and she thought carefully before she answered.

'Well, it's obvious that she's ill,' she admitted. 'I think she's the kind of person who puts on a front to hide the way she truly feels, but I'm sure you know that, Alice. I suppose it's something we all do at times. We all have private thoughts we'd prefer to keep to ourselves, don't we?' Helen smiled as she spoke, swinging Bobby around and making him shriek with laughter as she did so.

'You'd better be careful doing that, or he'll be having one of his accidents again. Lord knows I'm having a hard enough time getting him dry,' Alice warned, ignoring what Helen had just said. 'Anyway, Tilly's promised me that she'll try to come back for another visit in the summer, so that can't mean it's anything too serious, can it?'

'You're probably right,' Helen said, putting Bobby down.

'I'm sure you don't have thoughts you prefer to keep to yourself, anyway,' Alice went on, moving her own thoughts away from Tilly. 'You're the most open person I know.'

'But none of us knows another person through and through, do they? People only see what they want to see, and what people see when they look at me, for instance, is just a ruddy-faced countrywoman married to a country vet, who does her bit at the church socials and other village events. For all anybody knows, I might be a cauldron of jealousy and heaving emotions underneath this calm exterior.'

Alice burst out laughing, not thinking for a moment that

any of this could be true. 'For heaven's sake, Helen, I've never known you to get so philosophical!'

'Well, that's just what I mean. You didn't know that part of me at all, even after all these years.'

For the first time, Alice thought she detected a slight edge to Helen's voice.

'I know I'm as fond of you as if you were my real sister,' she said sincerely, 'and don't go implying that you're a frump. You're certainly not that, Helen, and Mick wouldn't have married a frump.'

'He might have married you if Walter hadn't got there first.'

Alice's heart thumped. For a few seconds she wasn't sure if she had really heard those words. Helen was showing Bobby how to put his wooden puzzle pieces together now, her face flushed as she leaned towards him on the rug. This conversation had suddenly become very tense, and how she answered it could mark an important moment in all their lives. She kept her voice light and amused, even though her heart was still thumping.

'Well, daft as that remark is, I daresay I might have married Mick, if he'd ever wanted me to, or asked me to, and if I hadn't fallen for Walter and known that he was the one for me!'

She could have said more, but that would only have made it all seem more of a possibility than Helen needed to hear. She was truly fond of Helen, and the last thing she wanted to do was to upset her by putting unwanted suspicions in her mind. Perhaps they had always been there beneath the surface, and that was something else Alice didn't want to think about either. When Helen continued playing with Bobby, she gave a small chuckle.

'Just listen to us, Helen. Two settled old matrons like us, talking about falling for young chaps and who we should have married, when we're all contented family folk. At our age it's long past time to leave all that falling in love nonsense to the young ones. You should be glad you've not got daughters to fret about. They can keep your thoughts too busy to worry about anything else!'

The hint of a bit of gossip was more than enough to catch Helen's attention.

'Don't tell me Rose is still pining over that Kelsey boy,' she said.

If she hadn't been able to rely on Helen being totally discreet when it came to family business, she would never have told her about Lucy's recent upset. As it was, she was careful not to say things too blatantly while Bobby was within earshot.

She explained about the incident at the Grange and had all Helen's sympathy over Lucy's bruised feelings. Then, before the afternoon descended completely into gloom, Alice told her about the new young doctor who was going to share the practice with his brother, Doctor Stacey.

'The old ducks in the village won't be too keen on having to see a young spark,' Helen said dubiously. 'They won't take easily to somebody new, either.'

'Well, according to Rose, he's perfectly charming. I think she's taken a bit of a shine to him, and you must admit, he'd be a better catch than a greengrocer's son. Mind you, I don't know that a doctor's son would think our Rose such a catch, being the daughter of a sawmill worker, no matter how much we think of her.'

Helen defended her at once. 'Rose would be a catch for anyone, and I'll not hear anyone say a word against her. Now then, let's have a cup of tea. I'm parched after all that talking, and I'm sure you are too.'

The rest of the afternoon passed amicably. Mick looked in on them when he came back from his regular rounds to the outlying farms before he went upstairs to wash and change. Alice found herself looking at him more quizzically than she usually did, as Helen pressed him to have a cup of tea first, saying he looked done in.

'I am a bit,' he admitted. 'There's a hard frost on some of the lanes, and it was a job to keep the old car on the road sometimes.'

'It's a pity you can't get an assistant like Doctor Stacey,' Helen said. 'You work too hard, my dear.'

She ruffled his hair as she passed him his cup of tea, and the smiles that passed between them were of pure affection. As if she was suddenly hit by a blinding light, Alice wondered how she could ever have thought, for one minute, that Mick Chase had feelings for anyone other than his wife.

Even more, how could she herself ever have thought seriously that she had feelings for him, other than brotherly ones?

Eleven

A couple of weeks later Tilly still hadn't done anything about getting another job, and she knew in her heart that she wouldn't bother. She'd saved enough out of her wages to last her for a while, and if she couldn't manage to keep body and soul together she'd think about it then. There were things she had to do, anyway, and something was driving her on, giving her small bursts of energy that could almost make her believe she was getting better.

Almost feverishly, she wrote the letters she had to write. She made lists of instructions, just as if she was a proper secretary in an office, even though she didn't have an inkling of what actually went on in such places. The next time her landlady popped in to her room to collect the rent, on an impulse she gave her a cheap picture of the seaside that had been hanging on her wall ever since she first went to Somerset. Mrs Coggins had always admired it. She was a good old dab, but privately Tilly thought Mrs Coggins could be a good model for a saucy picture, with her ample bosoms squeezing over the top of her dress and her fat little legs barely able to hold her up. The thought always tickled her.

'I don't know what you want to give this away for, gel,' she said to Tilly. 'Didn't your last visit to your old friend come up to your whatsits?'

''Course it did, but I've got too much stuff in me room, so I'm getting rid of some of it. Having a good clear-out like me dear old gran used to say when she gave me a dose of castor oil of a Friday night.'

Mrs Coggins shrieked with so much laughter that every bit of her buxom shape rolled and rippled like the waves in the sea.

'She must have been a caution, your old gran. What you

doing with all this stuff then?' she said, noting the cardboard box that Tilly was filling.

'I might take it to the church jumble sale on Saturday. The other lot on the chair's ready for chucking out. None of it's up to much.'

'Blimey, gel, you're getting in with the church a bit lately, ain't you? You ain't got a fancy for that new young vicar, have you?'

Tilly laughed back, suppressing a cough as she did so. 'Chance would be a fine thing. Just as if he'd ever look at an old has-been like me.'

'You ain't old. What are you, forty-five?'

'Forty-one, if you don't mind!' Tilly said indignantly, wishing the old trout would leave her now. She was starting to get exhausted with all this clearing out, and all this talking, and she could feel that the painful, stifling wheezing was going to start again, taking all her breath with it. 'Anyway, if I find anything else you might like, I'll be sure to bring it down to you.'

'You ain't thinking of doing a moonlight flit, are you?' Mrs Coggins said, suddenly suspicious. 'You've always been a good tenant, and I like a bit of notice before anybody leaves.'

'Don't worry, I'm not planning anything like that,' said Tilly with the brightest smile she could manage.

Armed with her picture, the woman left her alone at last, clumping down the stairs as fast as her waddling girth would let her. It wasn't fair, Tilly thought, suddenly savage. It wasn't fair that an old crone like her, obscenely overweight and living off the rent her tenants gave her, should look as though she'd go on for ever while Tilly was increasingly sure her days could be counted. There wasn't much to see out of her small window, and the East End was always pretty murky, anyway, but lately she often imagined she could see the vultures gathering, like angels of death. She shivered. Mrs Coggins was probably right and she was spending more time than she ever did at the church lately if she was getting so bleedin' fanciful. She didn't know if God made an allowance for a late sinner coming home to roost, or if she even believed in such things herself. She just liked the peace and quiet

inside the church on days when there wasn't a service or a
choir practice going on, and she could have the place to
herself. Just her and God.

Without warning, she felt something erupt like an earth-
quake inside her. She grabbed the only thing handy, which
was the cardboard box of stuff for the church jumble sale,
and the next minute she had fetched up an enormous quan-
tity of blood and mucous that left her gasping and weak.

She staggered back on to her bed, knowing she would
have to have a few minutes' rest before she felt able to cover
the lot with old newspapers and get rid of it all. So much
for helping the church, she thought, her head rocking fit to
bursting. Perhaps this was God's way of telling her he didn't
want an old sinner like her after all. But she didn't believe
that. She *wouldn't* believe that. Inside her head the words of
an old childhood hymn were going round and round in her
jangled brain.

'All things bright and beautiful . . . all creatures great and
small . . . All things wise and wonderful . . . the Lord God
made them all . . .'

Her gran used to bellow out that hymn at the top of her
voice when Tilly was a child. Not in church though. Her
gran always said you didn't have to go to church to be a
good person, because God would know you anyway. You
were all God's children, if you were young or old, fat or
thin or bald. Her gran had been going bald by the time she
died. For some reason the thought of that word started Tilly
giggling. The giggling brought on more coughing, which
produced a second eruption inside her, doubling her up with
excruciating pain, worse than ever before, so bad that she
simply slid to the floor in the middle of her own vomit and
knew no more.

It was four days before the smell in the house got so bad
that the other tenants got Mrs Coggins to go and investigate.
She had a key to all the rooms, and one of her male tenants
hovered behind her when she opened the door to Tilly Dilkes's
room. Once they stepped inside they both recoiled in horror
at what they saw.

The doctor was sent for at once, even though it was obvious

there was nothing that anybody could do for the poor woman. The police and the vicar came too, as if she deserved more dignified attention in death than she ever had in life.

'I only saw her four days ago when I collected me rent,' Mrs Coggins told them all tearfully. 'She was looking all right then, apart from that awful cough she had, but I thought it was a bit funny when she gave me a picture. I thought she was thinking of doing a moonlight flit, poor little devil. I never thought she was about to snuff it.'

Once the police had agreed that there was nothing suspicious about the death, and learned from the doctor that, judging from his recent diagnosis, this wasn't an altogether unexpected occurrence, the doctor took charge. Tilly had to be moved and taken to a chapel of rest. The disgusting room had to be cleaned and fumigated, and once the doctor had done all he could do there was another duty that he had undertaken to perform when the time came. There was a telephone number that he had promised to call as soon as possible.

There weren't many telephones in the village of Bramwell, but one of them belonged to the local vet. When the telephone rang in his surgery, Mick Chase was out on his rounds to one of the outlying farms where there was a problem with the sheep. It was ringing for quite a while before Helen heard it and hurried through from the connecting room.

'I need to speak to a Mr Mick Chase,' said a voice that she didn't recognize.

Assuming that it was a business call for Mick, Helen said swiftly that he wasn't here right now but that she would take a message. 'This is Mrs Chase,' she added.

'Then you'll be the person I want to speak to. It's about Miss Tilly Dilkes.'

Helen felt a shiver run through her. She didn't know the caller, and it took a few moments before she realized what the call was about. When she did so, her hand gripped the receiver more tightly, and her face blanched.

'There's no mistake, is there, Doctor?' she stuttered, as though a medical man would mistake the fact of a woman dying. But he had dealt with enough people in a state of shock to know how it took them.

'I'm afraid not,' he said. 'Miss Dilkes died five days ago now, although her body has only just been discovered. Her instructions were that Mrs Alice Chase should be told as soon as possible.'

Helen gulped. 'Alice is my sister-in-law, but I will let her know immediately, of course. But if it happened five days ago, has . . . has Miss Dilkes been buried?'

'Not yet, and I understand there are no relatives. So if you would pass on the message to Mrs Alice Chase, please.'

'Of course I will,' Helen said, still reeling but sensing that the doctor wanted to bring the conversation to an end.

She replaced the receiver as carefully as if she were dealing with a precious object. For all her self-assurance and common sense, she hated the thing, and always avoided answering it if she could. It could be the bringer of good news and of bad, and this would be the worst of news for Alice. But Alice had to be told, however painful it was going to be for both of them. Helen put on her outer clothes quickly and set out at once. She had gone halfway when she saw a familiar figure ahead of her, and felt a small rush of relief.

'Rose, hold on a minute,' she called out.

Rose turned around on hearing her aunt's voice. One of the pleasant duties of caring for the Staceys' baby was taking Mollie out in her pram and stopping to gossip with people she knew, just like a real young mother out with her child. She was too level-headed to fall into the trap of imagining that Mollie was her own, but taking Mollie out for her daily walk was a very enjoyable part of her day. She smiled as her aunt caught up with her, and then the smile changed.

'What's happened?' she asked, alarmed.

'I'm really glad to see you, Rose, and if you can spare the time, will you come and see your mother with me?'

'You're worrying me now. Has something happened to Uncle Mick or Jack?'

'Not them.' Helen's voice choked a little. 'It's Tilly. We've had a telephone call from her doctor. She's dead, Rose.'

Rose stood quite still in the middle of the street, oblivious to other people tut-tutting and skirting around the baby's pram. Her head was whirling.

'She can't be dead! She was here a few weeks ago. It must

be a mistake, Auntie Helen,' she said, repeating the word
Helen herself had used.

'I'm afraid it's not, my dear. It seems she was more ill
than any of us realized, and now I have to tell your mother,
and I just don't know how to do it.'

Rose took charge. 'It will be a terrible shock for her, but
we'll do it together.'

'I was hoping you'd say that. I've never been a coward in
facing up to things, Rose, but this was so unexpected, it's
really shaken me.'

They walked on towards the cottage where the smoke from
the chimney curled upwards into a clear blue sky. April morn-
ings could be chilly, and Alice always kept a fire burning in
the hearth until the sun got up. Today it was an idyllic scene,
with not a breath of wind anywhere. The leaves on the trees
were burgeoning into their lacy green foliage, heralding a
lovely spring day, and the woman inside the cottage had no
idea that her happy world was about to come crashing down.

Alice opened the door with a ready smile when she saw
the trio of visitors approaching. 'Well, this is a nice surprise.
It's not often I get an excuse to stop dusting the bedrooms
for a cup of tea and a chat.'

She had had no premonition of what was to come, even
though she wondered later if some instinct had kept her
talking to put off the moment when she heard the news. Her
voice finally trailed away as she saw the expressions on the
faces of Rose and Helen, and she knew that not even Bobby
hurtling across the room and begging to hold baby Mollie
was going to put off this moment. But in the end she was
more perceptive than Rose had been.

'It's Tilly, isn't it? I guessed that if she got worse, she'd
send a message through you and Mick. You'd better tell me,
Helen.'

'Sit down, Mum,' Rose said.

'I don't need to sit down. Just tell me what's happened.'

'I'm so sorry to have to tell you, Alice, but she's dead,'
Helen said shakily. 'Her doctor rang to tell Mick, but he was
out, so I took the call, and you know how I hate those telephones. I came to tell you straight away, and I ran into Rose
on the way.'

She was babbling too fast now, telling her everything, about the fact that Tilly had already been dead for five days, and that she hadn't been buried yet. By now Rose was holding tightly to her mother's hands. Alice was deathly pale, but she shook Rose off.

'I don't believe it,' she said, her voice stormy with grief.

'You have to believe it, Mum. Auntie Helen wouldn't make up a thing like this, would she?'

Alice automatically pulled Bobby back from leaning so far into Mollie's pram that he was in danger of going in head first on top of her. She felt bewildered, angry, and too shocked to even cry as yet.

'I *knew* she was worse than she said she was. She should have stayed here, or I should have gone back with her for a while. I could have nursed her. Why didn't she let me?'

'You had a family to care for, Alice,' Helen said gently.

'And she didn't,' Alice said. 'That's the point, isn't it? But there's nothing to stop me going to her now, is there?'

'You can't leave Dad and the boys to fend for themselves!' Rose said.

Alice had always been quick-thinking, and she was thinking quickly now.

'I need to see her for myself, and also to arrange a decent funeral for her. There's nobody else to do it, and I won't just let her disappear as if she never counted for anything. I'll wait until Walter comes home this evening to tell him what's happened, and by then I'll have thought out my plans properly. You can take Bobby to the Staceys' every day, Rose. Caring for two children instead of one won't hurt you. And Helen, if I can rely on you to cook for the family while I'm away for a week or so I'd be indebted to you.'

She rattled on as if she were organizing a military manoeuvre. There would be the usual household tasks to attend to as well – beds to be made, family washing to be done, Bobby to be reassured that his mum was only going away for a little while. All those things could be fixed, Alice thought, dismissing them as easily as if she had swatted a fly. Shock was still forcing her thoughts to race on, making plans, keeping her mind away from the awful truth that her dearest friend was dead. She was still talking in a high, rapid voice when she felt Helen shaking her.

'Stop it, Alice. You'll make yourself ill, going on like this!'

Rose must have been making tea all this time, because as Helen forced her to sit down, Alice felt a cup being thrust into her hand. She sipped the hot sweet liquid dutifully, and then her hands began to tremble so much Helen took it away from her quickly.

'Leave it a few minutes until you've had a chance to calm down, my dear,' Helen said. 'As for the things you've been saying, if you really do mean to go to London to see what can be done for Tilly, of course Rose and I will do everything that's needed here. You can rely on us, can't she, Rose?'

'Of course you can, Mum. I'm sure Mrs Stacey won't have any objection to my taking Bobby to work with me. We'll manage everything between us.'

In a strangely detached moment, Alice wondered if this was how it would be if she never came back, and just stayed in London for good, back in her old haunts, among the people she had grown up with and knew so well. They would all manage without her here. She would be like Tilly. Gone for ever, and no more than a memory. But just as instantly the feeling was gone. Didn't she want them to manage without her, for God's sake? They were offering their help in the saddest of times, not pushing her out!

'I think I can drink that tea now,' she said huskily.

Alice was nothing like Tilly, nor was she the girl she had once been, not any more. She had the love and support of a family around her, and that was more precious than gold. She caught Bobby's eyes watching her, huge and round and scared, and she made herself smile at him.

'You're dying to hold that baby, aren't you, Bobby? You sit here beside me and Rose will put her in your arms. Be gentle now, and mind her head.'

She fussed over him until he was settled with the baby, tickling her chin and making her laugh. This was normal. This was everyday life. This wasn't thinking about what had to be done for Tilly, not yet. This was putting it off, just for the moment, and pretending – just for the moment – that none of it had really happened.

But she wasn't like that. Whatever had to be faced had to be faced, and eventually she gave a deep sigh and sat up straighter.

'I'm all right now. Well, as right as I can be in the circumstances. I wonder if you can do one more thing for me, Helen. I know you don't like using the telephone, but can you find out the times of the trains to London for tomorrow morning? I'll want to go as soon as possible.'

'Of course I will, and you needn't fret about your family while you're away. I'll see that they don't starve, my dear,' Helen said, admiring her resilience.

It had taken a strong-willed person to leave her old home all those years ago and move to a new environment to marry the man she loved, and that strong will wasn't deserting Alice now. By the time Helen left the cottage, leaving Rose there for a while longer, she guessed that Alice would already be thinking about whatever clothes she would need to take. It wouldn't be a holiday, and it would be strange for her to return to the places she once knew, since she had never been back, nor wanted to do so. But this was different. This would be a journey of sorrow as well as love. Helen prayed that Alice would be up to it after all.

Walter and Tom came home from work that night to a very different reception from usual. Alice was normally preparing their evening meal by then, her face rosy from the heat of the kitchen, ready to welcome them with a hot cup of tea. Rose was always there before them, and tonight it was Rose who was setting the table for their meal, while Bobby played with his floor puzzles. A succulent rabbit and dumpling stew was simmering on the stove in the kitchen, and Alice was nowhere to be seen.

'Where's your mother?' Walter said at once, shaking off the wood shavings that clung to his coat before slinging it on the hook on the back of the door.

'She's upstairs,' Rose began.

'She's not ill, is she?' Tom said at once. 'She's never ill.'

Rose shook her head. 'No, she's not ill, but she's had a shock. Tilly died, Dad, and Mum's taken it very hard.'

Walter stared at his daughter as if she had gone mad.

'What do you mean, Tilly died? She was here a few weeks ago, and I know she didn't look fit to start jumping five-bar gates, but she wasn't that bad, was she? It must be some kind of joke. She was always one for teasing folk.'

'Don't go saying anything like that to Mum, Dad,' Rose warned him. 'Tilly's doctor phoned Auntie Helen to let us know, so it's definitely true. We've been here with her for most of the afternoon, and Mum's packing a case to go to London in the morning to see what she can do.'

Rose wished she hadn't had to give him the news like that. She wished her mum had been downstairs to say it all herself. But no matter who said it, how could there ever be a good for such news to be told?

'Going to London?' Walter roared. 'What the blazes does she want to do that for? She can't do anything for the woman if she's dead, can she?'

'Dad, for heaven's sake,' Rose hissed, but it was too late. Alice was already downstairs, her face white, her lips pressed tightly together.

'I know you didn't mean to be cruel, Walter, but Tilly's got nobody else, and I have to see her decently buried. You won't deny me that, will you?'

As her face crumpled she swayed as if she was about to faint, and in a moment she was held tight in his arms.

'God knows I've never denied you anything, Alice,' he said roughly now. 'I know Tilly never married, but you're not telling that in all the years you've been apart she's never had other friends. There's bound to be others.'

Alice shook her head. 'Workmates, I daresay, but I know I'm the one she'll want to be there to see her on her final journey.'

Tom cleared his throat. Too much talk about final journeys and the hereafters didn't sit comfortably in his mind. 'How long will you be gone, Mum? And what's happening about us?'

She looked over Walter's shoulder at him. Her practical son, who didn't always have his head in the clouds with his talk of aeroplanes and aliens from outer space, could always be relied on to bring things down to a proper level. She extricated herself from Walter's arms and told them all to sit at the table while Rose brought in the pot of stew and began ladling it out. She didn't think she could eat a thing, but she knew she had better try.

'I should think about a week, Tom. Rose will take Bobby to work with her each day, and Auntie Helen has said she'll cook your evening meals. Between them they'll see that everything goes smoothly, and you'll hardly know I'm gone before I'm home again.'

Even as she said it, she knew it was a daunting prospect to leave them all. It was so long since she had been to London, and she and Walter had never been apart in all the years of their marriage. As if he was thinking the same thing, she felt his hand reach out and cover hers. Walter, above all, knew how dear Tilly's friendship had always been to her, and she could see he had remembered it now.

'We'll all be glad when that day comes, Mother, so you just do what has to be done, and I'm sure we'll manage.'

That was a bit rich, considering he had never considered it a man's job to lift a finger to do anything in the house, thought Alice with a glimmer of humour. But with a surge of relief, she knew she could rely on her family. They would cope. She was the one who wasn't sure whether or not she could.

Helen and Mick turned up during the evening to say there was a train to Paddington at ten o'clock the following morning, and that they would drive Alice to Bristol Temple Meads station in good time.

'You're all being so good,' Alice said, feeling the weak tears stab her eyes again and dashing them away.

'We're just being your family,' Helen said, giving her a quick hug.

That night, cuddled up beside Walter in bed, the tears flowed at last, and once they started she couldn't stop them. So many memories flashed in and out of her head of all the times she and Tilly had spent together. Right from childhood they had been best friends, going to the same school, growing up together, working in the same factory, sharing secrets and fears, and becoming ever more excited about the wonderful work outing that was to take them to Somerset and would change their lives for ever. In Alice's mind now, Tilly was still the laughing girl she had always been, and not the sick woman who had breathed her last.

'She can't be dead,' Alice sobbed in Walter's arms. 'She just can't be dead, can she? I don't want to believe it, Walter.'

He felt helpless, knowing instinctively that there was no comfort, and even more certain that she had to do as she wanted. Without seeing Tilly for herself, however painful it would be, Alice would never be able to accept the truth that she was gone for ever.

'Hush, my dear,' he said clumsily. 'You'll do yourself no good by keening so, and you need to keep up your strength for the journey tomorrow.'

As her sobs gradually subsided, she knew it was his tacit acceptance of what she had to do. In all the confusion and upset she hadn't even asked his permission, like a good wife should. She had just told him she was going to London, but by now his initial anger had softened into tenderness. He was a big man in every sense of the word, and in that moment, she had never loved him more.

Twelve

Despite her resolve, Alice was dreading the moment when she would part from her family. She hugged Walter and Tom before they went off to the sawmills the following morning, but it was less easy to let go of Bobby, who clung to her and cried, and couldn't understand why he had to go off with Rose so early in the morning. It was only the fact that he would be allowed to play with baby Mollie all day and help to look after her that brought a smile back to his anxious little face. Then Mick and Helen came to take her to the station, and there was no more time to mope. Once there, they kissed her goodbye and wished her well, and urged her to try and telephone them to let them know when she arrived, and when she was coming home, so that they could arrange to meet her again.

It was all so strange. Alice hadn't been on a train for years, and as more passengers got into the carriage, she began to feel more and more like the middle-aged countrywoman she had become, rather than the eager young girl who had made the reverse journey. She didn't talk to anybody, and the hours seemed endless until at last the train steamed and puffed into Paddington Station, where she studied the underground map to find the train that would take her to Whitechapel.

This was where she and Tilly had grown up, and where Tilly still lived – and had died. It was familiar territory, or would be again, once she had found the platform and stopped being swept along with the crowds who all seemed to know where they going, and when her heart stopped banging so remorselessly with nerves. Were there ever so many people . . .?

'Lost your way, duck?' a woman asked her as she was still studying her ticket. 'Follow me, and I'll see you right.'

Alice did as she was told, just thankful to hear a friendly voice with an accent like Tilly's, which reminded her that she was home after all. The underground train was stifling and she hated it, but at last she had reached her destination, and she stepped outside into fresh air – or at least the freshest air that London could manage. Her mouth trembled, knowing this was the saddest journey she had ever made, and unsure which way to go for a moment. The woman who had helped her before was still hovering beside her.

'What place are you looking for, duck? A stranger, are you?'

Alice swallowed. 'I shouldn't be. I grew up around here, but I haven't been back for years. Do you know the way to Basin Street?'

'It's not far. You go down a coupla streets to the left and then you turn right, past the mews and the next one's Basin Street. Will that do you?'

Alice thanked her and followed the instructions to the house where Tilly had her lodgings. Her resolve was still strong. She wanted to see the landlady before she saw the doctor and found out where Tilly had been taken. There was a funeral to arrange and then she would go to the factory to make sure some of Tilly's workmates turned up on the day to give Tilly a proper send-off. She knew that some of them were still there from the time she and Tilly had worked there together. It seemed a depressingly long time.

The fat woman who opened the door of the shabby-looking house stared at Alice and her small suitcase. She wiped her hands on her overall, sensing a new tenant, and one that didn't look as scruffy as some.

'Are you looking for a room? There's two available at the moment.'

Alice felt the words sticking in her throat, but she forced herself to say them.

'I'm Alice Chase. I'm Tilly's friend.'

She felt so faint that she was hardly aware of the woman pulling her inside the house and sitting her down in a big untidy sitting room, nor of the cup of tea placed on the table beside her, the panacea for all ills.

'You look as if you ain't eaten in days,' the landlady said.

'I'm Mrs Coggins, by the way, so drink that tea and eat a biscuit, and then we'll talk.'

Alice realized she hadn't eaten anything since leaving home that morning and that her stomach was telling her so. She did as she was told, but all she wanted to know was how Tilly had died, and if she had been alone.

'I wish I could tell you different,' Mrs Coggins said sympathetically. 'There was nobody with the poor gel, but the doc said it would have happened so fast she wouldn't have known anything about it. Are you planning on staying? I could give you her old room, or the other one that's vacant. It's all cleaned up, of course.'

'I'll take the other one,' Alice said quickly, unable to bear the thought of sleeping in the same room where Tilly had died.

'Right you are. I'll show it to you now. I don't normally do food for my tenants, and you'll find two gas rings in your room, but you look famished, so if you want a bite to eat when you're ready, come back downstairs.'

'Thank you for being so kind,' Alice said huskily. 'I'll do as you say, and then I'll need the doctor's address, please.'

She wanted to do everything as quickly as possible. She needed to do what she could for Tilly and to see that she was decently buried. It was the last thing she could do for her. Walter had been generous in giving her what he could afford for her train fare and other expenses, but she didn't know whether Tilly had made any provisions for a funeral, or had even thought about it. You didn't, when you were young.

'Oh, and there's summat here for you,' Mrs Coggins went on. 'It was among her things, and I would have sent it on to you, but I ain't had a minute to meself yet. I had to get rid of all her stuff to pay for the extra cleaning and all. I reckon she'd been clearing things out for a while . . .'

She kept on talking as Alice took the packet and followed the woman upstairs to the room she'd been assigned. It was adequate enough, and the rent was modest. Once she was alone, Alice sat down on the bed weeping, only now realizing what an ordeal it had been just to get here. And the real ordeal hadn't even begun yet. She braced herself and

looked at the packet, addressed to her in Bramwell in Tilly's
scrawling handwriting. She swallowed the lump in her throat
and opened it.

> By the time you get this, I'll have popped my clogs,
> Alice. You'll know it by now, so it won't be any surprise.
> There's a bit of money here for your kids. It's not much,
> but you're all I've got to give it to, so be sure to tell
> them it's from their Auntie Tilly. The enclosed book is
> from the funeral club, so you can get the money out
> once you've got my death certificate from the doc. There
> should be enough to see me planted, and if there's any
> left, you're to keep it. Don't start bawling over me,
> Alice, 'cos I'll be up there looking down on you to see
> that you don't. That is, unless I'm sent to the other
> place. You were always the lucky one, gel, so you make
> sure you enjoy the rest of your life.
> Always your loving pal, Tilly.

If Tilly thought Alice wasn't going to bawl her eyes out after
reading that little lot, she didn't know her as well as she
thought she did, Alice thought now. But she finally straightened up, splashed her face with cold water from the jug on
the washstand, and went back downstairs to find Mrs Coggins.

'There you are, my dear,' the woman said, taking one look
at her. 'Now before you do anything else, come and sit down
and have some of this tripe and onions to line your stomach.'

Normally it would be enough to make her retch, but Alice
would have eaten almost anything at that stage. In any case,
she hardly tasted it, but she certainly felt better when she
was warmed inside.

'Can you give me the doctor's address now, Mrs Coggins?'
she asked. 'His name's Doctor Ryman, but I'm sure you
know that.'

'Why don't you leave it until tomorrow morning? You
look done in.'

Alice hesitated. 'I suppose it's the best idea, when my
head's clear. But I thought he may let me telephone home
to let them know I've got here safely.'

'You can do that from the telephone box around the corner.

I'll come with you and show you how to use it. You won't want
to be wandering about at night by yourself around this area.'

Alice suppressed a weird temptation to laugh. She and
Tilly had raced around these streets and alleyways as children with never any thought of danger. They had hung around
some of the local pubs and asked the regulars for pennies
to buy bags of chips and had been given them with a ready
smile for their cheek. But it was all different now. She was
a grieving woman, and felt more vulnerable than any child.
Mrs Coggins was right in guessing that she didn't even know
how to use a public telephone. She was almost ashamed at
her lack of knowledge, and she accepted the offer humbly.
The landlady might be a bit of a pantomime figure, but she
was a kindly soul. When they reached the telephone box,
Mrs Coggins asked the operator for Mick's number. After
what seemed like an age, Alice was handed the receiver, and
she heard Mick's voice at the other end of the line.

Her eyes smarted. She knew Mick would have answered,
but he sounded so much like Walter at that moment that she
could almost have imagined she was speaking to him. And
oh, how she wished it could have been him! But a private
telephone was not for the likes of them.

'Mick, it's Alice,' she said huskily. 'I wanted to let everyone
know that I'm here safely, and I've got a room to rent. Please
let Walter know, will you?'

'Of course I will. I'll go round straight away. And you're
all right?'

'I'm fine. I shall see about things tomorrow. I'm in a telephone box now so I can't talk for long, but would you ask
Walter to be at your place after supper tomorrow night, so
that I can call again and speak to him?'

'I'll do that. You take care of yourself, Alice.'

She sensed that he would have said more, but she had had
enough for one day and she hung up quickly, strangely
deflated. It was odd to be speaking to him at such a distance.
She liked him enormously. Well, if she was honest, she had
always felt something more than like for him, and yet she
had felt nothing for him just now. He was no more than a
connection between her and Walter, and she still wished with
all her heart that it was Walter she had spoken to just then.

'Come on, gel. Let's get you back,' Mrs Coggins said, noting her pinched face. 'You've had a long day, and you'll want to be up bright and early tomorrow morning. Do you know what's to be done?' she asked delicately.

'I'll find out tomorrow,' Alice said, having no intention of saying too much to the landlady. She remembered Tilly once saying what an old gossip she was, and the less she knew about Tilly's circumstances, the better.

On the way back to the house she bought a few necessities – bread and butter, milk and eggs, and a packet of cereal for her breakfast. Then she was finally alone in the unfamiliar room and, long before she normally went to bed, she was lying wide-eyed on the hard mattress, feeling a million miles away from home and missing her family. Missing the warmth of Walter's body next to hers; missing Bobby . . .

She had a restless night, tossing and turning, and going over everything she had to do a hundred times, so that when she woke up in the morning she felt worse than ever. This was no way to behave, she told herself feebly. She had come here with a purpose and she was going to see it through. She looked at her pale face in the cracked mirror of the dressing-table and sighed, hardy able to recognize the girl who had once been so excited at going on the outing to Somerset with her friend and their workmates.

'Buck up, and don't let yourself down,' she told the face in the mirror, and she imagined she could see Tilly's approving smile as she did so.

Later that morning she set out with the address of Tilly's doctor firmly fixed in her head. She used to know her way around the area, although many of the streets and businesses had changed considerably in the last twenty years. She reached the address at last and waited until she was invited into the doctor's sanctuary. She never liked these antiseptic places, but she swallowed her nerves and told the doctor who she was and why she was there.

'Ah yes, Mrs Chase,' Doctor Ryman said. 'Your friend's death will have been a shock for you.'

What was she supposed to say to that? The silly old buffer didn't need to state the bleedin' obvious, did he? Horrified, she suddenly realized she was slipping into Tilly's vernacular, as she used to call it.

'I need a death certificate to collect her money from the funeral club,' she said as steadily as she could, 'and I need to know where she is now so I can arrange the burial. I want to see her too,' she added, her voice choking.

'The certificate is ready, Mrs Chase, and I'll give you the address of Mr Jenkins, the undertaker where Miss Dilkes has been taken until they receive further instructions.'

What if none had ever been given? Alice wondered through a kind of rising hysteria. What if she hadn't even known about it, or been unable or unwilling to make this sad journey? Would Tilly have stayed there forever like some pathetic vagrant? Once she had got the information she needed she got out of there as fast as she could, her stomach churning. But this was only the first hurdle of the day. The next one, the all-important one, was to say a proper goodbye to Tilly.

Before that, she realized she needed sustenance. These last few days she had gone through a roller-coaster of emotions and it was beginning to take its toll. Nerves as well as hunger were gnawing at her stomach. The smell of hot onion soup and fresh-baked bread wafted out from a small café in a side street, and she found herself hurrying there, to sit down gratefully at a small table.

'Ready for a cuppa, love?' a waitress called out at once. 'You look like you could do with one.'

'Thank you, and then I'll have your onion soup and bread,' she said, glad not to have to make any other decisions for the moment.

An hour later, well fortified, she discovered that the undertaker's was a short bus ride away. It was in a quiet street conveniently near to the local churchyard and not too far from the factory where they had both worked. Alice thought that the women who had worked with Tilly until recently should have no excuse for missing her send-off. She braced herself as she went inside the undertaker's, and breathed in a fragrant aroma of flowers and herbs. The middle-aged woman seated at the desk looked up with the expected air of sympathy on her face.

'I'm here to see Miss Tilly Dilkes and to arrange for her burial,' Alice said huskily. 'I'll need it done as soon as possible as I have to get back to Somerset to my family, but I want it to be done decently and properly.'

'Of course, my dear,' the woman said.

She had spoken thoughtlessly, but Alice guessed that in this business, they were probably used to the remarks of grieving people.

'When I've taken you through for the viewing, come back to the front office,' the woman went on. 'My husband will speak to you, and then we'll see about the booking. I assure you it will all be as tasteful as you wish.'

Tilly would have said she sounded like she was booking a bleedin' music-hall act, Alice thought. No smut, no bawdy jokes, everything nice and tasteful . . . Then she forgot about such things as she was shown into a small side room with soft lighting. In the middle of the room was a trestle table draped in black cloth, on which there was a wooden coffin. Inside it, looking as peaceful as if she had just lain down for a bit of a snooze, was Tilly.

'There's no need to be nervous, my dear,' she heard the undertaker's wife say quietly. 'I'll be right outside the door if you need me.'

Alice had to admit that her nerves were all on edge now, because she had never seen a dead body before. It was still desperately hard to think of Tilly in that way, and her heart was beating painfully fast as she tentatively drew nearer. But her heartbeats slowly relaxed as she looked down at her. Tilly looked almost like a young girl again, her hair combed and tidied, her hands placed gently across her chest as if she was about to burst into a belly laugh at any minute. This was still her friend, her best pal, and nothing was going to change that.

'I'll do me best for you, gel,' Alice whispered. 'I'll see that you don't go out of this world alone, don't you worry about that.'

She remained in that little room a while longer, speaking in a low voice to Tilly, as if she could hear and understand all that she was saying about their old days and the memories that would never leave her. Finally she bent and kissed

Tilly's forehead, no longer afraid. She didn't turn back when she reached the door, but she took a long, deep breath, because now there were practical things to be done, and the sooner the better.

The undertaker was called Mr Jenkins. Alice felt obliged to show him the book with Tilly's funeral club details in it, to prove that there was money to pay for it all, and that she wanted the best that this amount could buy.

'Miss Dilkes had made good provisions for her funeral as you can see, and I'll be arranging for the money to be paid out as soon as possible,' she told him, 'but I can only give you a little on account until it comes through.'

'That will be fine, Mrs Chase. In any case you'll be sent an account after the event, which is how we usually do business. Now then, what day and what time would be suitable for you? If you wish, I can arrange everything with the vicar – and perhaps there is a favourite hymn to be sung at the church service?'

Alice realized how little she knew about the whole procedure, and was almost pathetically grateful for the undertaker's delicate suggestions. This was Tuesday, and she had already decided it should be on the Saturday so that the factory girls could be there. She was more determined than ever that they should attend. She asked for it to be arranged for two o'clock, and she would also ask Mrs Coggins to put on a little tea and cakes for the mourners, which she would pay for. It would give her Sunday to get over it and to visit the churchyard to see that Tilly was well settled, and on Monday morning she would go home. Never had the thought been more welcome.

Having got things started she felt a mite better, but it was enough for one day, and she decided the funeral club business and the visit to the factory could wait until tomorrow. It would be soon enough to give them the news, if they hadn't heard it already. It had never occurred to her before that they might have done so. Instead of taking a bus, she walked back to the lodgings through narrow streets that were not as familiar to her as she would have expected. Twenty years was a long time to have been away, and it struck her more and more forcibly that she no longer felt as if she belonged here.

Once she had given the latest information to Mrs Coggins, the woman agreed to put on a small do of tea and biscuits after the funeral for whoever wanted to come back and jaw over their memories of Tilly.

'I daresay the other lodgers will want to pay their respects,' Mrs Coggins said. 'We wouldn't want to see the poor young gel laid to rest without a proper how's-your-father, would we?'

She had a neat way of referring to things by avoiding the actual words whenever she could. Not that Alice was too keen to keep thinking of the day as Tilly's funeral, since the idea of it was still so unbelievable. But now she wanted to be alone, and she went back to her room, leaving Mrs Coggins satisfied that Tilly's 'how's-your-father' wouldn't cause her any personal expense.

She was exhausted. She lay down on her bed and closed her eyes, but much as she tried to resist them, the weak tears trickled down her face for the loss of her friend, and for all the lost opportunities that would never come again. The last few days had been traumatic, and she longed for the everyday to-ing and fro-ing of her daily life. She missed her children. She missed Bobby's baby softness, for all that he called himself a big boy now. Most of all, she longed for the comfort of Walter's arms, and she willed the hours to pass before the arranged time for her to go to the telephone box and speak to him.

She must have slept, because she felt chilled and stiff when she realized how long she had lain on top of her bed. It must surely be time for her to telephone Walter now. She washed her face and tidied her hair before leaving the house quietly in the hope that she wouldn't see anybody. Several of the lodgers had spoken to her now and had been so sympathetic they were in danger of making her weep all over again. She slipped out of the front door and walked to the telephone box, remembering all that Mrs Coggins had shown her. Even so, it seemed to take an age before she heard a familiar voice at the other end.

'Mick, it's Alice, like I promised,' she said breathlessly. 'Is Walter there?'

He was the one she wanted, and after Mick told her to hold on, she found herself doing do literally – holding the receiver as if it were a lifeline.

'Is that you, Alice?' she heard Walter bellow, and in the background she could hear Mick telling him not to shout.

'Of course it's me,' she almost sobbed. 'It's so good to hear you, Walter.'

'What's happening there? Is everything in order, girl? We've kept wondering how you were getting on.'

He was so unaccustomed to speaking on the telephone, just as she was, and she could tell he was finding it hard to know what to say. He didn't find it easy to talk about personal things at the best of times, especially as Mick and Helen were probably within earshot, so she had to be the one to do it.

'I've arranged everything, Walter. I'm staying in Tilly's old lodgings, and the landlady is very nice. The funeral's on Saturday afternoon, and Tilly had been paying into a club to pay for it all. I'm going to see the girls at the factory tomorrow in the hope that some of them will come, and I'll be getting a train home on Monday morning.'

She said the last bit all in a rush, knowing it was the best bit. The very best bit. It was something to hold on to throughout this terrible week. When Walter replied she could hear the relief in his voice.

'Well, that's good to hear, and I'm glad you've got things settled for Tilly.'

'Is Bobby all right?' she asked quickly. 'He's not fretting too much without me, is he? I hope he's not too upset.'

'You're not to worry about Bobby or any of us. We're all right. Bobby goes off with Rose every morning to play with the babby without any tears. Don't go wearing yourself out, Alice. You're a long way from home, so you just watch out for yourself.'

'Of course I will. Kiss Bobby for me, and I'll call you again in a few days when I've found out the time of the train home. It'll be the same time as tonight, Walter, so please be there.' She wanted to keep mentioning home, simply because it sounded so good.

'I'll do that, girl, and Mick and Helen will meet you on Monday.'

There didn't seem to be anything else to say, and so she said goodbye quickly and replaced the receiver. She was halfway between smiles and tears when she left the telephone box. She knew what he meant by telling her to watch out for herself. She was in the big, bad city, where Walter had never been, and which he mistrusted to the tips of his toes. But she knew she would be all right . . . But even as she had that thought, somebody lurched against her, and she smelled the foul stink of stale beer coming from every pore of the drunken lout.

'You going my way, pretty lady?' he leered at her, and in a sudden panic she pushed against him with all her might, sending him staggering into the wall. She heard the smash of glass as the bottle he'd been holding crashed to the ground.

'Bitch!' he yelled after her. 'Hoity-toity bitch!'

If she ever needed anything to tell her that she didn't want to be there any longer than she had to, that was it, Alice thought as she rushed off down the street. Her breath was tight in her chest as she reached the lodging house again and almost fell indoors, to be greeted at once by Mrs Coggins, who insisted that from the look of her she'd better come into her room and take a drop of her medicinal brandy in a good hot cup of tea.

Thirteen

Alice had always prided herself on being a methodical person. You had to be with four children and a cottage that was larger than some in the village, but still hardly a palace. But today she wasn't in the village, attending to normal domestic things. Today she was going to see about obtaining Tilly's funeral club money, or at least setting things in motion. And then she was going to the factory where she had once spent so many tedious hours.

They hadn't been all bad though. There had been plenty of banter and laughter among the girls and women working there, and at the end of the war, when everybody needing cheering up, they had all put their pennies enthusiastically into the factory holiday fund for the few days they were going to spend in Somerset, which had seemed as foreign a place then as going to the moon.

Later that day, Alice thought that she had come full circle. By then, with the proof of the death certificate, she had been assured that the funeral club account would be honoured before the end of the week. She was now retracing her steps through the grubby streets, and hearing people call out to one another in the old familiar accents as they went about their business. She stood outside Laver's Shirt Factory for a few minutes before she steeled herself to go inside. It all looked the same, and it was almost hard to credit that it was twenty years since she had set foot inside the place.

The minute she went inside she was assaulted by the noise of machinery and of people shouting to be heard above it. The woman nearest to the door looked at her curiously, and then her mouth dropped open.

'My good Gawd, it's Alice Butler that was, ain't it?' she said.

'It's Alice Chase now,' Alice said when she got her throat working. 'How are you, Vi?'

'Fair to middling, as ever,' the woman said. 'But what you doing here? You ain't looking for your old job in this flea-pit, are you? According to Tilly you was supposed to be living down in the sticks with a bundle of kids.'

Several other women whose faces were familiar to Alice were starting to take an interest. Younger workers who hadn't known her kept on with their work, knowing they'd be penalized if they were kept jawing for too long.

Remembering her errand, Alice felt her throat choke, but she had come here for a purpose and she wasn't going to be put off now. When she did begin to speak it all came out in a clumsy rush.

'I'm sorry to have to tell you this, but Tilly died last week,' she said.

'Don't be daft, you puddin'. Tilly ain't dead!' Vi said, half laughing. 'Some silly bugger's been having you on.'

'It's true,' Alice said desperately, holding her hands tightly together. 'I've come back here to arrange her funeral. It's on Saturday at two o'clock and I hope that some of her old workmates will come to see her off. There'll be a cup of tea and a biscuit back at her lodgings afterwards, so don't let her down.'

While they were still gawping at her and still arguing that it couldn't be true, it was too much to hope that the boss wouldn't appear to see what all the fuss was about. With his slept-in clothes and greasy hair, he looked the same as he'd always been, Alice thought, almost hysterical now at the sense that she was in some kind of time slip. Any minute now she'd be told to get back to her bleedin' machine and stop buggering about.

'Christ Almighty,' he said now, recognizing her. 'I thought you'd gone to live among the hay-seeds.'

'I've come to tell you that Tilly died last week, Mr Laver,' she repeated, remaining as dignified as she could while hearing her own voice grow shriller, and thinking how bloody embarrassing it would be if she fainted right there and then, the way she felt she was about to do.

'You'd better come and sit down a minute,' Laver said,

seeing how her face had blanched. 'I can't have you puking
up in here.'

He grabbed her arm and took her into the poky little cubby-
hole he called his office where he gave newcomers the once-
over and gave others the sack. Alice felt as if she was
somehow being sucked back into her old life, and fought to
hold on to her self-control.

'Now then. Take it slowly and tell me what happened.'

She managed to tell him as many details as she could, and
by then she was feeling so weary she just wanted to run
away and hide somewhere. She should have known what a
strain all this would be, but she hadn't even thought about
the toll it would take on herself. She had just wanted to do
the right thing by Tilly.

'I'm sorry,' Laver said when she had finished. 'She was
a good worker.'

Alice felt her eyes flash with anger. *A good worker?* Was
that the sum total of a human being's existence?

'Tilly was far more than that. She was a good person and
a good friend who never said a bad thing about anybody,'
Alice said tightly.

'Well, all that as well, I'm sure,' Laver said impatiently.

In such a small space, Alice felt stifled by the man. The
whole factory was full of dust from the fabrics as well as
the general lack of cleanliness that hadn't changed over the
years. No wonder Tilly had suffered in this atmosphere. It
was practically suffocating.

'I've said what I came to say,' she went on. 'I just wanted
to let people know, in the hope that some of them will come
to see Tilly off on Saturday.'

'Don't keep them yapping too long then,' Laver warned.
'Time's money and I'll be docking their wages if I see them
slacking.'

He was as mean-spirited as ever, Alice thought, but
somehow his very crudeness lifted her spirits, reminding
her that she didn't belong here any more. The thought of
still working in the factory after all these years like Vi and
the others – like Tilly – was enough to make her appreciate all that she had more than ever. She went back to
where some of the older ones now stood in a little huddle.

They looked up when they saw her, and Vi seemed to be the spokesman.

'Half a dozen of us will come to the funeral, Alice. It's knocked us all a bit sideways and no mistake, but the poor little bugger deserves a proper send-off. She always said you were a good pal to her, gel, so we'll see you on Saturday.'

She wasn't sure that she'd always been such a good pal, Alice thought, close to tears now as she left the factory and took in great gulps of air. She should have kept in touch more often, invited Tilly to stay more often, written to her more often. Common sense told her she was doing what everybody did when somebody close to them died; thinking of all the things they should have done, or could have done, and regretting all the wasted opportunities. And there was no point to it. You could never go back and undo the things you hadn't done, so where was the sense in wasting more of your life in useless regrets? She could almost hear Tilly saying so. In fact it was *exactly* what Tilly would have said, she thought with a wry smile.

Her nerves were gradually unravelling, and she could feel herself becoming calmer. She had done everything she could for her old friend, and once the weekend was over, she could think about going home. The word had never sounded more wonderful. She had hardly had time to think about the impact of all this on her family. But even though none of them had known Tilly the way she had, they knew how much she had meant to Alice. Tom hadn't bothered much about Tilly's visit, but Lucy, in particular, had built up such a glamorous picture of Tilly in her mind, and had been so crushed when the reality didn't live up to her dreams. She wondered how Lucy was feeling now, and prayed that her girl wasn't feeling unnecessarily guilty about the way she had mocked Tilly's brashness.

For Lucy, the memory of her disappointment with Tilly had faded, although she had previously regaled her roommate, Sophie, with details about the colourful and overly scented friend of her mother's. They'd had a good few laughs about Tilly. And then Lucy had gone home at the weekend to discover the news of Tilly's death and to find that her mother had gone rushing off to London. Once Bobby was out of earshot, Rose had explained everything to her.

Although Lucy had been completely shocked, she didn't feel like crying, even if she knew she probably should. Nobody had thought to go to the Grange to tell her before now, and why should they, anyway? All she could think of was how she had felt so let down by Tilly when she last saw her, but she knew that was unworthy and that her mother would be angry to know she felt that way.

'What did she die of?' she asked Rose.

'I don't know, but she was pretty ill when she was here, more than she let on, I think. Mum was in a state when we got the news through Uncle Mick, and we're all mucking in now to keep things going at home. I've been taking Bobby to work with me every day and he's been having a whale of a time with the baby, and Auntie Helen's been coming here every day to cook supper for everybody.'

'That's all right then,' Lucy said mechanically.

Rose realized she wasn't getting the reaction she had expected. 'Is that all you've got to say? Mum's lost her best friend, and you look about as interested as if I'd just told you it looked like rain tomorrow, you heartless little devil.'

'What do you expect me to say? I'm sorry she's dead and I know Mum will be upset, but she was different from what I expected when she came here last time.'

'Not so glamorous, you mean. People aren't, when they're ill.'

Lucy's face crumpled. 'I'm not heartless, Rose. I wish Tilly hadn't got ill, and I wish she hadn't died, and I wish Mum was here. It's not the same without her. Nothing's the same any more.'

Rose saw the growing uncertainty in her sister's face. Lucy was the one who hadn't been afraid to branch out and live away from home, finding her own sense of glamour in working at the biggest house in the area. But when it came to home, she never wanted anything to change. She wanted the stability of Alice's comforting presence here, as always. Just as they all did. Rose put her arm around her sister's stiff shoulders.

'Cheer up. Mum will be home on Monday and everything

will be back to normal. Meanwhile, I told Auntie Helen we'd do the cooking today, so you can peel the vegetables and help me make a pie.'

She didn't add that today was going to be even more of an ordeal for Alice, knowing that it was the day of Tilly's funeral.

The time drew nearer to two o'clock and Alice's hands were shaking as she put on her hat and coat. This was a day that came to everybody in the end, but for Tilly, fun-loving, bright and lively Tilly, it was far too soon. Mrs Coggins insisted on accompanying Alice to the church, for which she was grateful. Some of the other lodgers went along as well, and Alice was relieved to see a number of their old workmates waiting for the hearse to arrive. She knew some of them; others would have got closer to Tilly over the years. As close as she and Tilly had once been, perhaps. Time had moved on since those youthful days when they had told one another everything. It was a thought to make her cope with this day better than she had expected to do. These people all knew Tilly, and would have known her more intimately in her latter years than Alice had. With a little shock, she realized that she was the stranger here.

It was only when they all sang so lustily the hymn she had chosen, the hymn that she knew Tilly would have wanted, that the tears flowed.

All things bright and beautiful, all creatures great and small. All things wise and wonderful, the Lord God made them all.

Then, at last, it was all over, and she had dutifully thrown a handful of earth into the open grave on top of the coffin, and whispered her own goodbye to her old friend.

'Come on, gel, let's get back to the house and have a cuppa,' Mrs Coggins said briskly. 'There's nothing more to be done for her now.'

Alice let herself be led away, and less than an hour later she found herself laughing, actually laughing, at some of the tales the other lodgers and the factory girls had to tell about Tilly. None of them was malicious. They were all affectionate tales, sometimes a bit near the knuckle, but it was somehow reassuring to know that Tilly was never alone. She might not have had a family of her own, but she had a wider kind of kinship, and that was worth a great deal. There was also a lot to be said for friends gathering together after a burial, to remember the good times, and to put the sadness behind them, for a little while, at least.

Later that evening, she telephoned Walter again, and felt a huge rush of warmth at the sound of his voice. After she had told him of her day, and that she would visit the grave tomorrow to see that all was well, she asked eagerly for news of her family. Wanting to know of their doings, to bring them near. Asking after Lucy, and how she had taken the news about Tilly.

'Better than you might have thought. She's a hard nut, that girl,' Walter said.

'But with a soft centre,' Alice said softly, guessing that the reaction would come eventually. Lucy wasn't all hard, just learning to be self-sufficient, which was no bad thing for a young woman. 'How about the others?'

'The boy's the same as ever, and Rose is pleased that Bobby hasn't wet the bed all week. He's really taken to the Staceys' babby.'

'That's good.' *Didn't anybody miss her at all?* 'And how about you, Walter? Have you been managing all right?'

There was the smallest pause, and then he spoke gruffly. 'As well as I ever manage without you. It'll be a good thing when Monday comes.'

It was the most she could expect, especially as she knew that Mick or Helen would probably be within earshot, but it was enough to make her smile.

'Well, I'll see you then, and now I'm going back to have some supper with Mrs Coggins. The time will soon pass now, my dear.'

She left the telephone box with a lighter step than she had felt in the last traumatic week. Tomorrow she would pay her final visit to Tilly's resting place to make her private goodbye, and in her heart she knew she would never come back here again. Whitechapel had been her home for so long, but it had only been for half her life after all. The second half, the most rewarding and fulfilling half, had been spent with Walter and the home and family they had created between them. If she had ever felt the slightest yearning to be back in her birthplace, it was banished for ever in that moment.

Sunday was a strange day. Alice took some flowers and laid them on the fresh mound of earth that now covered Tilly's grave. She stood in contemplation for some time, then blew her a final kiss and turned away. Before she went back to the lodging house, she decided to walk around some of their old haunts; the back streets and alleyways where they had run as children; the old pubs where they had joked with the old men and the sailors; the barrow boys selling their whelks and jellied eels; the occasional flower stalls and the picture palace. It was still familiar enough, and yet because it was Sunday and people were either in church or staying indoors after being at work all week, it was almost like a ghost town. She felt as if she was seeing it all as if it was an old silent film. Nothing was quite the same, and that was because *she* wasn't the same.

Once she returned to the lodging house she packed her small case, ready for the journey home the following day. Packing her clothes again made it seem real, and never had the thought sounded so good. She found herself almost counting the hours, and the thought of being with Walter again gave her an almost girlish excitement that she hadn't felt in years. They had never been apart before, and whether or not it was unseemly to be thinking that way so soon after Tilly's funeral, she was darned sure Tilly wouldn't have minded. She was almost aware of a waft of Tilly's strong scent as she thought it. She could almost hear Tilly's voice in her head, teasing her . . .

Make the most of it, gel, you're a long time dead . . .

The train journey back to Bristol was as tedious as the one that had taken her to London, but the thing that made it more palatable was the fact that she was going home, plus the packet of thick ham sandwiches Mrs Coggins had insisted on giving her. The landlady had really taken her under her wing in the last few days, and she had been a real prop. But now she was going back where she belonged, and she leaned

back in the carriage and dozed on and off during the next
hours, lulled by the clacketty-clack rhythm of the wheels on
the train lines.

It was mid-afternoon when she stepped off the train at
last, feeling stiff and tired, but walking briskly towards the
exit of Brunel's magnificent station. She hoped that Mick
and Helen would be there to meet her and hadn't been delayed
at all, and once outside she looked around anxiously. There
were so many people milling about, some entering the station,
others, like herself, thankful to have arrived. She couldn't
see anyone she knew at first, but then she heard her name
being called.

'Mick, thank goodness,' she said involuntarily, so thankful
to see a familiar face. She couldn't see Helen for a moment,
and before she knew what Mick was doing he had caught
her in his arms and kissed her soundly.

Her reaction to that kiss shook her. It was too passionate,
too familiar, too everything she didn't want from him. In a
fraction of a second, she knew it. All her romanticized ideas
about the other brother disappeared like a will-o'-the-wisp,
as if they were nothing, and had always amounted to nothing.

She broke away from him, giving a small embarrassed
laugh.

'My goodness, Mick, people will get the wrong idea about
us in a moment. Where's Helen, anyway? Is she waiting in
the car?'

He picked up her case and steered her through the throng
of people to where his car stood outside the station entrance.

'She's at your place, Alice. You know how she likes to
cook, and she was sure you'd be hungry for some good
Somerset food when you got home. She wanted to prepare
a special meal for your homecoming, so she sends her apologies.'

He sounded awkward now, as though he knew that in those
few seconds there had been a subtle change in their relationship, even if he wasn't entirely sure what it was. But
Alice knew. She felt as if she had been released from some
affliction that had bothered her for years, and like a miracle,
she was completely free of it.

'She's a good sister-in-law, Mick, and you're the best

brother Walter could have. We do appreciate you both, even
if we don't always say it.'

It must be the emotion and tension of the last week that
was making her more free with her words than usual. Or it
could be something deep inside her that wanted to make him
see exactly what she now saw – that there was no place for
him in her life other than being her husband's brother.

'Let's get you settled in the car, Alice,' he replied after a
brief silence, and she was thankful that the moment was
covered by so many folk chatting and jostling them. 'This
week must have been an ordeal for you, and I'm sure you
can't wait to get home.'

She nodded, saying that she couldn't wait to see Bobby
and hope he hadn't fretted too much while she had been
away. What she really meant was that she couldn't wait to
see Walter, but she wasn't going to add any more slushiness
to the conversation by saying so.

Somehow the awkward moments passed, and they chatted
about ordinary things on the journey home. It was a relief
to Alice when the village finally came in sight, and Mick
stopped the car outside her own cottage. There was a small,
delicate silence, and then Mick spoke gruffly.

'I'll just come in with you to see if Helen's still there,
Alice, and then we'll be getting on home. You'll be wanting
to spend time with your family, and you won't want us
around.'

'You know you're always welcome, Mick,' Alice said automatically. 'But Helen and I will have plenty of time to jaw
together once I've got settled again. I'll bring Bobby to see
her as usual very soon. I'm really grateful to you both for
looking after Walter and the children this last week.'

The emphasis on their relationship had settled back to
normality. For Alice, it was an enormous relief, and she felt
a weird sort of gratitude to Tilly for making her see where
her rightful place was. This enforced parting from her family,
allied with the grief for her old friend, had finally swept
away any lingering doubts about herself and Mick. What
might have been would never have been, she saw that clearly
now, and absence didn't just make the heart grow fonder. In
many cases it could diminish what was there, but in her case,

absence had simply reinforced the love she had for her family, and for Walter in particular.

She walked into the cottage purposefully and was immediately enveloped by its warmth and the homely smell of cooking. Helen was flush-faced from the stove, and seeing Alice's bright eyes, she gave her a quick hug, rather than add to the emotion of the moment.

'It's good to have you home, Alice, but I'm not going to stop and ask you how it all went, because you'll be exhausted from the journey. Besides, there are other folk you'd far rather see than Mick and me, and Walter said he was going to get home early today,' she added with a smile. 'There's a stew simmering on the stove, so come and see me tomorrow and tell me all about it.'

She was already reaching for her hat and coat as she spoke, and Alice had never loved her more. Helen was a good and understanding woman, and within minutes she and Mick were leaving, and Alice was alone.

For a few seconds she stood exactly where she was in the middle of her home, absorbing the atmosphere with the thought that she never wanted to leave this place again. Already London seemed like another life to her, one that she remembered with affection, but was content to leave to her memories.

She gave a deep sigh and then took her suitcase upstairs and unpacked it quickly until everything was back in its rightful place again, as she was. And then she heard noises downstairs, and turned eagerly as she heard Bobby's childish voice calling out to her as Rose brought him home. She flew down the stairs and caught him up her arms, breathing in the sweet, baby smell of him, and caressing his soft sandy hair.

'Are you staying here with us now, Mum?' he said tremulously. 'I don't want you to go away again.'

She gave a soft laugh. 'I'm not going anywhere, sweetheart. I'd much rather be here with you than anywhere else.'

She caught sight of Rose's eyes over the top of Bobby's head, and smiled back at her. If ever there was an apt moment for thinking that home was where the heart is, this was it, she thought thankfully.

A child was the icebreaker everyone needed when emotions ran high, and Rose insisted that Alice sat down with him while she got the table ready for their evening meal. Bobby didn't have too many vibrant memories of Tilly and was more interested to know about the big city where the king and queen lived, and if Alice had stayed in the palace with them. She felt relaxed and calm by the time the door opened again, and Walter and Tom burst in.

Everything was instantly as it was before. With the exception of Lucy, the family was all together again, and even though Tom considered himself too old now to give his mother a demonstrative hug, Walter felt no such restraint. He strode across the room and clasped Alice in his arms, and her world righted itself again.

'We've missed you, Mother,' he murmured against her cheek.

For some crazy reason, Alice felt a wild urge to giggle. Surely she shouldn't be so flippant, having just returned from her friend's funeral! But the friend was Tilly, who had always insisted that prolonged mourning was a waste of energy for those who were left behind, that you were a long time dead . . . she still couldn't get those words out of her head.

'I'm not your mother,' Alice murmured back, and then she pressed a fervent kiss on her husband's lips, just to remind him that they were both alive.

Fourteen

When they went to bed that night, Walter was guarded with her, treating her with kid gloves as if afraid that he would say the wrong thing, do the wrong thing, upset her all over again by being insensitive about wanting her when she was still grieving over Tilly. Much earlier, once Bobby had been put to bed with many assurances that his mother would still be here in the morning, they had spent the evening talking about Tilly, getting everything out in the open about how sad it had all been, and how Alice had rallied their old workmates to give her a good send-off. Tom hadn't been there to hear it. He couldn't be doing with any more grown-up talk about death and dying, and had gone off to see Jack. But the three of them – Alice, Walter and Rose – had talked quietly and calmly about Tilly, and Alice had found it cathartic to talk about the early days when she and Tilly had been girls, and how they had both eagerly anticipated the wonderful few days in Somerset all those years ago that had ended with one of them staying for good.

'I've heard Doctor Matt say how often life hangs on a chance. He's quite a deep thinker, and he says a lot of clever things that folk like us never think about,' Rose commented, startling Alice.

'You seem to know a lot about Doctor Matt,' she said, forcing herself to remember that he was Doctor Stacey's brother.

Rose blushed. 'We've talked quite a bit, and he's very nice.'

And you're falling for him, thought Alice, and prayed that her girl wasn't going to he hurt by this clever young man who was a doctor, and might not look twice at the daughter of a sawmill worker. At least, not with marriage in mind . . .

'Be careful, Rose,' she said automatically, at which Rose smiled.

'Don't worry about me, Mum. I was courting one young man that turned sour, and I've no intention of doing so again. I just like him, that's all.'

All the same, she couldn't hide the lights in her eyes whenever she spoke of him, Alice noted, and if Rose believed that this Matt was the one for her, then she hoped he knew it too. She had yet to meet him, but apparently he was very good with young children, and the next time Bobby had a sniffle, Alice had every intention of taking him to see the young doctor, rather than Doctor Stacey, and giving him the once-over at the same time.

But all that was forgotten when she felt the strength of Walter's arms tightly wrapped around her in their bed that night. She lay against him, as close as spoons in a box, and felt his heartbeats against her, warm and alive. His breath was soft on her neck, and even though she knew very well he was holding back from any physical need for her out of respect for Tilly, Alice was consumed with the desire to be a part of him, and he of her.

Somehow, just as before, she could imagine Tilly's voice. *Bleedin' hell, Alice, don't hold back because of me. You're a long time dead, gel, so you just make the most of it.*

Her own voice seemed to echo gently and sweetly inside her head.

Enough now, Tilly. Some things are only meant to be shared by two.

As Walter moved slightly in the bed, she twisted around to face him. She clasped his face in her hands, running her finger gently down the jagged scar on his cheek, and murmured softly against his mouth.

'I'm not your mother, Walter. I'm your wife, and I've missed you so much.'

He couldn't mistake the invitation in her voice, and he needed no other urging. With a smothered oath, he clutched her to him, rucking up her nightgown to feel her soft flesh, and she in turn was instantly aware of his arousal that never failed to awaken her own response.

'God knows I've missed you too, girl,' he whispered back against her mouth. 'Don't ever leave me again.'

And then he was inside her, filling her with life, with

passion. He was everything she had ever wanted, and she had never loved him more.

Even that was only a brief respite from her sadness. She took Bobby to see Helen the following afternoon. Helen had been fond of Tilly for that brief time, and she deserved to know what had happened while Alice was in London. It wasn't that Alice wanted to forget it, or that she ever would, but every telling was like the twist of a knife in her heart, and the sooner it was done, the better. So, once Bobby was busy with his crayons and colouring book, Alice related it all to her sister-in-law.

'It was such a sad end for Tilly,' Helen said sympathetically. 'It must be terrible to die alone. You and I are the lucky ones, Alice, to have our family around us. And providing this blessed Hitler doesn't start a war and kill us all, we'll have them with us for ever.'

Alice's heart jolted. All this time, worrying about Tilly and dealing with her funeral, she had given little thought at all to the wider implications of what was going on in the world. None of it seemed as overwhelming to her as the death of one woman Alice had known all her life.

'I suppose you saw the air-raid shelters they were putting up in London,' Helen went on, as if to take her mind off Tilly.

'Oh yes,' Alice said vaguely. Of course she had seen them. But Londoners were hardy folk and had always taken things in their stride, and hardly anyone she knew had been talking endlessly about air-raid shelters or the likelihood of war. Not that she had invited anyone to talk about anything but Tilly. She hadn't given a thought that if the worst did come, some of them might even be thinking as Tilly had once thought, about getting away from the target of the big cities to the safety of the country.

'Our Jack and his mates talk of nothing else now, seeing only the excitement of it all, but he won't have to go,' Helen went on. 'He'll be safe, working on the farm. People will always need food in their bellies, won't they? Unless he volunteers, of course,' she added uneasily.

Alice stared at her. For some reason her gut was churning.

She had just emerged from a personal tragedy, but Helen was talking of a much wider one, and one that could even involve her own son. She felt a flood of guilty relief that Tom would be far too young to be involved, providing it didn't go on for too long.

'I think it's time I took this boy home,' she said hastily, as Bobby began to get fretful. She was suddenly stifled by this talk of war. You couldn't bury your head in the sand if it became reality, but until it did there was no sense in getting too wound up about it.

She put Bobby into his pushchair and bade Helen goodbye. The April air was warm and balmy in the afternoons, but it was still cool at night, and she didn't like to keep Bobby out any later than necessary. She was glad of his chattering company. A child of his age had no concept of the real meaning of death, and a good thing too. Very soon he would hardy remember Tilly at all, while Alice's head still seemed full of so many memories, and no matter how she tried, she couldn't shake them off entirely. Nor would she want to, of course. But it was no good to dwell on the past and Helen was right. They were the lucky ones, with families of their own to care for and who needed them.

'Morning, Mrs Chase,' she heard someone say, and she realized she was hurrying past Kelsey's shop with her head down, lost in her own thoughts.

'Good morning, Mr Kelsey,' she said automatically. She went to walk on, but he barred her way.

'Heard about your friend. Bit of a shock for you, I daresay.'

'Of course it was,' she snapped. What did he think? That she would have sat down calmly and not thought any more about Tilly?

'She was a smart woman,' Kelsey went on. 'If she'd stayed down here longer, I'd have given her a job in my shop any day. She'd have brightened up the place all right.'

Alice couldn't think why he was making this small talk with her. She didn't want to talk to him. She couldn't stand his roving eyes and odious voice.

'Well, my friend has gone to a better place now,' she said coldly, hoping he would get the irony of her remark.

'Ah well, there's them that think so, and there's them that

don't deserve the good Lord's forgiveness. Not that I'm pointing a finger in any direction, mind. I'm just saying.' His voice was full of hidden meaning. But his words dwindled away and he stepped back a pace as Alice rounded on him, fury in her eyes, her own voice tight enough to be menacing.

'Mr Kelsey, I suggest you keep such insinuations to yourself unless you want my husband to come here and silence you, and make your nasty little remarks public. My family is well respected in this village, and I'm sure your business wouldn't be so profitable if folk got to hear how you harassed a grieving woman.'

She stared him out. She had never spoken to him so forcibly before, and although she was shaking inside, she was determined not to show it. After a few seconds, he shrugged.

'I'm sure none of us want any unpleasantness between neighbours, Mrs Chase, and I apologize if I've offended you. I only meant to offer my condolences, nothing more.'

She kept her lips tightly shut until he moved aside and she walked on towards the cottage with her head held high and her nerves on edge. Whatever he had meant to imply about Tilly, she was sure it had also been directed at herself, but by standing up to him, she hoped she had got the better of him at last.

'Was that man being mean to you, Mum?' Bobby said.

Alice gave a forced laugh. 'He was just being himself, my love, and we don't need to bother any more about him.'

She fervently hoped it was true, and in her heart she was sure of it. Whatever else Henry Kelsey was, he thought more about his precious shop than anything else. He wouldn't risk folk staying away by any suggestion that he had upset Alice Chase through any snide remarks he had made about her old friend. It was a thought to make her heart feel a mite lighter.

Lucy came home at the weekend, and Alice was anxious to see her girl again. Lucy had once been so enamoured of Tilly, almost hero-worshipping her, and it had been a blow to see that her idol wasn't as perfect as the image in her mind. It was soon clear to Alice that Lucy was more jittery than usual. She was glad when Rose took Bobby out for a walk, and that Walter and Tom were out, so that she could have her younger daughter to herself.

'What's wrong, love?' she finally asked, when Lucy could do nothing more than roam about the cottage aimlessly, picking up a magazine and throwing it down again; fiddling with the buttons of her cardigan until she was in danger of twisting them off; curling a strand of hair around her fingers. Lucy flopped down on the sofa, her arms folded, a stormy look in her eyes.

'Why did she have to go and die?' she said angrily, catching Alice completely off guard.

Alice sat beside her daughter, aware of the trembling in her slight body now. She caught hold of Lucy's hands, feeling how cold they were, despite the warmth of the day. She spoke carefully, knowing that this was something very important to Lucy.

'Everyone dies, darling. You know that. We're born, we grow up and live our lives as best we can, and then we die. It's something none of us can escape, but we don't waste our time worrying it every minute of the day. If we did, we'd go mad, and we wouldn't be getting the best out of the time we have.'

'Did she get the best out of her life then?'

Alice became more alarmed at the increasing aggression in her daughter's voice. 'She has a name, Lucy. Why can't you say it?'

'All right then. Tilly. Did Tilly get the best out of her life? It didn't do her much good, did it? What was the point of it all?'

She tore her hands away from her mother's, wrapping her arms around herself as if to ward off any intrusion into her feelings . . . her misery. As clearly as if a light dawned on her now, Alice realized that this reaction was a manifestation of guilt on Lucy's part. The last time she had seen Tilly she had been so disappointed in her. Tilly was so much less than the glamorous image Lucy had built up around her. Lucy had been less than kind about her appearance, her over-scented clothes, her brashness . . . and now Lucy was wracked by guilt.

'Do you believe in the afterlife, Lucy?' Alice asked her quietly.

They rarely spoke of such things, but her children, like herself, had been brought up to respect the church and its teachings. They had gone to Sunday school, and even if they weren't exactly regular churchgoers, they were all believers. Or so Alice had hoped. But the great hereafter was one of the greatest mysteries of all. If you didn't believe there was something to attain at the end of your life, then what was it all for? She realized she was echoing Lucy's own words.

'I don't know,' Lucy said sullenly. 'I know you want me to say that I do, but I don't. How do you know, anyway? How does anybody know?'

Alice put her arm around the girl's shaking shoulders. 'Well, I think Tilly knows now,' she said matter-of-factly.

Lucy stared at her. 'You shouldn't say such things, should you?' she said uncertainly.

'Why not? If anybody knows, Tilly does. So do my parents, and your dad's parents, and all the others who have already gone on the great adventure.'

She was aware that Lucy was looking at her now as if she was crazy, but at least she had got her attention. She was no longer looking like the little lost soul who had come drooping into the house that day, so unlike her usual bubbling self.

'It's not much of an adventure to die,' Lucy muttered.

'Me and Tilly thought so once,' Alice mused. 'When we were kids in Whitechapel we used to drive the living daylights out of the Sally Army when we hung around the pubs at night making fun of them. They drummed something into us kids though, whether they knew it or not.'

Lucy's mouth had dropped right open now, and Alice knew she was seeing a side to her mother that she had never seen before. She laughed gently.

'You should have heard Tilly sing,' she went on deliberately. Never mind that her heart was breaking at the sweet, half-forgotten memories. 'She had a voice like a fog horn and she could never keep in tune, but we bellowed along with the rest of the raggle-taggle kids who followed the Sally Army around on a Saturday night as if they were the Pied Piper. Tilly's favourite was always "Jesus wants me for a sunbeam", and that's how I think of her now. Sitting up there on a cloud, trying to play her bleedin' harp – pardon my language, Lucy – and bellowing out that Jesus wants her for a sunbeam. Well, I reckon He's got her now, and knowing her, she'll be the brightest sunbeam of them all. So you don't need to be too sorry about Tilly. She'll always come up smiling wherever she is.'

She stopped for breath, and despite Lucy's determination to be furious, since it conveniently blotted out any other emotion, the girl couldn't stop her lips twitching at the thought of Tilly sitting up on a cloud trying to play her harp and bellowing out the words of 'Jesus wants me for a sunbeam'.

The image was so real that the next moment they had both started giggling helplessly, and Rose and Bobby came home to the unlikely sight of their mother and sister holding on to each other on the sofa, laughing and crying at the same time.

'And by the way,' Alice told them a long while later, when they had all calmed down a little. 'Tilly thought the world of you all, and although she didn't have much, she didn't have a family either, so there's a small amount of money for each of you to remember her by. It would please me very much if we all went to church on Sunday to say a prayer for her, and I'm sure she'd know.'

She said it to assure Lucy that whatever mean thoughts Lucy might have had about Tilly, they would all be forgotten and forgiven now. And seeing the girl's small nod, she knew that Lucy understood.

Having sorted out Lucy's problems, Alice decided that she should see this young wonder doctor that Rose mentioned every time she could slip his name into the conversation. It was obvious to an observer that she just wanted to say it over and over. Rose might not even be aware herself that she was falling for Doctor Matt, but Alice knew so well that feeling of trying to bring someone close by proxy. After that first visit to Somerset, Tilly had teased her constantly about the number of times Alice had mentioned Walter's name. She had even kept a tally of it at one time, until she had driven Alice mad with her teasing.

Just remembering it could make her smile, and after a few weeks, it dawned on her that she could remember so many things about Tilly now without the acute sadness she had felt at first. Arranging her funeral had been the best thing she could have done, Alice reflected. Despite the trauma of it all, it was right and fitting that she should have been the one to do it.

So now she was taking Bobby to see Doctor Matt. There wasn't really much wrong with him, but he was her excuse. She sat waiting to be called, and immediately wished she wasn't there. It smelled far too medical, too clinical, too everything she preferred to forget, after Tilly . . .

'Mrs Chase?' said the fresh-faced young man in the white coat who came out to greet her. 'I'm very pleased to meet you, and this young man and I know one another already, don't we, Bobby?' he said, ruffling Bobby's hair. 'Come on into the surgery and let's have a look at him.'

As she followed him, holding tightly to Bobby's hand, she felt such a fraud. She wasn't really here to check up on Bobby's sniffles, just to see who was the object of her daughter's affection – and to wonder if he even knew it.

She liked what she saw, and he obviously had a way with children. By the time he assured Alice there wasn't much wrong with Bobby, and that a healthy dose of sunshine and fresh air would do him as much good as anything he could prescribe, she felt comfortable in his company.

'Can I see Mollie now?' Bobby asked eagerly.

Doctor Matt laughed. 'I think she's having her sleep right now, but I'm sure Rose will bring you to see her again soon.'

Alice wasn't sure if she was imagining things, but did his voice linger over Rose's name a little? Did his eyes sparkle a little bit brighter? She found herself hoping so, as she liked this young man more with every moment. She thanked him for reassuring her about Bobby, and when they were halfway home her son spoke with the innocent candour of children.

'Do you think Doctor Matt and our Rose are going to get married, Mum?'

After a stunned moment, Alice laughed out loud. 'What a thing to ask. I'm sure Doctor Matt is far too busy to think about marrying anybody, and you're far too young to think about such things.'

'Well, I'm not going to be a pageboy if they get married,' he went on more belligerently. 'There was a picture of a pageboy in one of Lucy's magazines, all dressed up in frilly clothes. Our Tom said he looked more like a *girl*.'

The way he said the word was damning in itself, thought Alice with a smile. And of course, it was never going to happen. Their Rose marrying a doctor! Highly unlikely . . . but nothing was impossible, and you never knew.

She had more to think about a few weeks later when Walter and Tom came home from the sawmills in a fever. She knew something was up the moment she saw them. Walter seemed to be unduly agitated, and Tom was jumping about as if he had fleas in his pants.

'What's happened?' she said at once, thumping a pot of tea on the table. Walter still looked at her uneasily.

'Now don't get all hot and bothered; it's nothing to fret about.'

Alice folded her arms. 'Well, if anything's going to get anybody hot and bothered, it's hearing something like that. And you're not getting any supper until you tell me what it's all about.'

Tom sniggered. He was obviously bursting to come out with it, but Alice guessed that whatever it was, he had been warned to let his father do the talking.

'You'd better sit down, Mother. We'll all sit down.'

'I'm *not* . . .' she began. But oh, what did it matter? It wouldn't make any difference to the conversation whatever he called her, and if it was something bad, the sooner she heard it the better. She sat down heavily on the sofa. Walter sat beside her and Tom sat on a chair, as tense as a kitten. At that moment she didn't know how significant the distance was between them.

'You remember Mr James Conway, don't you?' Walter said.

'Well, I've never met him, but I know the name. He's one of your biggest customers at Wakeman's, isn't he? From up Bristol way? Makes furniture or something. What's he got to do with anything?'

Before Walter could say anything more, Tom had burst
out with the news.

'He only wants to offer me an apprenticeship, that's all,
Mum! He's been looking for a young man to learn the trade,
and he says he's had his eye on me for some time, knowing
how I love the feel of the wood and understand the grain
and all, and he thinks I could be the one – if you'll let me.'

Walter frowned at his son. 'Now, just let me tell your
mother what Mr Conway is proposing, boy, before you go
off half-cocked.'

'I think somebody better had,' Alice snapped.

Her head was suddenly whirling. Everything she had
always thought was safe and secure in her life seemed to be
spinning away and she could do nothing to stop it. Lucy had
left home long before Alice had expected her to, although
she couldn't begrudge her position at the Grange, and she
hadn't gone far. But then Tilly . . . Tilly, her life-long friend,
who, even though they didn't see one another very often,
had always seemed to be the anchor in her life. Now Tilly
had gone to a place that no one could follow, leaving her
adrift, and she realized she was still too vulnerable after
losing Tilly to cope with the thought of Tom leaving home.
He was too young . . . far too young.

'I think you had better calm down, Mother,' Walter began
uneasily, seeing how her face was suddenly burning.

'I am *not* your mother,' she almost screamed. 'Tell me
what this man said to you, Tom, and then I'll tell you why
I'll have none of it.'

She heard herself, cantankerous and spiteful, treading on
Tom's dreams. But these dreams would be just another fad,
like the ones he had so often, of flying an aeroplane, or of
aliens from outer space. Nothing lasted with Tom. He was
still a boy with childish dreams. Until Bobby had come along,
Tom had been her baby, Walter's cherished boy that he'd
wanted for so long, and now it seemed that even Walter was
being carried away by an ambition that Tom never even knew
he had until some man called James Conway had put it into
his head.

She had never met the man, but already she hated him.
She closed her eyes for a moment, as if to shut out the whole

world and what was happening in her small corner of it. When she felt somebody take her cold hands in his, she opened her eyes again to look at her son, sitting beside her now. Her young, strong son, who had been growing up despite his mother's efforts to keep him safe by her side, regardless of the risks he took in his working life or the threat of war. Common sense told her she couldn't keep him safe for ever, but for just a little while longer, she pleaded inside her head. Just a little while longer.

'Mum, I really want to do this,' Tom said in the husky grown-up voice she seemed to be registering for the very first time. 'Mr Conway had a long talk with Dad before they came to me with the idea, but it's a great chance to be offered an apprenticeship and learn to be a craftsman. You never know – one day there might even be tables and chairs with the name Thomas Chase stamped on them somewhere. You'd be proud of me then, wouldn't you?'

Alice felt a great lump in her throat. Young as he was, he saw far into the future in a way that she never did. She only saw what was here and now, and what was important to her family.

She stroked his hair, and for once he didn't jerk away. 'I'm proud of you now, Tom,' she said, taking a shaky breath. 'We'd better all have a cup of tea and then you can tell me properly what this Mr Conway said to you and your father.'

She couldn't look at Walter. He had always favoured Tom so much over the girls, and Bobby wasn't yet old enough to be much more than a pet to him. But Tom, his boy, had been a part of him for so long, sharing the work he did, and going off with him each morning. Father and son, working together. And now she was seething inside, feeling that Walter had somehow betrayed that trust, regardless of how eager Tom was about the whole idea. It was Walter who was sending her son away from her, and she would never forgive him for that.

Fifteen

Alice told herself not to be so feeble, obliged to recognize that there were two men in this house now, not just one. Tom was more eloquent than his father, and able to say what was in his heart more readily than Walter ever did. It was Mick who was the expert in that, Alice thought with momentary bitterness, recalling the love letters she had received all those years ago.

But she didn't want to think of that now. She didn't want to think of anything but how important this new plan really was to Tom, and to be sure for his sake that it wasn't going to be just a nine-day wonder.

'And this Mr Conway suggests coming here to see us all to discuss it?' she said now through dry lips.

She wasn't keen on this idea. It would seem to be an honour for him to make the journey especially to see the parents and be sure they were happy with his proposal for Tom, but Alice was the sort of woman who wasn't comfortable with strangers in her house. It wasn't that she kept an untidy house – far from it – and nor was she ashamed of the fact that they were working-class folk and always had been. It was a feeling of exposing herself, her family and all they stood for to the outside world. Maybe that was being too insular as well, she admitted, hearing how Tom was looking forward to leaving home and making his own way in the world. Hadn't she done the same thing after all, when she had left familiar ground and come to live more than a hundred miles away from all that she knew best? She forced herself to listen to what Tom was saying now.

'Mr Conway is anxious to meet you, Mum, to get your full approval, of course, and when he comes here you'll see what a decent man he is. He's got a son a few years older than me but he's got something wrong with him and he's not too bright, so he's not able to go into the furniture business. Mr Conway says that his mother cares for him at home.'

'He's a family man, then,' was all Alice could think of to say at that moment, listening to her son who suddenly seemed so much more older and wiser than she was, and could speak so calmly about a boy less able than himself.

'So what do you say, Alice?' Walter said, aware that she was displeased with him more than with Tom, and unable to fathom out why. All parents wanted the best for their children, and this chance for Tom had come out of the blue. And if Alice didn't think he'd be devastated when his boy left home, then she didn't know him as well as she thought she did, he thought belligerently. But a man didn't shed woman's tears at such an event, and it was right that a boy should make his own way in the world.

'I won't say that this hasn't taken me by surprise, because it's been a bit of a shock,' Alice said carefully, still preferring to speak to Tom rather than his father. 'But if your heart is really set on it, Tom, then this Mr Conway had better come here as he suggests, and let us know all the details. It's a big step for you to take, so we all have to be sure that it's the right one. I'll say no more than that for now.'

She was rewarded by a hug from her son, and his whispered words that he wouldn't let her down. Her heart softened; she'd never thought he would for a minute. She knew she had to let him go. She had always known this day would come. He wasn't the one she was angry with, and when her eyes met Walter's, both of them were stormy and distant.

Tom said he wouldn't stop for a drink of tea and that he'd have his supper later. First of all, he had to run down to Jack's house and tell him the news.

'Just remember that nothing's settled yet,' Alice said sharply, but by then she was talking to thin air.

She poured out two cups of tea and pushed one towards Walter, unable to contain herself any longer. All her ideas about letting Tom go had vanished the moment he went out of the door.

'How could you let this happen?' she burst out.

'Let what happen?' he said angrily. 'Did you want to keep him tied to your apron strings for ever, woman?'

'But he's not a man yet. He changes his mind about things all the time. He's still a boy. *Your* boy, or so you always said. You couldn't even call him by his name half the time, could you? How can you bear to let him go?'

'I'll let him go because it's the way things happen. You stick to your babying with the young 'un, but it's time to let Tom become a man, whatever we feel about it. Now I'm going out to my shed to cool off before I say summat I'll really regret.'

He stumped out, limping quite badly; either he was putting on a show for her benefit, or his foot was playing up with the gout. Well *good*, she thought savagely, hoping it was the latter, and then felt instant remorse at such a petty thought.

She had no taste for her cup of tea either, so she threw the contents of the cups down the sink.

How had they come to this? The year had started out with such hope, the way every new year did. Rose had had a boyfriend, even if Alice had never really approved of Peter Kelsey; Lucy had still been at home; Tom had his daydreams; and Tilly had still been sending her letters and cards, the way she had done for years. Now everything had changed, and even though Alice knew she was letting herself drown in self-pity, she couldn't seem to help it, and didn't know how to stop it.

By the time Rose came home for supper Alice was in a foul mood. It wasn't often that she let things get on top of her, but Rose found her banging pots and pans about while Bobby sat morosely on the sofa playing with his toys.

'You look as though you've lost a tanner and found a penny,' Rose said.

Alice never cried. Not in public, anyway, and never in front of her children. But Rose's words were the last straw, and right now it took all of her self-control not to do so, even while she was calling herself all kinds of a fool for letting this affect her so much. If it hadn't come so soon after Tilly, she was sure it wouldn't have affected her so much, but everything she'd thought safe in her world now seemed to be turning upside down.

She wouldn't give in to the luxury of crying in front of her children, but her hands were shaking so much that Rose took the dish of stew from her in alarm.

'I'm sorry if that was thoughtless, Mum. I know you're still upset over Tilly, but I didn't know how much. I've been so wrapped up in myself lately, and you did seem to be getting over it.'

That was the difference between feeling the death of a friend so sharply, and still being young enough to think that life went on for ever, Alice thought. It was right and proper that it should be so, but it didn't help when feelings were so bruised. It wasn't even all about Tilly any more, although Tilly was the catalyst that had made Alice's own world so uncertain.

Rose put the dish of stew on the table and drew her mother to sit beside her and Bobby on the sofa, ignoring his grumbles at being squashed.

'Why don't you tell me what's wrong, Mum?' she said quietly.

Bobby piped up before Alice could draw breath. 'Our Tom's going away to make tables and chairs and our Mum don't like it, and I'm having a bedroom all to myself,' he announced.

Alice gasped. 'You were listening, you little wretch! You were supposed to be upstairs tidying your toys.'

'I'm still having a bedroom all to myself, aren't I?' he said.

He looked so indignant that before she could stop herself, Alice began laughing. Actually laughing, which she didn't think she had done to any degree since the moment she had heard about Tilly.

'What's he talking about?' Rose demanded. 'And what's so funny?'

'Trust him to get things right,' Alice said, still laughing in that shrill, strange manner. 'He's getting a bedroom to himself like the big boy he is, and that's the most important thing to my baby.'

She grabbed him to her, burying her face in his, and

breathing in the sweet baby smell of him, even while he tried to get out of her clutches.

'I'm not a baby!' he howled.

Walter came into the room to the incongruous sight of them all. Rose was still looking bewildered and trying to make sense of it all, and Alice and Bobby seemed to be virtually fighting with one another, with tears streaming down Alice's face.

'Who's murdering who in here?' he asked unnecessarily.

Walter was already feeling uneasy at the way he had stamped out of the house, and it cut him to the heart to see Alice looking so flushed with tears on her face. He cursed the moment James Conway had ever mentioned the bloody apprenticeship for the boy, even though he knew it was the opportunity of a lifetime, and one that couldn't be ignored. But he hadn't reckoned on how it would affect Alice.

A woman saw things differently from a man, and felt them more keenly. A woman needed to be handled with more care than a man with rough hands whose pride depended on sawing and planing a piece of wood to perfection. He'd missed his last cup of tea, and he made them all a fresh pot now, ignoring the fact that it was woman's work to do so. It took a while before they had all calmed down sufficiently for Rose to find out what had brought on her mother's tears, and what Bobby was babbling about. Once she understood, Rose squeezed Alice's hand.

'I can imagine your feelings, Mum, but this is such a great opportunity for Tom, isn't it?' she said, echoing her father's thoughts.

'Don't you think I know that? Of course it's a great opportunity, and I'm sure I wouldn't want to be the one to stand in his way. It just seems that my family is breaking apart – and before you say anything else, I know it's healthy and natural for young ones to leave the nest and go their own way. It just seems so soon, that's all. Far too soon,' she finished lamely, aware of how pathetic she sounded, so unlike the strong woman she had always believed herself to be. She looked at Walter, his face so troubled now, and thought how stalwart he had always been through the years of their marriage. He had never let her down for a moment, and she wasn't about to let him down now. From somewhere deep inside she forced herself to take a deep breath and gave them all a weak smile.

'Listen to me going on, will you? I'm just having a mothering moment, that's all, and although it took me by surprise, I wouldn't deny Tom his chance if this is what he really wants. How could I deny Bobby the chance to have his own bedroom? I'd never hear the end of it if I did.'

Bobby immediately began jumping and down and chanting, and it wasn't hard to see that the thought of Tom going away wasn't bothering him a bit. She didn't miss the look of relief on Walter's face at her words, though.

'Well, let's get on with drinking this tea and then have some supper. I'm starving, Mother.'

He grinned sheepishly at her then, expecting the usual sharp retort that she wasn't his mother. Instead, she put her arms around his neck and kissed his cheek.

'I'm not your mother,' she whispered jerkily in his ear so that only he could hear. But it was as good as saying that all was well between them.

A short while later Tom practically flew indoors, just in time for the stew and dumplings to be ladled out, and only a fool would not be able to see how excited he was at having passed on his news to the rest of his family.

'Our Jack's as jealous as heck that I'll be moving up Bristol way,' he said gleefully. 'I told him there's plenty of farms up there if he wants to come with me.'

'It's not settled yet,' Rose warned him, glancing at her mother.

Alice spoke calmly. 'Oh, I daresay it's as good as, providing this Mr Conway can assure us it's all above board. I've got to meet him yet, mind.'

But they all knew she was giving her silent consent.

'Why should Jack be jealous, anyway?' Rose said curiously. 'I always thought he was a bit of a stick-in-the-mud with his farming job.'

'It's because one of his mates left the village a while ago, and came back looking swanky and with money in his pockets from some new job he's got. Our Jack's got itchy feet, despite what you think, and he's only been biding his time until the war comes. Then he'll be off.'

He said it so matter-of-factly, so thoughtlessly and so cruelly, thought Alice, that it almost took her breath away.

'Does his mother know he feels that way?' she demanded.

Tom shrugged. 'I suppose so. I don't know. He's never made any secret of the fact that he wants to be an airman.'

'I thought you did too,' Rose teased him. 'But that little dream soon faded away, didn't it?'

'Well, now I'd rather make furniture,' Tom retorted.

Amen to that, Alice thought silently. At least it was better than imagining him risking his life in one of those flimsy aeroplanes. Not that he would, or could, at only fourteen, she added with some relief.

Helen came to see her the next afternoon to share her thoughts on the matter.

'You've got to let him do this, Alice.'

'Don't worry, I'm already resigned to it, but I want to see this Mr Conway first. He's a family man, and Tom will be living in his house, so I want to be sure that he'll be taken care of.'

'He's a young man, Alice. Younger boys than Tom have run away to sea or gone down the coal mines and made their own way in life. You can't mollycoddle your children for ever.'

'Oh no? Jack's still living at home, isn't he? I haven't noticed him wanting to move away and be without all his home comforts.'

She knew she was sounding ungracious, but now that she was reasonably settled in her own mind that Tom would be leaving home, she didn't need her sister-in-law giving her a lecture on the subject. They so rarely disagreed, but this was her family business, not Helen's.

'I know you're upset, Alice, so I won't get angry over what you just said,' Helen said after a moment. 'I was only trying to help, but I can see I'm not helping at all, am I? I would say you should be glad you've still got Rose close at hand, and Lucy comes home every weekend, and Bobby's a little love, but that won't help either, will it?'

Alice didn't miss the tiny barb, even if it was a blatant reminder of how lucky Alice was to have four children, when Helen and Mick had always wanted more, and it had never happened.

'You know you can have a share of Bobby any time,' she said, 'especially when he gets in one of his moods!'

Helen laughed. 'I'd take him, even like that,' she said. Then she spoke more soberly. 'I know it's only a matter of time before Jack leaves home for whatever reason, and then there'll be just Mick and me rattling around in that big house. You're the lucky one, Alice. You've always been the lucky one.'

'I know I'm lucky to have Walter, and how he puts up with me sometimes I don't know. We've both got good marriages, Helen, and I'm not going to allow us to sit here and wallow any longer, so let's take Bobby for a walk instead.'

James Conway came to the house on Saturday afternoon, driving up in a big car that made Alice nervous at once. She knew he was arriving that day, and she had polished the house so much that Walter grumbled that it wasn't the king and queen who were coming, and that he'd be afraid to sit down on his own chair in a minute for fear he'd slide right off. With the girls, she had been the one to go and see their prospective employers, and although it had been unnerving, at least her home hadn't been invaded by strangers, which was how she thought of this situation. She couldn't help thinking that this time *she* was the one who was being inspected.

'There's a woman with him,' Lucy said, home for the afternoon and curious to see who thought her brother's talents could be so wonderful that they were taking him away from home. 'She looks all right, and there's a boy who looks a bit odd.'

'Come away from the window, Lucy,' Alice said at once. 'I didn't know he was bringing his family, but that will be the boy who's disabled, so don't stare.'

The boy was called Graham. He had one leg shorter than the other, which meant that he had to wear a surgical boot. He was also rather slow in manner, and he didn't say much, but apart from that, he was a pleasant young man. It was obvious though, that his hand–eye co-ordination wouldn't allow him to do the fine work required of a furniture maker.

The moment Mrs Conway smiled at her, Alice relaxed. They were both mothers, after all, and both wanted the best for their children. From the way Graham was cared for, it was obvious that Tom would be in good hands, and although they had an awkward beginning to the afternoon, by the end of it everything was settled. Tom would give in his notice at the sawmills, and James Conway would be back to collect him in two weeks' time.

That was the moment when it really hit Alice. In two weeks' time, she would be losing Tom. The once busy house would be reduced to just herself, Walter, Bobby, and Rose. Some other woman would be cooking Tom's meals, washing his clothes, hearing how his day went.

'I'll make sure he writes to you every week, Mrs Chase,' she heard the other woman say. 'I know it's what I would want in your position.'

She smiled, and Alice smiled back as best she could. Mrs Conway was a good and understanding woman, nobody could deny that, but she was still taking Alice's son away from her. She felt a shaft of jealousy, similar to the one she'd felt when Tilly had gone to stay with Helen, and was ashamed of herself. She'd never thought of herself as a jealous woman before, nor even known that she could be.

'Thank you for that, Mrs Conway' she replied steadily. 'Tom's father and I will naturally be anxious to know how he's faring.'

'And you're lucky enough to still have another little one to keep you company,' the woman went on, reminding Alice that she had other compensations even if it felt as though the heart and soul of her family was being ripped out.

She felt resentful of the implication, and then she caught sight of the look in Mrs Conway's eyes. It was the same yearning she sometimes glimpsed in Helen's eyes when Helen played with Bobby. It told Alice in an instant that this woman would also have wanted more children. For whatever reason, she only had Graham, and his affliction must have caused his parents plenty of heartache.

There were details to be sorted out between the men,

but by the time the Conways were on their way home everything was arranged for Tom's departure, and a contract of apprenticeship had been signed between the interested parties.

'You're a lucky devil to get such a good job, Tom,' Lucy told him when they had waved the big car away and the family were able to relax properly.

'I know,' he said gleefully. 'But don't worry. By the time you find yourself a chap to marry you, I'll be such an expert I'll make you a nest of tables for a wedding present.'

'Now don't you get too cocky, boy,' Walter told him. 'Our Lucy's too young to be thinking of anything like marriage, and you've got to learn your trade first. A craftsman ain't born overnight.'

There was no doubting his pride in the situation, though, and Alice could see it every time she saw him look at Tom. He was going to miss him like the clappers, she thought irreverently. Anyway, in the right order of things, it would be Rose thinking of marriage long before Lucy, and she couldn't help thinking that neither of them would be doing so for a long while yet.

But for now they were all together, and the house was full of babble and noise, and Bobby's voice could be heard above the rest, still shouting that he was having a bedroom all to himself as soon as Tom was gone.

'Oh, Bobby, you've gone and wet yourself now,' Rose scolded him as she noticed all the excitement had become too much for him, and he could no more stop the pee running down his legs than stop himself breathing.

'I couldn't help it!' he shrieked. 'It just happened.'

'Never mind, love,' Alice said, scooping him up in her arms. 'Let's take you upstairs and change your drawers.'

She didn't care that he had peed himself. He'd been trying so hard to be dry, but he was still vulnerable, still her baby, still going to be with her for years and years, and a pair of wet drawers was a small price to pay for the joy that a small child could bring. And these moments when they were alone, when he needed her, while the presence of the family below was muted, were still precious to her. She cleaned him up, kissed his flushed face and took him back downstairs, thinking how strange it was that a moment like this could make her stop and take stock.

It wasn't as though Tom was going away for ever. Bristol wasn't the other side of the country, like London. She was sure they could go and visit him now and then, and Mrs Conway had assured her that he would some come home for a weekend every month, so she was making a stupid fuss over nothing.

'All right?' Walter said when he saw her, his eyes still uneasy. She nodded at him over Bobby's head.

'All right,' she said.

They all kept determinedly talking for a while longer, and then it was as though a silent signal had arrived for the party to break up. Rose said she would take Bobby down to the village shops for a bit of fresh air; Lucy decided it was time she went back to the Grange; Tom was so eager to go and continue crowing to Jack about his new job that they could practically see his head swell, and then Alice and Walter were alone again.

'What are you really thinking . . . Alice?' he asked.

She knew him so well. He had restrained himself from calling her Mother at the last instant, and for all that she railed against the word, it was exactly what she was. Not *his*, of course, but she was mother to all their children, the most precious role a woman ever played in her life. Her heart stirred. Without Walter she would never have known the joys of motherhood, nor all the pains and anxieties it could sometimes bring too, but this was the life they had chosen for themselves, and she would never have wanted it otherwise.

'I'm thinking that I'm glad we've got each other,' she said simply. Which was her way of saying that she loved him.

'That we have, and now that we've all done enough jabbering for one day I'll leave you in peace for a while. Call me when supper's ready, my dear.'

He stood up and pressed her shoulder in passing – which was as good as saying that he loved her too. She watched him stump out to his shed, limping a little, and felt a fierce rush of passion for him at that moment. He was prepared to let Tom go, knowing it was to the boy's benefit, but also knowing he would miss Tom so much. Working with his boy every day, and knowing Tom shared his love of the work they did, had been a real fillip to Walter, and soon that daily closeness would be gone. Knowing him, he would bear it stoically, and she must do the same. Right there and then she made a silent vow not to let either of them down.

Sixteen

Two weeks had never passed so quickly, and Alice's resolve began to falter as the day of Tom's departure approached. She had to keep reminding herself that this was for Tom's good, and that she couldn't keep him safe for ever. Though why she should think that sending him to a good apprenticeship was less safe than working in the dangerous environs of a sawmill was probably ridiculous. All the same, she found herself with damp eyes as she washed and ironed his clothes for the last time. The scent of his body rose from the heat of the flat iron as she smoothed his shirts into shape, and she told herself to stop being maudlin, and not to send him off with the sight of his weeping mother to remember.

The Conways arrived, and Mrs Conway had brought a bouquet of flowers for Alice. It was sweet of her. But Alice couldn't help thinking the flowers were in exchange for her son, and it was a blooming poor exchange, she thought with a stab of her old spirit. But then the woman gave her a brief hug, and whispered that she'd insist Tom write to her the very next day to let her know he was all right.

Alice knew how foolish she was being. If there was a war, like the warmongers had been saying for so long now, then plenty of mothers would be saying goodbye to their sons, possibly forever. She gave a small shudder, and put a brave face on. At the last minute, Tom put his arms around her and held her tight.

'Don't you worry about me, Mum. As soon as I can I'll make you something, and then you'll be proud of me,' he said, his young voice wobbling just a little.

'I'm already proud of you, so don't make me blubber now. You go and learn a trade and make your fortune!'

She wanted them gone now. She couldn't bear all this

lingering about; it wasn't helping anybody. But at last they had loaded all Tom's things into the big car and the moment had arrived. The rest of the family had said their goodbyes, and they stayed indoors while Walter went outside to wave them off. He didn't turn back for some minutes, and even though he would never admit it, Alice knew how difficult this was for him. She decided to make his favourite rabbit pie for supper that evening. It wasn't such a silly remark that the way to a man's heart was through his stomach. It gave him comfort as well as sustenance. Besides, she already had his heart, and she hoped that cooking for him now would tell him – in more than words – that she knew just how he felt about losing Tom.

She often thought of Tilly nowadays, and she knew that Tilly would have told her to look on the bright side, and not to be so bleedin' lily-livered. Tom wasn't gone for ever, and they had the summer to look forward to. It was already April and the days were getting warmer. Wild daffodils were blooming in the hedgerows, and the winter snowdrops had long since come and gone. Trees were burgeoning into new life with a network of spring green, and it was time to feel hope, not sorrow. Alice made herself think it. Besides which, Bobby was now beside himself with excitement, because of the bedroom he now had all to himself.

Despite it all, she knew Water was grieving inwardly, even if he never said as much. That first night, in the closeness of their double bed, when she didn't quite know what tentative words to say to him that wouldn't make things worse, their bedroom door suddenly opened. A small, wraithlike figure stood in the doorway and then came hurtling across the room, sniffing loudly.

'Can I come in with you?' Bobby sobbed. 'I don't like it all by myself.'

'Come on, sweetheart,' Alice said at once. 'In you get.'

She threw back the bedclothes and he climbed in, snuggling against her, his warm little body tacky with sleep, his arms holding on to her fiercely.

'Just don't pee in the bed,' Walter grunted. 'And don't think you're going to make a habit of this, my son. You're the boy of the house now, mind.'

Alice wondered if saying those words made him feel any better. It was true, of course. Bobby was the boy of the house now. It wasn't that Walter had ever overlooked Bobby, just that he and Tom had always been such good companions, and Bobby was still a baby in his eyes. But when Bobby climbed in between then and she felt Walter's arm go around him, she felt a tiny sliver of hope that things would work out for them all. But she kept her fingers crossed as she thought it.

True to his word – or maybe Mrs Conway's – they soon had a letter from Tom, describing the big house that he was living in now, and how he was cautiously getting to know Graham, and how wonderful the furniture workshops were.

'I don't think I'm likely to be making proper furniture for a while just yet,' he wrote. 'There's a lot to learn, and Mr Conway says I've got to take things slowly, because that's the way true craftsmen are born.'

Walter guffawed when he read that part of the letter. 'That'll be the day when he takes things slowly. He was always the impatient one.'

'He'll have to do as he's told,' Alice said, 'and it will be good for him. It's a different kind of life to the one he led at the sawmills, I'm sure.'

'Oh ah, and I'm sure Conway's a good teacher.'

Alice was reading the rest of the letter. 'He says they're going to Bristol to some furniture exhibition next week. I had no idea this Mr Conway was such an expert, but Tom says there will be some of his work on show too.'

'Maybe some day it will be some of our Tom's as well. That will be a feather in his cap for us, eh, Mother?'

She didn't miss the pride in his voice now, and she knew he had accepted the new situation – more easily than she had, really. After a week, Bobby had reluctantly gone back into his own bedroom again, once Alice had promised that if he woke during the night, she would lie in Tom's old bed for a while until Bobby dropped off to sleep. Not that she would be doing that for long, Alice thought keenly. It wasn't much fun to climb into a cold bed after the warmth of the double bed she shared with Walter. But Bobby was gradually learning to be the boy of the house now, just as Walter had told him.

'I knew he'd settle down,' Helen told her complacently, as though she had a dozen children of her own and knew exactly how to handle them. As if she had been the one to endure broken nights while Bobby got used to the idea that the bedroom he'd coveted so much wasn't as much fun as he'd thought it would be.

Alice couldn't explain why Helen was starting to irritate her so much. She had always been her friend and confidante as well as her sister-in-law, and until recently Alice had never fully realized how lordly Helen could be, especially when it came to country matters. It was as if she considered herself to have superior knowledge over the upstart who had come here from London to live – which was ridiculous, since Alice had lived here for more than twenty years now, and considered herself as much of a countrywoman as anyone in Bramwell . . .

Except in her speech, she conceded. Her accent may have mellowed over the years, but there was no disguising where she came from – and why should she try? She was who she was, and she was damn proud of it.

'Are you all right, Alice?' Helen said more sharply when she didn't reply.

'Well, about as right as I can be, knowing my son's left home at fourteen. You've still got that joy to come, remember,' she added, knowing she was being sarcastic and not knowing how to stop it.

Helen stared out of the window. Her voice was full of a quality Alice couldn't quite follow. 'It won't be any easier for me than for you, Alice. Harder, in fact, because then Mick and I really will have nothing left to talk about.'

'What do you mean? You and Mick are always chatting to one another. There's nothing wrong, is there?' For the first time, she realized that her sister-in-law looked unusually down in the mouth. Alice had been so wrapped up in her own family that she hadn't even noticed how the years were taking their toll on Helen. Older than Alice, she looked quite pinched around her mouth now.

'It may seem as though we chat all the time, but we don't say anything of any importance to each other. Not like you and Walter do.'

Alice began to laugh. 'Good Lord, we don't say anything that would put the world to rights, Helen. It's mostly family stuff, that's all.'

'I know, and I'm just being silly, aren't I? I suppose it's seeing your Tom go off like that and wondering when it's going to be our turn. Jack's always saying he'd have left home long before now if he wasn't so comfortable there.'

Alice didn't like this conversation at all. 'Well, there you are then. You know what I think? It's all talk. It doesn't mean anything. He may say he wants to leave home, but I bet he never will until he gets married and gives you grandchildren. You won't have a minute to yourself when that happens.'

'I daresay you're right. I'm just being silly, aren't I?' Helen said, making a determined effort to be more cheerful.

Neither of them mentioned the fact that the decision for Jack to stay at home might be taken out of their hands if the meddling governments had their way.

'Anyway, I'm quite happy for you to take Bobby off my hands any afternoon you like while I get on with my belated spring-cleaning,' Alice said. 'The whole house needs a good spruce and I can't do much with him under my feet all the time.'

'I'll take him now, if you like, and bring him back in time for supper,' Helen offered, far too eagerly.

It wasn't really what Alice had intended, and nor was she in the mood for turning bedrooms upside down, but she had made the suggestion now, and Bobby was already clamouring to go and stay with Auntie Helen for a couple of hours where he knew he'd be spoiled. She watched them go, then went upstairs with a sigh, ready to tackle relining dressing-table drawers and sorting out clothes that had had their day and were to be sent to the next church jumble.

She knew she shouldn't grumble, but it came to something when a woman was so lonely that she wanted to take another woman's child for a few hours, just for the company. She'd never thought of Helen as lonely before, but now she realized that was the case. She wondered just what kind of husband Mick had become, if he and his wife seemed to have drifted apart so much. She shivered, knowing that it could have been her. Mick had been the articulate one in the past, but now it was mostly with his clients, she realized, and especially the animals he cared for. It was Walter, the head of a busy household, who was the family man, and who sometimes had to bellow at length to be heard above the rest of them! Somehow he'd always managed to keep them all in order with a rod of iron in a velvet glove.

Christ Almighty, Alice thought with a girlish giggle, *I'm a blooming poet and I don't know it . . .*

'I think Helen's lonely,' she announced to Walter that evening.

He stopped eating and gave a guffaw. 'Don't be daft, woman. How can any woman with a family be lonely?'

'That's just it. She doesn't have the kind of family we have, does she? I know I've sometimes grumbled about having them all under my feet, but that's how families should be. For Helen, there's only Jack, and he's hardly ever there. And Mick – well, I don't know that he's much company nowadays.'

Walter looked at her strangely now. 'I thought you liked Mick.'

'I do like him. But it seems to me he's happier with animals for company than people. You two don't spend much time together any more, do you?'

'We don't live in one another's pockets, if that's what you mean.'

'But when I first met you, you were closer than Siamese twins.'

Walter finished his supper and pushed his plate away. 'People change, Alice. You're not the girl I met, are you?'

'What's that supposed to mean?' Her heart began beating faster, and she wished she had never started this conversation. She had certainly never meant it to take this turn. Then she heard him laugh.

'Well, my girl, you're a sight more buxom than you were then, not that I've any objection to that! You and Tilly were all skin and bones when me and Mick first laid eyes on you.

It made no difference, though. I still knew you were the girl for me and always would be.'

'Did you?' Alice said, astonished – not that he meant it, but that he should actually put it into words.

''Course I did. I reckon our Mick took a bit of a fancy to you back then too, but I was the lucky one, and don't expect to hear me saying such daft things too often, because I won't. That's quite enough complimenting for one day,' he finished with a grin, seeing how her face had gone pink.

She got up from the table, and put her arms around his shoulders.

'And that's quite enough complimenting for me, you old softie,' she said with a catch in her throat. 'All the same, I think I shall see Helen a bit more often until she gets over her gloom. It's the least a good sister-in-law can do, isn't it?'

It must have been no more than a gloomy patch, she thought later, since Helen seemed to have recovered herself perfectly well during the next few days. Perhaps she was on the change, Alice thought suddenly. Whatever it was, when the woman who did the flowers for the church decided to retire, Helen offered to take on the job, and she was definitely more cheerful once it had been settled.

'I've been sitting around the house too much,' she declared, which was nonsense in itself, since Helen had been for ever dusting and polishing in places that were totally unnecessary in Alice's opinion. Alice's annual spring-clean was almost a monthly ritual in Helen's house, but she understood now that it could also be a kind of substitute activity for not having a clutch of children to care for.

But all thoughts of Helen's problems vanished a few weeks later. Tom was writing home regularly, and was full of enthusiasm about his new job, putting his mother's mind at ease. He and the reticent Graham Conway had struck up a rare friendship, which Alice was sure was due to Tom's ability to deal with young Bobby, as well as living in a house full of siblings. Alice was thanking the Lord for a relatively calm summer now, refusing to think too seriously of any prospect of war ahead, despite the government's continued warnings and rumblings. However, her complacency came to an abrupt end one night when she heard noises coming from Bobby's bedroom, and her heart stopped for a moment.

She scrambled out of bed and rushed into his room to find him sitting up in bed, his face beetroot-red as he tried to catch his breath between gasps and awful coughing. She gathered him up in her arms, ignoring the heat coming from his sweat-soaked little body. The coughs were racking him from head to toe, and Alice's heart throbbed as rapidly as Bobby's own as she recognized the signs.

Whooping cough could be deadly in a baby or young child. It was also highly contagious, and among the thoughts whirling around in her head was the fact that Rose was working every day with the Staceys' baby. She often brought the baby home during their walks, and Bobby loved playing with her, so the disease could so easily have been passed on to her already. Alice tried to stifle her rising hysteria, knowing she must be the one to stay calm, however difficult it might be. But just as she thought it, Rose appeared in the bedroom behind her.

'Get out, Rose,' Alice croaked. 'Don't come near Bobby.'

'What's wrong with him?' Rose said, taking a step forward.

'Do as I say!' Alice almost screamed. 'I think he's got the whooping cough, and if so, then baby Mollie could be at risk, and I'll never forgive myself.'

'It wouldn't be your fault, Mum!' Rose said, but she automatically began backing away, just as Walter came blundering in, his hair awry, annoyed at having his sleep so rudely disturbed.

'What's all the rumpus in here? Can't you keep the child quiet, Mother?'

It was too much for Alice. She rocked Bobby back and forth in her arms, as if she was afraid she was about to lose him at any minute.

'Can't you see the child's very sick?' she almost shrieked. 'If he dies, I won't ever forget that you called this night nothing but a rumpus.'

Walter stared at her, completely taken aback by this reaction. 'What the devil are you talking about?' he said harshly.

Rose answered him fearfully. 'Mum thinks Bobby's got the whooping cough, Dad.'

'Then he needs a bloody doctor, not to have you two females twittering and blubbing over him. Get dressed and go and fetch him, Rose.'

'I can't go,' she said, as choked as Alice now. 'If it is whooping cough, I could have passed it on to Mollie Stacey. They won't want to see me in the middle of the night with such news!'

'Then I'll bloody well go,' Walter said, anger and fear for his child making him lose control of his words. 'You women do what you can for the boy and I'll get down to the village and knock the doctor's bloody door down if I have to.'

He blundered out again, and Alice calmed down a little. None of the other children had suffered in this way, but somewhere in the back of her mind she recalled Tilly telling her of her own childhood bouts of asthma and chest infections, and what her grandmother had done to relieve them.

'Rose, go downstairs and boil a kettle. Fill a jug with the boiling water and bring it back up here. Bobby needs to breathe in the steam to relieve the symptoms. I'll put him in dry pyjamas and sponge his face to make him more comfortable.'

Rose flew downstairs to do her bidding, pulling her dressing-gown tightly around her in the cold early hours of the morning. Her hands shook, hoping desperately that she hadn't unwittingly passed this illness on to the Stacey baby. Whooping cough was often fatal, and a household full of doctors were of little use if fate decreed it otherwise. She prayed as she had never prayed before that it wouldn't be as bad as they feared.

Walter soon came storming back to the house, and he had Doctor Matt with him. The women had expected to see the older doctor, and it was clear from Walter's face that he had expected it too.

'I'm sorry it couldn't be my brother,' Doctor Matt said at once. 'He's been called out to attend to a dying woman, so you'll have to make do with me, I'm afraid.'

'That's not the kind of remark to make us feel any better,' Walter growled. 'Just see to the boy, will you?'

Matt Stacey glanced at Rose encouragingly, and in any other circumstances Alice wouldn't have missed the way her girl blushed at being seen in her dressing-gown, even if it covered her from head to foot. She wouldn't have missed the way Walter was now referring to Bobby as 'the boy' either, as if he had transferred all his filial feelings towards his younger son now that Tom was safely settled. She didn't think anything of it then, but it all came back to her later.

'You've done the right thing in giving him steam to breathe, Mrs Chase,' Doctor Matt said approvingly. 'A mother's instinct usually knows what to do.'

Alice knew she couldn't take the credit for that, and she wondered if Tilly was hovering over them all somewhere, guiding her from whatever bizarre heaven she was in. She also wondered if she was getting light-headed or even going slightly mad, to be thinking such things at a time like this. All the children had had various childhood ailments in the past, and she had always coped, but never with anything as potentially fatal as this.

The three of them stood back silently while the doctor sat on Bobby's bed. He listened to Bobby's chest, took his temperature and felt his pulse, and took away a sample of phlegm for testing. Bobby obligingly coughed and spluttered and spat, and finally the doctor straightened up.

'You're not feeling too well, are you, old chap?' he said soothingly to Bobby. 'But never mind, we'll soon have you on the mend again.'

He smiled at Alice. 'It's not whooping cough, Mrs Chase. I know it was alarming to hear him trying to catch his breath like that, and that's what made him whoop, but it's no more than croup. That's bad enough in itself, but we can give him some medicine, and some Friar's balsam in the jug of hot water will help to ease his chest. Keep his bedroom warm, because the change of temperature from downstairs is likely to start him off again. But you did the right thing to be cautious, and I'll be round to see him again in the morning.'

Alice could have wept with relief, and Walter started clearing his throat, with nearly as much rattling in his chest as Bobby. The parents stayed with him as Rose saw the doctor out of the house, and at the front door she thanked him tearfully.

'It's what I'm here for, Rose.'

He pressed her hand as he left, and she felt the warmth of it long after she had finally gone back to bed, reassured that Bobby was going to be all right.

Alice slept in Bobby's room again that night. Even if she hadn't wanted to be on hand to change the jug of hot water and Friar's balsam when it grew cold, she knew she needed to stay near him, just to be sure. She had been more fearful than anyone could have guessed, truly thinking her baby had contracted the whooping cough, and knowing that there were a number of small graves in the village churchyard from other young children who had succumbed to the disease.

She would never admit to Walter that all her emotions over Tilly's death had come flooding back as well. For a few moments, holding Bobby's hot little body close to her, she had even imagined she could smell Tilly's strong scent wafting about the room, and wondered fearfully if Tilly had been sent for Bobby, to guide him from this world into the next. But he wasn't *hers*, Alice had thought fiercely. He didn't belong to Tilly, and she wasn't going to have him. They had been no more than wild, foolish fancies, but even now, listening to Bobby still rasping, but sleeping at last, she couldn't quite rid herself of them.

Walter didn't like her sleeping in Bobby's room every night, but she told him it wasn't going to be for ever, just until she was sure he was over the worst. Doctor Matt had reassured them when he came to visit on several occasions, and he told Alice that she too should get proper rest or she would be the next one to fall ill, but she pooh-poohed the suggestion. Her place was to hold the family together, and she had no intention of cooking less than her usual nourishing meals, washing and ironing their clothes, and keeping a clean and tidy house.

'You know, I think Matt's right, Mum,' Rose told her after a week, when Lucy had been home to hear the news, and Tom had written to say he was glad all was now well. They were both a little detached, Alice thought sadly, but that was what happened to families when the young ones spread their wings.

Rose went on: 'You don't need to fret over Bobby now, and perhaps you could do with a tonic yourself.'

'Are you turning into the mother now?' Alice said, more sharply than she intended. 'And anyway, since when did you call the doctor by his Christian name?'

'Since he asked me to,' Rose said simply.

Alice immediately remembered the way they had looked at one another when the doctor came to see Bobby. She knew that look so well.

'Be careful, Rose,' she said without thinking.

'What do you mean?'

'Well . . . a doctor. They're different from the rest of us, aren't they? They've had proper education and learning, and all that kind of thing. I wouldn't want to see you get hurt, Rose.'

'It's not what I want, either, so don't fuss, Mum. I'm not a child, and I do know how to look after myself. Just because Matt comes from a family of doctors it doesn't mean he looks down on us – far from it, in fact. And if he did, I certainly wouldn't want anything to do with him. We're as good as anybody, aren't we?'

Alice smiled at her indignation. 'Of course we are, love.'

All the same, she couldn't help wondering what Matt Stacey's family would say if they suspected he took more than a normal interest in the Chase girl, who had only been hired as his sister-in-law's baby minder. Or perhaps they did know, Alice thought with sudden weariness. Right now, it seemed too much of a bother to think about. For once in her life she was going to take it easy that afternoon and take advantage of Bobby resting. She went upstairs and lay down quietly on the bed opposite him. The pungent scent of the Friar's balsam was strangely soothing. That, and the sound of Bobby's snuffling, lulled her into a fitful sleep.

Seventeen

Bobby responded quickly to Doctor Matt's medicine and treatment. Once he was on the mend, Alice began to relax, until Walter's words made her jittery all over again.

'We can't ignore what's going on any longer, Mother,' he said one evening at the end of April.

'What's going on?' Alice asked, too busy with folding sheets and pillowcases ready for ironing to take much interest in what he was saying, or to have noticed that he'd been perusing the newspaper for far longer than he usually did.

'At the beginning of the month Chamberlain announced his plans for evacuating thousands of children to the country as soon as the war begins, and now he's talking about conscription for military service for men aged twenty. They've already doubled the number of Territorials and ordered more supplies of boots and uniforms and military supplies. If that's not a threat for us all I don't know what bloody well is. Bastard politicians,' he added grimly.

Alice's hands stilled over the linen. 'Language, Walter. Politicians do nothing but talk. It won't ever happen. All these preparations are like kids playing make-believe with toy soldiers, and they're not even grown men at twenty. They're still boys, playing with pretend guns, not real ones.'

Walter swore beneath his breath. 'Don't be so daft, woman. It will happen, I tell you. No blasted government throws all this money into such widespread preparations unless they're damn sure we're heading for war. It's time to stop hiding your head in the sand, Alice.'

'And you can stop scaring me! I know our boy's too young to be conscripted, and so is Jack at the moment, but I don't want to think of the other young boys in the village having to be forced into something that's none of our business.'

All the same, she felt more than a tug of fear in her heart, knowing she was doing just as he said and burying her head in the sand. She and Helen always determinedly kept any talk of war out of their afternoons together, as if it would go away if they just ignored it. But neither of them was stupid. Alice had read the newspaper reports and listened to the dour voices of the wireless announcers. She knew the possibility of war was becoming ever more real. She just wanted to keep her family safe. To keep everybody's family safe, because that was the way women felt. It was only the men – and the young boys – who wanted to be comic-book heroes.

'There's nothing ordinary folk can do about it, anyway,' she went on firmly. 'Men in high places will decide what's to be done, and it's folk like us who will have to bear the consequences.'

Walter realized how upset she was becoming, and he slapped the pages of the newspaper together. 'Well, let's just be glad that our children have got sensible jobs – not that the girls would have anything to worry about. Tom's all right up Bristol way now, and the babby's too young to know what's going on. As for young Jack, they'll still need farmers to produce food, so I doubt that he'd have to go.'

'Unless he volunteered,' Alice said, echoing a thought that had long been in Helen's head, as she very well knew from the rare occasions when they felt obliged to discuss what was really men's talk. Only when it affected family life did the fear really touch them – because for all that in wartime it was countries fighting other countries, it was families who suffered in the end.

'He wouldn't be such an idiot as to volunteer,' Walter said, but he didn't meet her eyes, and they both knew that if it was a case of do or die for their country, there would be plenty like Jack Chase who wouldn't waste a moment.

'Well, I don't want to talk about it any more,' Alice said quickly, hearing Rose at the front door as Walter went stumping out.

She knew that all this talk of wars and conscriptions was starting to have an unpleasant effect on her. Her own family might be safe from going to war, but others wouldn't be so lucky. People she knew would send their sons and loved ones to fight, and some of them might never return. Would Doctor Matt enlist, even if he was older than the required twenty? Wars produced casualties, and doctors were the first ones who were needed. What about Peter Kelsey? A grocer's son wasn't going to be exempt. Alice would hardly call him military material, but he'd no doubt think himself a flash fellow in a uniform.

It was all Walter's fault that the thoughts whirled sickeningly in her head now, and she desperately wanted them out. She turned to Rose with some relief to hear about her daughter's day, and she couldn't miss her girl's bright eyes, or the hint of nervousness around her mouth.

'I don't know what you'll say about this, Mum, but Matt's asked me to the pictures with him on Saturday evening. I've said I'll think about it. Should I go?'

'Do you want to go?' Alice countered.

'Well, yes, I think so.'

'What's all this?' Walter said, coming back into the room to catch the gist of the conversation.

'It's Doctor Matt,' Alice said, giving him his full title. 'He's asked our Rose out to the pictures, and she wants our opinion.'

Rose hadn't actually asked Walter for his opinion, but they all knew he'd have to have his say on it. Alice saw him frown.

'He's not our sort, Rose, and you'd do better not to get involved with the likes of him.'

Rose burst out laughing. 'Not our sort? What do you mean? You know how good he was with Bobby when he was ill, and how he kept coming round to check on him. He's clever and funny, and the children in the village all love him, and he's had more learning than anybody around here!'

'Well, that's exactly what I mean, girl. What would a clever young doctor with more learning that anybody else around here want with a sawmill worker's daughter? You tell me that.'

Rose's face scalded. 'Perhaps he just likes me. Most people wouldn't see anything nasty in two people just enjoying one another's company.'

She put too much emphasis on the words *most people*, and Walter didn't miss the implication.

'Well, maybe most people are too simple-minded to see

that when folk of different classes try to mix, nothing good ever comes of it,' he snapped.

'Matt is a decent young man, Dad, and you're being beastly to see anything wrong in our having an innocent evening together. You understand, don't you, Mum? Don't let him spoil it for me.'

What Alice understood was just how important this was for Rose. She had only ever been courting with Peter Kelsey, who Alice had always thought too coarse for her daughter. Matthew Stacey might be of a different class socially, but anybody could see he was a well-brought-up young man, and that he also had an eye for her daughter. It wasn't as though Rose was some young flibbertigibbet. She was sensible and proud, and Alice was quite sure she had always kept herself clean and decent.

'I think if you and Doctor Matt like one another, and if he wants to take you to the pictures, then there's nothing wrong in it at all. You agree with that, don't you, Walter? After all, I was only a factory worker in the back streets of London when I met your father and I'm sure he thought he was a cut above me, but we turned out all right, didn't we?'

She hadn't intended making a speech of it, nor to fix Walter with such a steely glare, but if he thought he was going to mess this up for Rose, he would have her to deal with. She heard him grunt, and then he gave her a wry smile as he digested her words.

'Anybody who thought they were a cut above your mother didn't know what they were in for,' he said directly to Rose. 'And seeing as how you're your mother's daughter and know how to conduct yourself, I daresay it's all right.'

He was rewarded with a hug, and he breathed in the sweet fragrance of his daughter's fresh young skin, reminding him of why he'd fallen in love with the girl's mother in the first place.

That night, thankfully, Bobby slept through the night, and since Walter had always believed that actions spoke louder than words, he proceeded to show his wife why he still loved her as much as ever, after all these years.

*　　*　　*

Tom was coming home on the first Friday in May for the first time since moving away, and there was great excitement in the Chase household. Alice had made his favourite chocolate cake and filled it with buttercream, just the way he liked it, quite sure that however domesticated Mrs Conway was, she couldn't bake a cake for her son the way that Alice could. James Conway was to drop him off at the house during Friday afternoon, and would collect him on Sunday morning, as he had a number of weekend business appointments in the area.

Bobby was full of excitement, fully recovered now, and ready for Tom to share his bedroom just for the night, now that he was used to having it all to himself. It was a joyful homecoming, but all Alice could think was how her boy had changed in so short a time. He was still her Tom, but once they had done all their noisy chattering at seeing one another again, she couldn't mistake how he seemed to have grown in stature and maturity.

She knew that Walter saw it too, but he viewed it all with pride, rather than the slight sadness Alice felt in realizing that her boy had subtly grown away from them in more than distance. But she wouldn't let it blight this homecoming, and by Saturday morning she had overcome her feelings as Tom said he was off to see Jack to tell him all that he was doing now. He got out his old bike from the shed and rode through the lanes until he reached the farm where Jack worked, knowing that was where he would be on this fine May morning.

He saw Jack before Jack saw him. He was across the fields, mending fences with the farmer. The scents and smells of the farm and the surrounding countryside mingled in Tom's nostrils, and for a moment he felt a huge sense of nostalgia for this place that would always be home. But it wasn't a lasting regret, because it would for ever be somewhere to come back to from his new and interesting surroundings. His mother had been born and raised in a city, and he knew exactly why she would have loved it so much, because to him Bristol was just as vibrant and exciting as he imagined London to be.

'Jack! Hey, Jack!' he yelled out, and was rewarded by

seeing his cousin in quick consultation with the farmer, before he came striding across the fields to meet Tom halfway.

'Hey there, kid, given up on the furniture-making already, have you?' Jack said with a grin. 'I knew it was only one of your fly-by-night ideas.'

'That's where you're wrong then. I'm just home until tomorrow for a visit, that's all. I see you're still doing the same old thing, farm boy,' he added, quickly falling into their old style of banter.

'Cheeky sod,' Jack said, giving him a playful punch on the shoulder. 'You like playing about with bits of wood and sticking them together, do you?'

'It beats stinking of cow shit every time you go home,' Tom said.

Jack laughed. 'My mother's used to it, what with all the smells coming out of my dad's surgery. Anyway, it looks like we've got a big job on here soon. Farmer's said I can bugger off for today if I'm willing to start early on Monday morning.'

'Oh yes, what's that then?' Tom asked, not really interested as he picked up his bike from where he'd thrown it down, and waited for Jack to collect his from the farmyard.

'We've got to start digging for victory,' Jack said with a snort. 'A bit bloody daft to call it that since there isn't even a war on yet. We're going to plough up several of the fields and start re-seeding pasture land. Farmer's all for it, as the government's going to pay two pound an acre for the privilege.'

'Best of luck,' Tom said absently as they started cycling away from the farm towards the village.

Jack glanced at him. 'Don't worry; I shan't be here for much longer. Keep this under your hat, mind, our Tom, but I intend to join the Territorials soon.'

'What would you want to do that for, when you're in a cushy job?'

'Christ, you've changed, haven't you? What happened to all that talk of wanting to fly aeroplanes?'

'What happened to yours?' Tom retorted. 'Anyway, now I'm more keen to make furniture and be famous.'

Jack laughed again. 'That'll be the day. Anyway, I decided

against flying. I'd rather take my chances with the army
instead.'

'You think it's really coming then?' Tom asked.

'Of course it's coming. The sooner the better, I'd say. We'll
soon beat the buggers – but remember, not a word about me
joining up. Nobody else knows about it yet, so you'd better
keep your mouth shut.'

'Of course I will. You know you can trust me. What
about that girl you were seeing?' he asked casually,
wondering if he was going to hear a juicy bit of gossip on
that front.

'Got fed up with her,' Jack said briefly. 'She was a bit like
a clinging vine, and I'd rather stick with my mates any day.
A few of us are hanging around at the back of the church
hall. You could come – if your mother would let you out, of
course,' he added with a mocking grin.

'Don't you worry about that!'

Despite the barb, Tom felt an enormous burst of pride,
knowing they were talking more as equals now, and that Jack
was treating him more as an adult than as his young cousin.
He was definitely one of Jack's proper mates now.

By the time they parted company and he was cycling back
to the village he felt like a heck of a swell. He had a job
that fascinated him; he was living in a household that was
a bit more refined than his own – although he meant no
disrespect to his family in thinking so, he thought swiftly –
and he felt more of a grown-up than he had ever done. He
had never thought that his dad was holding him back in any
way, but living and working with Walter for twenty-four
hours a day wasn't the way to grow into an individual. He'd
had to move away from the family to achieve that, and
already he felt that he was changing.

'You don't mind if I go out tonight, do you, Mum?' he
asked Alice casually. 'Rose is going to the pictures, and she
didn't have to stay in just because I'm home, so I don't have
to stay in and chat all evening, do I? Me and Jack are meeting
some of his mates.'

'I don't know about that, Tom,' Alice began. 'We've hardly
seen you yet!'

Walter had other thoughts. 'Don't fuss over him, Mother.

And don't you go drinking, boy. I know what young lads are like when they get together.'

'I won't! They're only hanging around together.'

Tom hadn't even considered drinking. It was an odd place to meet, at the back of the church hall, but on Saturday nights it would be quiet enough to gossip about anything they liked without being overheard. The occupants of the adjacent church-yard weren't going to object, he thought with a shivery grin.

He'd never been invited out with Jack and his mates before, and he assumed the talk would be all about girls and the secret things that boys a few years older than himself talked about. He was excited at the thought. He'd never had a girl-friend, and he knew his dad would box his ears if he thought his boy was even interested in such things.

But he had stirrings like anybody else, and he'd seen the film stars at the pictures and in Lucy's magazines, all curves and red lips, and legs that seemed to be twice as long as those of normal girls. He was just as curious as any boy of his age to know what it was all about, and maybe Jack and his mates were just the folk he needed to enlighten him.

He would have felt mortified if he'd heard Jack's mates ranting at him for inviting him. They were as aggressive as ever and Jack knew it had been a mistake to mention it at all.

'Can he be trusted not to go blabbing to his daddy?' the local blacksmith's son said with a scowl.

'He's all right,' Jack said defiantly. 'Just go easy on him. He's only home until tomorrow morning, and then he's going back to Bristol. Anyway, I didn't exactly invite him, and I don't expect him to come.'

'He'd better not then. Bit of a namby-pamby job, making tables and chairs, ain't it?' another youth said with a deri-sive hoot.

'Could you do it, Skinner?' Jack demanded, and was met with a quick cuff about his head, which he easily matched. 'Oh Christ, shut up, the lot of you, and give the kid a chance,' he added, as Tom's bike slewed to a stop beside the group.

There were six of them, all larger and broader than Tom, and apart from his cousin, he didn't know any of them, except

by sight. Jack reeled off their names, but they merely acknowl-
edged Tom and then ignored him. This wasn't the way he
had expected it to be.

'What are we doing then?' he asked boldly after fifteen
minutes of feeling as though he was invisible, even by Jack.

The one called Skinner looked him up and down, and then
drew something from his pocket. He leered at Tom.

'You can try this for a start – if you're not too chicken.'
He added insult to injury by flapping his arms and squawking
in a fair imitation of a farmyard fowl.

Tom looked at the golden liquid in the bottle Skinner had
produced. 'What is it?'

'You'd better lay off, Tom,' Jack warned.

Skinner brushed him aside. 'Let the kid decide. If he wants
to join in our games, he'd better start now. It's only a drop
of cider, boy. It won't kill you.'

Several of the others were grinning at him now, and one
of them was restraining Jack as he attempted to grab the
bottle out of Skinner's hand.

'Leave him alone, Skinner.'

'Why should I? You brought him here. Let him make up
his own mind.'

Tom grabbed the bottle and opened it. The strong, apple-
sweet smell of scrumpy rose to his nostrils, coupled with
something more pungent. He had only ever had a drop under
supervision before, but he saw now that the others had similar
bottles in their hands, and he thought *why not? Why bloody
not?*

He tipped the bottle to his mouth and took a great gulp
of the stuff. Far too big a gulp. The next minute he was
spluttering and gasping as the golden liquid ran down his
throat and the sky swam.

'What the hell was in that?'

'Just a drop of spirit to give it a kick,' Skinner laughed.
'Have some more.'

'No thanks.'

'I said have some more.' The voice was uglier now, and
Tom found himself held by a couple of strong arms as the
bottle was thrust into his mouth and he was forced to swallow
what was inside it.

The next minute it was as if all hell had broken loose.
They were all laughing and yelling, including Jack, even
though he was fighting to get the bottle away from Tom, and
then everyone was brawling together. Tom found himself
knocked to the ground, hitting his head on a rock and feeling
the hot sting of blood on his skin. His head felt like cotton-
wool, wondering how Jack had ever got in with this wild
crowd, and knowing he was completely out of his depth.

He scuffled along the ground away from them, knowing
he was being a coward and not caring. He scrambled on to
his bike and rode as fast as he could away from there, with
catcalls following in his wake. He wondered viciously if his
Auntie Helen and Uncle Mick knew what their precious son
was up to, and in those head-spinning minutes he lost all
respect for the cousin he'd practically hero-worshipped all
his life. He rode blindly, almost sobbing with the shame and
humiliation he felt. He hardly knew where he was going,
except that he couldn't go home yet until his head felt better
and he had cleaned himself up, knowing his parents would
be furious at the sight of him. Without warning he suddenly
crashed into someone walking towards him, and for the
second time that evening he was knocked off his feet and
he landed on the ground, completely winded. He was instantly
hauled to his feet and found himself looking straight into a
pair of murderous eyes.

'What the devil have you been up you, you young bugger?'
Walter roared. 'And is that drink I can smell on your breath?'

'I didn't know, Dad,' Tom croaked. 'I thought they were
just going to be larking about.'

'Jack's old enough to know better,' Walter snapped. 'I'll
have something to say to his father about this.'

'Oh, don't tell Jack's dad, or he'll get into trouble, and
he'll know I've betrayed him.'

After a moment, seeing how abject his boy looked, and
given the fact that he himself was on the way to the Pig and
Whistle, Walter's heart softened a mite. All the same, the
boy needed to learn a lesson.

'Come with me,' he ordered, yanking his son's arm.

Tom had no chance to do anything else, wheeling his bike
with one hand as he was frogmarched towards the pub by

his father. When they reached it, Walter sat him down on one of the wooden benches outside.

'Sit there and don't move, or I'll have your hide,' he threatened.

Tom wasn't sure he was ever going to be able to move again. He didn't think he'd drunk very much, but the fiery mixture of scrumpy and spirits was raking his gut now. Minutes later, Walter came outside with a jug of rough cider and thrust it into Tom's hand.

'Drink it,' he ordered.

'I can't!' Tom spluttered. 'The smell's already turning my stomach and I'll puke if I have to swallow a drop more.'

'That's the idea. If you think you're a man, my son, you can act like one, and take your drink. If not, then let's hope you've learned a valuable lesson this night, and we'll say no more about it.'

Tom knew he had no option but to do as he was told. It was purgatory to put the jug to his lips, and his hands were shaking so much he spilled half of it. But half was enough. Long before it had reached his stomach, the contents of it revolted, and he clapped his hand to his mouth as his father marched him around to the grassy yard at back of the pub where he threw up his guts.

'That's enough to put me off drinking for life,' he gasped eventually, tears streaming down his cheeks in a most unmanly way.

'I doubt it,' Walter said dryly. 'But I'll wager you'll remember it. Now, calm down and we'll get you cleaned up before we get you home to your mother.'

'She'll kill me!' Tom said in a panic.

'No she won't. She'll hear that you had an accident on your bike and she'll fuss over you the way she's always done.'

Tom felt more and more humiliated, knowing that his father was covering the ugliness of this night for him. His voice was choked. 'I don't know why you're doing this for me.'

Walter pressed his shoulder for moment.

'Because you're my boy, that's why.'

Eighteen

If Alice was unsatisfied by the tale Walter told her, she kept her counsel. She was too concerned about the state of her son to ask too many questions, thankful that Walter had seen him coming home and had taken him to the Pig and Whistle to give him a drink to settle his nerves. It wouldn't have been her remedy, but it seemed to have calmed Tom down, and that was what mattered. She still tut-tutted at the state of his clothes. There was no time to wash and dry them before Mr Conway came to fetch him in the morning, so he would have to wear some of the others that were still in his wardrobe, and leave these dirty ones until he came home next time.

'How was Jack?' she asked. 'I haven't seen him lately.'

He flinched as she dabbed at the cut on his head, relieved to learn that it was only a scratch.

'Jack's all right, but I don't like his mates. Next time I'd rather see him at his house than with them,' he said, avoiding Walter's look.

'Well, it's best to find friends of your own age, and Graham Conway's a steady enough lad, isn't he?' Alice suggested.

When they went to bed that night, Alice lay in the darkness next to Walter. It was comforting to know that all the members of her family, except Lucy, were under the same roof again, but she needed to say what was on her mind.

'I don't know exactly what went on tonight, Walter, nor do I know how you came to find Tom in such a state, and it's probably best if I don't know. My instinct tells me it wasn't as straightforward as you said, but it also tells me that you dealt with it, and for that I thank you – even if it did involve giving him something to drink.'

He didn't answer for a moment, and then he put his arms

around her. 'Then let's leave it at that, my dear. He was hurt, and I put things right. That's all there is to it.'

She nodded thoughtfully, but as well as the smell of drink, she knew the smell of vomit on a young lad's clothes. She guessed there had been more than a sip of cider passing Tom's lips that evening, but if Walter said he had dealt with it, that was good enough for her.

It was obvious that James Conway was going to show some concern when he saw Tom's puffed cheek and the scratches on his face and head. Tom was pale-faced, and his head throbbed like fury, but he remained as dignified as he could, and assured everyone that he wouldn't be so foolish the next time he rode his bike around the lanes. He gave his father a special look when he said it, and was rewarded by a small nod from Walter.

Alice couldn't quite put her finger on the reason, but for all his pallor, her son seemed to have grown in stature and solemnity after whatever had gone on between him and his father the night before. She didn't question it. It was the way things happened when a boy grew into adulthood.

All too soon, the visit was over, the goodbyes were said, and on Monday morning Alice added Tom's soiled clothes to the pile of family laundry, to be ready for the next time he came home. At least she was still needed, she thought with the ghost of a smile, and her hands paused, wondering why such a thing had even entered her head. Of course she was needed. A mother was always a mother, no matter how old the children were, or how far away from home they strayed. And she still had her little one.

Right on cue, Bobby came hurtling out into the garden when she was pegging out the clothes to dry on this fine May morning.

'Is Rose bringing baby Mollie to see us today? She said she would,' he shouted, never able to talk quietly when he was excited about something.

'She said she might,' Alice corrected him. 'It won't be until this afternoon, anyway, so you'll just have to be patient, love.'

It was like asking the sun not to shine. She brushed her hand across her eyes, feeling suddenly a bit limp and a bit woozy, and decided it must be the anti-climax after having her family all around her again.

'When I've finished out here, we'll go indoors and make some fairy cakes, Bobby,' she said, knowing they were his favourites.

'Oh, all right,' he replied, scuffing his boots as he went back indoors.

The thought of it obviously hadn't thrilled him, and it would be a good thing when he was old enough for school, she thought – and then she would have the house to herself all day. Her heart turned over. How would she feel then, to be by herself all day long? And what kind of a turnip was she turning into now, to be falling into such melancholy! She picked up the washing basket and marched back indoors, hardly knowing why she felt so out of sorts.

It was a relief later, when Rose came with baby Mollie as she had promised, and Bobby spent an hour amusing the baby and making her gurgle.

'You look tired, Mum,' Rose said eventually. 'Why don't you go and have a lie down while I watch these two for a while?'

Alice looked at her in astonishment. 'When did I ever have a lie down in the middle of the afternoon? I've got a bit of a muzzy head, that's all, but it'll pass, and I'll be as right as rain soon.'

'You do too much. It wouldn't hurt to get Doctor Stacey to check on your health sometime.'

'Listen to you!' Alice said with a smile. 'Have you turned into a doctor's assistant now?'

She saw Rose blush as she laughed, and knew at once that it wasn't just a doctor's assistant Rose wanted to be. She hadn't mentioned Doctor Matt, but she didn't need to. By now they had already arranged to go to the pictures again on the following Saturday evening. Rose's eyes had shone when she told her mother, and Alice knew love when she saw it.

'I just want you to be well, Mum,' she said simply.

'And there's no reason why I shouldn't be, my dear. I shall probably live to be a hundred and become the old crone of the village.'

They both laughed, but even as she said it, it was as though a shadow had fallen over the room and Alice shivered in the sudden chill that ran through her. It was just the kind of thing people said. It didn't mean they thought they *were* going to live to be a hundred, and she wasn't sure that she wanted to. It was the kind of thing she and Tilly had said when they were young girls, laughing behind their hands at some of the old biddies who were still working in the factory, and the gory tales they told. But now Tilly was dead, and she had hardly got beyond forty.

'Mum?' Rose said. 'That's the second time Bobby's asked you when we're having one of your fairy cakes.'

'Right now,' Alice said determinedly, wondering why she should be feeling so lacklustre today.

During the week the postman delivered a small packet. Alice thought immediately that it must be from Tom, but even though the postmark was smudged, she saw at once that it wasn't his handwriting, and when she opened it her heart gave a huge jump as a silky object slid out of the envelope into her hands. She recognized it at once, just as she recognized the unmistakably lingering odour of the strong scent wafting up from it.

'Tilly,' she whispered, her lips dry.

Her head swam for a moment, and then it cleared as she told herself that of course it hadn't been Tilly who had sent the scarf. Tilly was dead . . . Her heart was beating rapidly now as she realized there was a note inside the envelope, and she drew it out with shaking hands. It was from the landlady of Tilly's old lodgings in Whitechapel, and Alice quickly read the words she had written.

It seemed that there had been a new tenant in Tilly's old room, and when the landlady was giving it the once-over, she had found this scarf of Tilly's lodged at the back of a drawer, and she thought that Tilly's old workmate would like to have it as a keepsake.

Alice remembered when Tilly had bought the scarf. It was so like her, a bit flamboyant in shades of blue and green, and ignoring the old notion that *blue and green should never be seen*. Tilly always said she thought that was daft, anyway, since blue flowers had green leaves, didn't they, and why should she have any objection to what nature provided!

Alice's eyes were damp with tears as she read the note from the landlady, and then pressed the scarf to her face, as if to breathe in the essence of her old friend one last time. Just as quickly, she tossed it down on the sofa, but the smell was still in her nostrils, and without warning she had the most extraordinary sense of something not quite of this world. It was just the same as when Bobby had been so ill, and she had fancied that Tilly's ghost was hovering near, ready to guide him into the great unknown if that was to be his destiny.

Now, she felt a momentary sense of panic. It may have been nothing more than a kind gesture for the landlady to send her the scarf. Or it could be a sign that her time was coming, since Alice had been feeling less than her usual self lately. And if so, then Tilly was waiting for her.

'I must be going mad,' she said out loud, startling Bobby from where he was playing with his toy soldiers on the rag rug.

'Can I have a drink, Mum?' he asked plaintively.

'Of course you can, my love,' she said, scooping him up in her arms, despite his protests that he wasn't a baby, and pressing a kiss on his tousled head.

She was being ridiculous in letting her imagination run away with her, she thought as she fetched him a drink of milk. But when she returned with the drink, she found Bobby draped in the scarf and playing at being a bandit, and it was all she could do not to snatch it away from him.

When Walter came home he said she should throw it away because it made the whole house stink.

'Mum can't do that,' Rose told him. 'It was Tilly's, and so it means something to her. Besides, it's too pretty to throw away.'

'Do you want it?' Alice asked her without thinking.

'Only if you don't,' Rose said uneasily, wondering why her mother was taking such an odd attitude about a simple thing.

'I don't need a scarf to remind me of Tilly, and if you like it, then you have it,' Alice said, forcing herself to sound more natural than she had a moment ago. 'I'll wash it first, though, to get some of the smell out of it.'

'I'm surprised it's lasted so long,' Walter grumbled. 'But Tilly always had strong taste when it came to scent, as I recall. I prefer a woman to smell as nature intended, not cover herself in perfumes and paint.'

'You don't mind a bit of soap, though, Dad?' Rose said with a laugh.

'Oh ah, soap's all right,' he grunted. 'I always said a bit of good old carbolic never hurt anyone.'

He couldn't understand why his womenfolk burst out laughing at that, but he let it go. Rose wasn't the only one who had noticed Alice acting a bit strangely lately, and a bit of laughter usually worked wonders.

Alice didn't mention her odd feelings to anybody. She told herself firmly it was only the recent upheavals that were making her go a bit doolally, what with Bobby's illness that had frightened her so much, Tom moving away from home, and then coming home looking so much the worse for wear from his night out with Jack. It was nothing more than that . . .

Helen turned up at the house one afternoon, looking far from her usual serene self. She was red-eyed and shaking, and it was obvious that something was badly wrong. For a dreadful moment her heart stopped. Helen and Mick hadn't been getting along so well lately, but surely Mick hadn't done something so stupid, after all these years, as to hint at anything happening between himself and Alice? Especially as there never *had* been anything between himself and Alice, and never would be!

'I don't know how he could have done such a thing,' she burst out as soon as she got inside the door. 'How could he have been so cruel?'

Alice had no idea what she was talking about, but she shooed Bobby out into the garden to play before he overheard something he shouldn't.

'Sit down, Helen, and tell me what's happened,' she said quickly, her heart pounding.

'It's our Jack! He's gone and joined up without a by-your-leave or discussing it with his father and me. He's volunteered for the Territorials, if you please, and left a note saying he'd be in touch again when he was settled and could give us an address.'

'You mean he's just *gone*?' Alice said, not sure whether to feel upset at the sight of Helen's real distress, or relieved that it wasn't anything more personal involving her.

'That's what I said,' Helen almost snapped. 'Oh, he was eloquent enough in his note, of course. He's got his father's gift for saying what he thinks folk want to hear, and it was all very noble about being patriotic and getting into uniform before he was forced to do so. But he's still a baby, Alice. My baby.'

Her face crumpled, and Alice swallowed hard. But being sentimental at such a time wasn't going to help anyone.

'He's not a baby, Helen. He's a man, and I have no doubt that Mick's very proud of him.'

'Oh yes, of course Mick's proud of him. It's what men do, isn't it? Go off and get themselves killed at the first sign of war, even if it hasn't even happened yet!'

'He won't get killed. Don't be so melodramatic, Helen, and don't go putting such ideas into his head, either. You and Mick should be supporting his choice.'

She didn't know where these words were coming from, nor how she would feel if it was Tom who had gone and signed up . . . But Tom was still only fourteen, so she could afford to be complacent about that. She heard Helen give a shaky sniff, and then she blew her nose hard and straightened her shoulders.

'We do support him, even if we don't like it, and I know Mick was really as cut up as me at first.' She gave a wan smile. 'The funny thing is, Alice, that ever since this happened last night, Mick's started talking to me more than he has in ages. In fact, we stayed up half the night talking, and somehow it seems to have brought us closer. I don't understand it, but at least I'm not worrying about that!'

Alice had her own ideas about why that might be. Because of her shock and distress over what Jack had done, Helen was obviously leaning on Mick more than usual. She had always been a forthright and independent woman, and sometimes a man needed a woman to be a bit softer. Alice knew better than to say so right now, though, and risk Helen flaring up at her again. But if Mick and Helen were finding themselves growing closer through this, then she was glad. Really glad, without a single reservation.

'Let's have a cup of tea,' Alice said, resorting to her panacea for all ills.

Helen followed her out to the kitchen. 'You know I love your brood, Alice, but Mick and I are both agreed that it's a good thing we never had more children. I couldn't bear to be worrying over them all the time, especially in these uncertain times, so I'm glad now that it was never meant to be.'

It wasn't the most tactful remark she could have made, but Alice let it go.

Walter was astonished when he heard the news that Jack had gone.

'Good for him. I always thought that boy had a lot of backbone. He'll sort out the enemy if it ever comes to it.'

'Single-handed, I suppose,' Alice said dryly.

'Well, with a bit of help,' Walter conceded. He glanced at her. 'You're not worrying about our Tom, are you? I know what you women are like when it comes to mollycoddling your sons, but he's far too young to be doing anything so daft, and he seems to be doing fine now.'

'Well, that's exactly what I was thinking,' she told him, her fingers crossed.

Although Walter was never going to say so, he was a bit uneasy as to why Jack had made such a sudden decision, and he had a fair suspicion that it might have something to do with that night when Tom had come crashing into him, his face bloodied and strong drink on his breath. That Jack had been involved, he had no doubt, but if this was his way of dealing with it, he wasn't sure that it was the best way, nor was he sure how Mick would have taken it. He found out when he met his brother in the Pig and Whistle that night, where some of their cronies were buying a round of drinks for Mick on account of his son Jack.

'This is a turn-up,' Walter said with a grin. 'These old buggers have usually got mothballs coming out of their pockets, not coppers to throw around.'

'Jack's the first in the village to go,' Mick said, 'so that makes him special. Besides, it's carrying on our old man's tradition of being in at the beginning.'

'He died for it too,' Walter muttered before he could stop himself.

'Well, that's something we're not going to think about,' Mick said determinedly. 'So if that's all you've got to say, go and sit somewhere else, Walter.'

'What, and miss out on free drinks in my nephew's honour? Not bloody likely,' Walter said. 'I'll raise a glass to him like the rest of you.'

But when he went home that night, he looked in on his snuffling younger son, and couldn't help looking at the second empty bed in the room. After a moment's heart-tugging, he imagined Tom sleeping soundly in his bedroom in Bristol, content with his new life. He listened to the varying creaks and whispers of his house as it settled down for the night, and thanked God for it all. Then he went to bed and wrapped his arms around his wife, thanking God for Alice most of all.

Alice knew there was definitely something amiss. It wasn't like her to be off her food, or to pick at meals she had always enjoyed. She was a touch uneasy that there might be something wrong with her, but she wasn't a woman who went scuttling off to the doctor on the slightest pretext. If it was nerves – that mysterious complaint that seemed to cover a multitude of other, hidden ailments – then she had no truck with it.

Besides, she wasn't a nervous person. She had always considered herself able to cope with anything, just like her sister-in-law. After Helen's first bout of anxiety over Jack, they had now heard from him with detailed information of how he was settling into a new routine, and she and Mick were bristling with pride for him now. Alice didn't blame them for that. It was preferable to wallowing in self-pity.

But Alice had had several big upsets in the few months since the start of this year. The most dreadful shock of all was hearing that Tilly had died, and that had happened afterwards, when she had gone up to London and suffered the anguish of seeing her old friend leaving this world. She had never felt as alone as she had at that time. Before that, Lucy had left home, Rose had broken up with Peter Kelsey – but had thankfully found another satisfying new job. There was nothing to worry about there. But Walter had been involved in his accident at the village meeting; then there was Bobby's illness and Tom leaving home . . . and now the news about Jack.

She dismissed all the silly notions she had once had for Mick, because none of it compared with the gratitude she felt to have Walter by her side. Alice knew – as she had always known, she thought with a sudden rush of love – that the one constant in her life was always Walter.

But she still felt a weird restlessness inside that she couldn't explain. When she and Tilly had been girls they had always thought they would live for ever. Not that they had actually put such a thought into words, but you didn't need to when you were young and full of confidence about the future. She felt a shudder run through her, and she didn't like this uneasy feeling of mild panic. Perhaps she should ask Doctor Stacey for a tonic bottle when she took Bobby for his regular visit, but she knew in her heart that when the time came she wouldn't ask him about such a trivial thing.

'This young man seems to be improving with the sunshine,' the doctor said with a smile, after giving Bobby a thorough check-up. 'Is he sleeping better at night now?'

'He's much better, thank goodness,' Alice said.

The doctor looked at her thoughtfully, his trained eyes sensing the words Alice couldn't say. 'And how about you, Mrs Chase? Are you sleeping well at night, after all your upheavals these past few months?'

To her horror Alice felt her eyes blur with tears. She was shocked at having such a reaction to a simple question, but the doctor noted it, and just as swiftly he pressed a button on his desk and asked his assistant to take Bobby away and give him some milk and a biscuit.

'Now then, why don't you tell me what's wrong?' he said gently.

How could she tell him, when she didn't know herself? There were genuinely sick people waiting, who needed his attention far more than she did. How could she say that she simply felt out of sorts, not quite herself, missing her old friend, her son, wishing that she could turn back the clock? A sensible, forty-year-old married woman couldn't waste his time by saying anything so foolish . . .

Seeing that she was almost unable to speak he began asking her more pertinent questions in his calm and deliberate manner. She answered numbly, praying he wasn't going to tell her something awful. But after he'd scribbled a few notes on a pad she saw that he was actually smiling.

'Don't you know what's wrong with you, my dear?' he asked.

'I thought you were going to tell me,' she mumbled.

'I thought an intelligent woman like yourself, who had already had four children, would have recognized the signs by now . . .'

Already had? Alice looked at him blankly for a moment, and then her heart thumped, stopped for a moment, and then raced madly on.

'You think I'm expecting another baby?' she whispered.

'Well, unless I'm very much mistaken, I'd say that's a fair assessment. Your food has made you feel nauseous at times, you've missed your regular cycles, which you put down to anxiety, or maybe even the start of the change, but it's far more likely to be otherwise in a healthy young woman like yourself. Come back and see me in a month and we'll confirm it, but meanwhile, let me be the first to congratulate you, Mrs Chase.'

Alice's head was still whirling when she left the doctor's surgery, holding on tightly to Bobby's hand. She hardly heard any of the boy's excited chatter about how he was going to be a doctor when he grew up, or fully registered any of the people who passed the time of day to her as they walked home. She was too full of the momentous thing that was happening to her and to Walter and to all of them. It was the best news of all, and something that hadn't even crossed her mind as a possibility.

Her heart was bursting with the joy of it. She wasn't ill, and she wasn't dying, and she couldn't wait for Walter to come home from work. Her face glowed. He had to be the first to know that there was going to be another little one in the family, and she was already anticipating his reaction when she told him. At the start of this year, he'd said he thought 1939 was going to be a good year for them all. Instead it had had more than its share of sadness and anxiety – until now.

But on this wonderful early summer's day Alice felt so young and alive that she felt like skipping along with Bobby now, imagining the look on Walter's face, his beloved face, when she told him that, for them, 1940 was going to be even better.